HAMLYN JUNIOR STORY LIBRARY

EXCITING STORIES FOR BOYS

Dr David
Hewitt

HAMLYN JUNIOR STORY LIBRARY

EXCITING STORIES
FOR BOYS

by well-known authors

*Selected
and edited by*
PETER ROLLS

HAMLYN

London · New York · Sydney · Toronto

First Published 1975
Published by the Hamlyn Publishing Group Limited
London · New York · Sydney · Toronto
Astronaut House, Feltham, Middlesex, England
© IPC Magazines Limited
Printed in Czechoslovakia
51115

Contents

CONTRABAND

by Lee Mayne

Superintendent Bill Downs had torn London's underworld apart to capture a smuggling organization, but it was only when he asked The Hawk to help him that the gang's success was broken.

Superintendent Bill Downs was a very worried man. He stood by the window of his office, teeth clamped hard on the stem of his empty pipe as he stared out into space. From here, high up in the New Scotland Yard building, there was a fine view over the Thames. Usually, the sight of the bustling river traffic, the imposing building of the County Hall across on the other bank, and busy Westminster Bridge to his right, brought a gleam of appreciation to the Superintendent's eyes. Now he looked at them unseeingly. He was up against one of the toughest problems he'd been called on to face, and it had turned sour on him.

He moved away from the window and picked up a message slip from his desk. It was from the Questura in Rome and it contained four words: "Temple missing. Details follow." Downs stuffed the useless pipe into his pocket. Detective Sergeant John Temple was one of his best men – if anything serious had happened to him . . .

The Superintendent's face set grimly. He tossed the message on to the desk, reached forward and flipped the switch of the intercom.

"Get me Interpol Headquarters, Paris," he said, tersely. "I want to speak to Inspector Jean Collet – personally!"

The Hawk closed the folder he had been reading, leant back in his seat and let his eyelids droop shut. He was on the B.E.A. Comet flight to Rome, having managed to get a seat at very short notice. He smiled slightly. Scotland Yard, in the bulky shape of his old friend Bill Downs, had asked for quick action. In the flight schedule, the Comet left Paris – Orly (Nord) Airport – at 12.10 hours, and was due to arrive at Rome – Ciampino Airport – by 14.20 hours. What could be quicker than that!

His keen brain switched to a review of the case that was causing Scotland Yard – and the Questura – such grave concern. Some weeks previously, the British Police had raided a house in London which the Customs and Excise Office believed was used as a store-house for contraband goods. The officers had been hoping for a reasonable haul, but they expected nothing like the veritable treasure trove they unearthed. Jewellery, gold watches to the value of £ 12,000 were found in the house! The discovery sparked off a full-scale investigation by Scotland Yard, with Superintendent Downs in charge of the operation. Within a week, the Superintendent had reached an inescapable conclusion. A brilliant smuggling organization was at work, bringing contraband into the country on an unprecedented scale – and the bulk of it came from Italy!

In the days that followed, the Superintendent had almost torn London's underworld apart in an attempt to get a lead on the gang. He had no success – either the underworld knew nothing, or it just wasn't talking! Worse still – despite redoubled precautions, a steady flow of smuggled goods was continuing to enter the country. It seemed that the organization had devised a method of getting the stuff through which was so unique that it was outside the knowledge of even the most experienced Preventive Officers.

Faced with a blank wall, Bill Downs had decided to try tackling the problem from the other end. He had sought, and obtained, full and immediate co-operation from the Italian Police. With their approval, he had sent one of his best men – Detective Sergeant Temple – to Rome with instructions to work independently and undercover. Now the Questura had informed Scotland Yard that Temple had completely disappeared!

"Will you fasten your safety-belt, please, sir." The quiet voice of the Air Hostess cut across the Interpol agent's thoughts. "We shall be coming in to land in a few moments." She smiled, cheerfully, and moved off along the aisle. The Hawk's eyes narrowed, shrewdly, as he snapped the two ends of the belt together. A sixth sense warned him that the landing at the end of this journey spelled trouble!

Half an hour later, The Hawk's instinct was confirmed. Captain Riccio, ace detective of the Questura, stared stonily across his desk at the Interpol man.

"I had one of my own men working with Temple," he said. "Carlo Mazza – one of the slickest operatives I've got." He paused. "He's disappeared, too!"

The Hawk said nothing, sensing that there was more to come.

"As soon as I was certain something was wrong," Riccio went on, "I sent Sovera to check up. Sovera is my second-in-command." His face grew even bleaker. "Or rather – he was. They pulled his body out of the Tiber two hours ago!"

The Hawk's expression became hard and ruthless. "So now it's murder as well as smuggling!" He looked keenly at the Italian detective. "How did you find out that Temple and Mazza were missing?" he asked. "Couldn't they have just gone off somewhere to follow a lead?"

Riccio shook his head. "I had made a strict arrangement. Independently, each of them had to make personal contact with me every day between nine o'clock and midday."

The Hawk nodded. "Had they been getting anywhere with their investigations?" he asked.

Riccio pursed his lips, thoughtfully. "The fact that they've disappeared seems to indicate that they'd got too close to something," he said. "But up to their last contact, they had nothing to report. The only clue I can give you is something Temple said just before he rang off."

The Hawk raised his eyebrows, questioningly. "Yes?"

Riccio stood up. "He said: 'It's surprising what you can learn in this city if you keep your shoes clean.' It sounded as if he was just joking at the time, but now I'm certain he wasn't."

"I've heard that the shoe-blacks in Rome provide a pretty good information service," said the Interpol man, seriously.

"That's right," nodded the Italian. "For us – sometimes. For the underworld – *all* the time." He looked at The Hawk. "But you're on the right track," he said. "I told Sovera to check around the shoe-blacks!" His eyes blazed with anger. "I'll find out who killed him if I have to choke the truth out of the whole bunch of them with my bare hands!"

The Hawk put a sympathetic hand on Riccio's shoulder. "No," he said. "Just find out where he was last seen."

The other looked at him, sharply. "And then?" he enquired.

"If the shoe-blacks are more willing to talk to crooks than they are to the police," said The Hawk, easily, "I suggest we give them the opportunity." He paused. "I'm not known in Rome. I could very well be a Swiss dealer in expensive watches – looking for a ready market!"

The Hawk stood with his foot on the old shoe-black's box listening to the rhythmic slapping of the polishing rag as the man worked on the already gleaming toe. He seemed to be deeply immersed in his newspaper, and was apparently just another sightseer.

"Know anything about watches?" The Interpol man murmured the question without looking up from his newspaper. He spoke so that only the old boot-black could hear, and his usually perfect Italian had suddenly acquired a slightly guttural accent. He could easily pass as a German or Austrian Swiss.

"Si signor," answered the old man. "You want to buy?"

"I want to sell – at the right price," said The Hawk from behind his paper.

"It is more difficult, signor – but not altogether impossible. The watch must be good – and new."

"Like the one I'm wearing?" The Hawk eased his left wrist forward so that his watch was visible to the other.

"Si – I could get you a fair price for that one."

"And how many more like it?" The Interpol man dropped the question gently.

"All things can be arranged, signor," answered the boot-black, cagily.

"I would like to discuss a deal of, say, three or four million lire!" murmured The Hawk, gently.

For a moment there was a pause. Then . . .

"Your other foot, please, signor." The old man's voice did not change expression. The Hawk changed feet and the shoe-black started working on the second shoe. Before he did so, he rapped his brush against the side of the box three times with a peculiar rhythm.

Moments later, The Hawk felt rather than heard someone move up behind him.

"Do not turn around, signor," hissed a voice in his ear. "When your shoes are finished, go and take coffee at the Café Luna, in the Via Corso."

Seconds later, The Hawk knew that he and the shoe-black were alone again. He also knew something else – the Via Corso was very close to the river. The Questura detective – Sovera – had been pulled out of the Tiber!

The Hawk sat at a little table under the tattered pavement-awning outside the Café Luna. To a casual observer, he appeared engrossed in his newspaper but, in fact, his keen eyes were shrewdly assessing the occupants of the other tables around him. A scruffy-looking waiter came out of the café and moved across to him.

"Si, signor?" The man idly flicked a napkin over the table top.

"Coffee," growled The Hawk in guttural Italian. In his rôle of a German Swiss he kept up a hard, terse manner. Now he eyed the soiled cloth in the waiter's hand with obvious distaste. "And I want it in a *clean* cup," he snapped.

The man shrugged carelessly and turned away, leaving the Interpol agent to his appraisal of the other customers. They were a mixed bunch – some husky-looking men he judged to be market porters, a couple of mechanics in oil-stained dungarees and a few indeterminate loafers. He wondered which of them was his 'contact'.

"Signor!" The Hawk lowered his newspaper at the sound of the shrill, eager voice beside him. He found himself looking into a pair of dark, intelligent eyes, set in the grubby, grinning face of a diminutive street urchin. "You want to buy picture postcards, signor?" The boy spread a pack of brightly-coloured views of Rome over the table top. "I sell the best cards in all Italy," he said, proudly.

The Hawk grinned inwardly at the lad's cheeky, self-confident approach, but he kept a pretence of ill-humour. "Clear off!" he grunted.

"They are very good, very cheap, signor," persisted the boy. He shuffled the cards around. "Only thirty lire each." He shot a calculating glance at his prospective customer. "You see one you like, maybe I let you have it for twenty."

"I said – clear off!" barked The Hawk.

"All right, all right – I'm going!" The youngster hastily swept the cards together. "But you're missing a big chance, signor." He held out a gaudy picture of the Coliseum. "Only twenty lire, and it is so beautiful!" He lowered his voice. "As beautiful as a Swiss watch, signor!"

So this was his 'contact'! The Hawk's eyes narrowed – with the sharp eyes of street urchins and shoe-blacks working for them, he began to understand how the gang managed to keep a jump ahead of Captain Riccio and his men.

"Here," he said. "I'll take it." He tossed twenty lire on to the table and held out his hand for the card.

A stream of angry Italian from behind him made The Hawk turn his head. The waiter was bearing down on the table, shouting furious threats as to what he would do to the youthful postcard seller if he ever caught him annoying his café patrons again. The Hawk felt the card thrust into his fingers and turned in time to see the boy grab the money, thumb his nose cheekily at the waiter then run like a rabbit to lose himself amongst the passers-by. The Interpol man frowned as he stared at the brightly-coloured postcard. "Now what?" he thought. Then, as he turned the reverse side uppermost, his expression cleared. Hastily printed in Italian was a brief message: 'Follow him.'

Unhurriedly, The Hawk finished the indifferent coffee the waiter had brought him. He knew the boy would wait, and he wanted time to think. His every instinct warned him that when he moved away from the café he would be heading into danger. He ought to let Captain Riccio know what had happened, but if he was spotted making contact with the Questura it could spoil everything. He shrugged to himself – he'd have to play it through alone. As he stood up to leave, there was a gleam of anticipation in The Hawk's eyes. Maybe he was walking into a trap, but at least he'd be ready for it! After following the young 'guide' for twenty minutes, a less experienced man than The Hawk would have been hopelessly lost. Since he had picked up the Interpol agent a hundred yards away from the Café Luna, the boy had led the way through a bewildering maze of back streets, passageways and alleys. It was only by keeping a careful check on their over-all direction that The Hawk knew they had been doubling backward and forward within a relatively small area. Now, as the ragged youngster stopped at last by the entrance to a narrow passage between two derelict warehouses, The Hawk grinned to himself. Unless he was very much mistaken, they were no more then a few hundred yards from their starting point.

"Down there, signor." The boy jerked a thumb towards the passage. "Second door on the left." Then, before The Hawk could say a word, he turned and ran off down the deserted street as fast as his wiry little legs could carry him.

Cre-ee-eak! Rusty hinges whined in protest as The Hawk cautiously pushed open the battered door. He wrinkled his nose in distaste as a wave of dank, musty air assailed his nostrils. For a few moments he stood in the doorway, letting his eyes become accustomed to the gloom inside the abandoned building. After a while, he was able to make out the dim shapes of broken packing-cases, battered oil-drums, heaps of rotting canvas and a whole clutter of unidentifiable rubbish strewn around the huge floor space. Obviously this had once been the main packing and dispatch area. Suddenly, his keen eyes noticed something much more significant. The dust on the floor immediately in front of him showed signs of considerable disturbance! Others had been using the place frequently – and recently!

The Hawk knew it was vital that none of his actions, either conscious or subconscious, should betray his years of police training. He slouched forward into the dimness of the warehouse.

"Anybody here?" he called, gruffly.

Cre-ee-eak! Slam! The badly-hung door behind him swung shut, and the dimness became almost complete darkness. The Hawk felt in his pocket, and there was a rattle as he found a box of matches. Suddenly, the brilliant beam of a powerful electric-torch flashed through the blackness, blinding him as it pinpointed his face.

"Do not move, signor!" rasped a coarse Italian voice.

The Hawk lifted his hand to shield his eyes. "What's all this?" he blustered, angrily. "Who are you? I came here . . ."

"Sure you came here," cut in a quiet voice behind him. "But *why –*

13

that's what I want to find out!" Something hard jabbed viciously against his spine. Every nerve in The Hawk's body tingled – not because of the gun in his back, but because of the second man's voice. The accent was English! Here, at last, was a link between the organization in Rome and the wide-spread contraband problem facing Superintendent Bill Downs at Scotland Yard!

"I was told I would find someone here interested in dealing in Swiss watches," he growled.

"Maybe you will – if you're genuine," said the quiet voice. "We like to be quite sure. What's your name and where are you from?"

"Weber of Zurich," answered the Interpol man.

"Right – stand quite still! Remember you're still being covered!" The gun ceased to press into The Hawk's back; then, swiftly and expertly, the man behind him began to search him systematically from head to toe.

"Well, Mister Weber of Zurich," said the unseen man, when he had finished his search. "You are a most unusual character. There is not one single thing on you which could confirm your identity!"

"I know that," snapped The Hawk. "It's the way I like to operate."

"I'm quite sure it is," answered the other, softly. "But only two kinds of people would go to so much trouble – a big-time professional – or a police agent!"

The Hawk shrugged. "I'm tired of all this stupid play-acting," he growled. "Do you want to talk business or not?"

"Not with you, Mister Weber," came the answer. "You see, if you *were* big-time, like you say you are – we'd know about you already. That only leaves one alternative, doesn't it?"

The words were spoken in an almost gentle tone, but the Interpol agent sensed the underlying menace. In the same way, he sensed rather than heard the quick movement behind him as the man aimed a blow at the back of his head. Automatically, his body swayed as he partially 'rode' the vicious chop of the gun butt. If he had taken the full force of it he would have blacked out for a very long count. As it was, his knees buckled and he collapsed half-conscious, fighting the waves of nausea that swept over him. Summoning all his will-power he forced himself to lie limp and apparently lifeless.

A toe prodded him roughly in the ribs. "Tie him up and put him with the other one!" It was the quiet man speaking. "Tonight he can take a permanent bath in your convenient and historic River Tiber!"

Thud! The Hawk stifled a grunt of pain as his bound body was dumped carelessly on the hard wooden floor. The man who had carried him handled his dead weight as easily as if he were a sack of flour – and he felt just as helpless.

"How's the other one?" The Hawk sensed the big Italian moving away from him. At the same time, he became conscious of the sound of heavy, laboured breathing close by him.

"Still in a coma." It was the softly spoken English voice that gave the reply. "Doesn't look as if he'll last much longer, though."

"Why don't we dump them *both* in the river – tonight!" growled the Italian.

Taking a chance that the two men were, for the moment, preoccupied, the Interpol man risked a quick look through halfclosed eyes. He was in time to see the torch beam flick up from a second prostrate figure and pin-point the face of the last speaker. It was one of the two tough-looking market porters he had seen sitting outside the Café Luna!

"Is that a question – or are you offering me advice?" The soft voice of the man who was holding the electric torch held deadly menace.

"No – no, signor!" The big Italian sounded scared. "I just thought . . ."

"You're not paid to think!" snapped the other. The torch beam dropped to the unconscious man again. "His body must be found where it will confirm the false trail."

The Hawk anticipated the man's next move and shut his eyes quickly. A second later, from the brightness he could sense through his closed lids, he knew the spotlight was on his own face.

"Then maybe we'll have no more of these interfering snoopers." Floorboards creaked as the two men turned away. "Tie him in a sack and make sure it's properly weighted." A door slammed, the sound of footsteps died away across the main warehouse floor outside, and The Hawk was left alone with his unknown, unconscious companion in the little, windowless store-room.

For a while, he lay relaxed and still, assessing the situation. He had deliberately walked into a trap – and he had been caught! Now what?

15

Certainly he had learnt a good deal, but it was not enough by a long way. It was equally certain he couldn't improve on the situation while he lay there, trussed up like a chicken. Slowly and methodically, he started to exert pressure on the ropes that bound his wrists and ankles. There was no 'give' – the big Italian knew his job. Suddenly, The Hawk tensed – something about his surroundings had changed! In a flash, he realized what it was. The breathing of the unconscious man had lost its rasping, stertorous quality and had become even and regular.

"Signor!" A weak voice called to him through the darkness.

"Here," answered The Hawk, softly.

"Who are you?"

There was a pause, as though the man had to gather strength for his reply. "Mazza . . ." he spoke with an effort. "Mazza of the Questura."

The Hawk took a deep breath. Carlo Mazza – the Italian detective who had been working with Temple, the Scotland Yard man, and who had disappeared at the same time!

"I'm Jean Collet – Interpol. Are you badly hurt?" Again there was a pause. "If you can roll over to me – maybe – I can – untie you." Mazza's speech was slow and laboured.

The Hawk sensed that the man was at the limit of his endurance. He made no attempt at further questioning but, instead, started to inch his way across the floor to where the other lay. Moments later, when he wriggled alongside the Questura man, he got another shock – the hands that reached out to start work on his ropes were unbound!

"How did you manage to get free?" he asked.

"I was never tied up," answered Mazza, through clenched teeth. "There was no need – I can't move, anyway – my back is broken."

The Hawk's hands came free. He sat up and began working at his ankle ropes. "There'll be an ambulance down here just as soon as I can get out to a 'phone," he grunted.

"No!" Mazza's voice was scarcely audible. "Listen, signor . . ." The Hawk had to put his ear close to the injured man's lips to catch the whispered words that followed. " . . . Temple is dead. They shot him. I tried to get away across the roof – the coping was rotten – it gave way – I finished up down in the yard." There was a pause, as the Italian struggled for breath. "They dragged me in here – I've pretended to be unconscious ever since – thought I might learn something – no good." Again he paused. His last reserves of strength began to ebb away. "Only clue from Temple – before he died – he said: 'Fruit in the garden' . . ." Suddenly, Mazza's hand gripped The Hawk's arm with fierce strength. "Get them, signor! Get them for both of us!" he whispered. Then his grip relaxed and his body went limp. The Questura man was dead! The Hawk stood up slowly. Mazza's magnificent courage and endurance was something he would never forget. For three days he must have lain there, suffering great pain, knowing he was fatally injured, yet forcing himself to act a part in the hope of gaining information about the gang. The Interpol man's lips tightened into a thin, hard line – the Italian detective's life, together with the lives of the policemen Temple and Sovera, made a debt he was going to see paid, even if it cost him his own!

He turned towards the door, then paused, abruptly. If the gang came back and found he'd escaped, the whole organization would be alerted. On the other hand, if they thought they had disposed of him, as planned . . . Swiftly, he went through his pockets – they were empty. He knelt beside Mazza's body. Maybe they'd been less careful with an injured man. A sharp grunt of satisfaction escaped him as he eventually found what he was looking for – a keenbladed pocket-knife. Working quickly, he slit a long strip of cloth from the lining of his jacket and used it to bind the open knife to the inside of his left forearm. Then he slipped his jacket back on and, having made sure he could get the knife quickly and easily, he moved back to the spot where he had been dumped and set about tying himself up again. When he had finished, he looked as tightly bound as he'd ever been, but he knew he could twist free of the ropes in a matter of seconds. Now all he had to do was wait!

It was just after midnight when the big Italian shipped the oars of the little dinghy and let the boat drift quietly along with the current. For a moment, he stared at the canvas-covered figure in the stern, and his face twisted into an evil grin.

"From now on," he growled, "you're going to do your snooping among the fishes in the Tiber!"

He rose to his feet and stood straddlelegged for a moment,

calculating the balance of the boat. Then, with one powerful heave, he bundled The Hawk's inert body over the stern. *Splash!* Weighted by two large pieces of pig-iron, the canvas sack sank like a stone. But, almost before the water had closed over him, The Hawk had the concealed knife in his hand. He had already slipped the ropes on his wrists during the row out from the warehouse jetty, and it was only a matter of seconds before he was ripping a long slit up the length of the sack. In another few moments he was fighting his way out of the clinging canvas that was to have been his shroud; then, with a powerful kick from his bound legs, he shot towards the surface.

He broke the water as silently as an otter and lay for a moment, gulping in great lungfuls of life-giving air. Then, as he started to free his ankles, he permitted himself a grim smile of satisfaction. With *him* out of the way, the gang would be feeling pretty secure now – and overconfident criminals become careless!

Captain Riccio's face was expressionless as he sat listening to The Hawk's story. Only the fierce gleam in his eyes betrayed the emotion he felt as he heard of the death of Carlo Mazza. The Interpol man finished towelling himself and reached for a dry shirt.

"And they got the Yard man, Temple, as well," he said. Riccio stirred slightly. "I know," he nodded. "There was a message from Interpol. The Swiss police found his dead body this afternoon in a ditch, just on the outskirts of Lausanne."

The Hawk paused in the act of putting on his tie. "In Switzerland!" he exclaimed. "Why should they take his body all the way there?"

Riccio looked at him, sharply. "His *body*?" he queried.

The Hawk nodded. "Mazza told me he was shot three days ago."

Captain Riccio stood up. There was a curious look on his face as he took a message from out of his pocket and passed it across to The Hawk.

"Then how do you account for *this*?" he asked, in a strained voice.

The Hawk glanced at the slip of paper. It was a copy of the Interpol message. Suddenly, his eyes narrowed as the full import of the contents registered. According to the medical examination by the Swiss police doctor, Temple had been dead *less than six hours* when his body was found!

Captain Riccio paced his office, restlessly. "It just doesn't make sense," he growled. "Temple was shot here, in Rome. Mazza saw it happen. Yet, *three days* later, when the body turns up in Lausanne – five hundred miles away – he's only been dead for *six hours!*"

The Hawk stared at him, thoughtfully. "I wonder where poor Mazza's body will turn up," he said.

Riccio frowned. "Why do you say that?"

"Because the Englishman said he wanted it found where it will *confirm the false trail.*" The Hawk's eyes narrowed. "I think it'll be Lausanne again."

"Meaning that Temple is the false trail," said Riccio.

"Exactly," nodded the Interpol man. "If I was still at the bottom of the river, where I'm supposed to be, what would your reaction be if both Temple and Mazza were found in Switzerland?"

Riccio shrugged. "I'd think they'd been following a lead that took them there."

"Right!" said The Hawk. "And you'd think it must have been a red-hot lead, too, if they were killed because of it. So would, everyone else . . ." He paused, significantly. ". . . and the whole contraband investigation would switch there!"

"Leaving the gang to carry on with 'business as usual' in Rome. Pretty smart," he conceded. Then, as an afterthought: "But it still doesn't explain the mystery of Temple's death."

"No," said The Hawk. "Nor the message he passed on to Mazza." He repeated the words. "Fruit in the garden."

"What fruit? Whose garden?"

. Suddenly, The Hawk sat up. "I think I've got it," he said. "Temple was investigating smuggling on a large scale. Suppose we treat his message on a large scale. A lot of fruit – a big garden!"

Riccio stared at him, blankly.

The Hawk stood up. "Italy has a lot of fruit – so much that they are able to export it. England has a big garden, where they import fruit – Covent Garden!"

The Questura man's eyes gleamed. "It's the perfect set-up. Fruit shipments as a cover for smuggling!"

"Now we've got to find out – who." The Hawk's lips tightened as he thought of the three policemen who had died at the hands of the gang.

It was some hours later when a messenger hurried into the room with a top priority radio from Interpol Headquarters. It contained information which The Hawk had requested – details of every export and import firm dealing in the fruit trade between Great Britain and Italy. It also contained a vital clue. The Hawk let out a shout of triumph.

"Got it!" He slapped the paper on Riccio's desk. "Look at the second group of names. All four companies deal in 'quick frozen' produce, as well as fruit. *And* they transport their stuff by road – in refrigerator trucks!"

"Direct from the farms to Covent Garden market." The Questura man nodded. "Sounds like the answer."

"It *is* the answer!" said The Hawk. "They proved it for us – with Temple's body. Soon after he was shot, they must have put it in the deep-freeze plant. Later, it was taken to Lausanne by a refrigerator truck. When it was found, it had thawed out and gave the appearance of having been dead only a few hours!"

The Italian slammed his fist on the desk. "Ghouls!" he snarled. "They're not fit to be called human beings!"

The Interpol man put a sympathetic hand on the other's shoulder. "Take it easy," he said, quietly. "Remember – we can't move an inch until we've got the London end tied up as well. Then we'll hit 'em both ends simultaneously!"

For three days, both the Questura and Scotland Yard worked at top pressure to narrow the possible suspects among the produce companies. Their investigations were not made easier by the need for absolute secrecy – one wrong move and the birds would fly.

It was on the evening of the third day that Captain Riccio leant wearily back in his office chair and pushed a slip of paper across to The Hawk.

"This has to be the one," he said, "All the other companies have impeccable reputations. We've checked on their staffs, too – they're all clean."

The Interpol man looked at the name on the piece of paper. "Stella – Frozen Food Specialists. Anything definite?"

Riccio smiled, grimly. "That depends on you." He opened a folder and passed a photograph across. "Recognize him?"

The Hawk stared at the hard, vicious face of the man in the photograph. "I'm not likely to forget the man who tried to drown me." He looked up. "He was at the Café Luna and at the warehouse."

"He also drives a refrigeration truck for the Stella Fruit Company! Your very accurate description of him was a great help." He stood up and gave a satisfied yawn. "Well – now we know, we can move in and grab the lot of 'em!"

The Hawk shook his head, thoughtfully. " 'Fraid not," he said. "Superintendent Bill Downs just 'phoned through from the Yard. He's checked on every firm that handles frozen Italian produce. They're all absolutely in the clear!"

The Questura man's Latin temperament got the better of him. "Then his men have had their eyes shut!" he exploded. "There *must* be an outlet that end!"

The Hawk grinned. "Take it easy," he said. "Bill's men are among the finest policemen in the world. If those firms weren't on the square, they'd have been spotted in a second." He rubbed his chin. "But you're right – obviously *somebody* receives the stuff at the London end. Also, I'm convinced that the man behind the set-up was the Englishman who slugged me."

"I wish you'd got a good look at him," grunted Riccio.

"So do I," said The Hawk. "But I did hear his voice – I won't forget that!"

"Right now, that doesn't help us," shrugged the Captain. "What we want is a lead to the London contact."

The Hawk stood up. "Well, there's one way to do that. I'm going to follow their next shipment every inch of the way from Rome to Covent Garden – and back, if it's necessary!"

Brrrrm! Brrrrm! The exhaust of the little Italian sports car gave a healthy crackle as The Hawk changed down before swinging into the tight, almost right-angled bend. Rome, Florence, Bologna, Milan, were all behind him. Now they had left Stresa, after skirting the South Western side of Lake Maggiore, and were heading for the Italo-Swiss border. The last town before the border, Domodossola, had been a good place to stop for a quick snack. With the twisting Alpine roads ahead, The Hawk could afford to let the heavy refrigerator truck have plenty of start, otherwise he would almost certainly arouse suspicion

"Every inch of the way from Rome to Covent Garden . . ."

if he was forced to sit on the lorry's tail. "Give them plenty of rope," he thought, with grim humour. He had been using the same system all the way from Rome – sometimes letting his quarry get as much as 10 miles ahead before burning the road to close the gap.

Suddenly, as he flicked the car round the last few yards of the long bend, The Hawk gave a gasp of surprise. Fifty yards ahead was the Stella truck – and it was stationary! He stamped hard on the brake and tyres screamed as the car slid to a halt. The Interpol man jumped out.

Crack! Simultaneous with the sharp report, The Hawk collapsed in the centre of the road, motionless.

"What now?" The smaller of the two Italian thugs asked the question as they stood over The Hawk's body.

"It's him all right – Mister Weber of Zurich he called himself. I don't know how he's done it, but he's supposed to be dead. I dumped him in the river myself!"

"Let's get him out of here. Somebody might come any second!" The first man was starting to panic.

"I'll handle it," growled the other. "You get in the truck and carry on. First place you come to, telephone the boss in London – tell him what's happened. Here . . ." He passed over a slip of paper . . . "You'll want the number. I'll catch you up in his car!"

Moments later, the huge refrigeration truck rumbled out of sight round the next bend. The big Italian bent down to lug The Hawk's body to the side of the road. It was his last conscious action! The Hawk's hands shot out and grabbed the man's lapels – a second later he was flying headfirst across the road from a powerful stomach throw. His head hit a rock and he lay still!

The Hawk dumped the unconscious man into the passenger-seat of his car. The Italian thug was no better at shooting people than he was at drowning them – the bullet had missed him by inches. He slid lithely into the driver's seat and started the engine. He had to stop the Stella truck before the driver could telephone London. Once the gang boss knew he *hadn't* died in the river, he would realize the police must know much more than he believed, and would probably cease operations! The Hawk's toe pressed harder on the accelerator and swept on to where the Alpine road dropped sharply in a series of hairpin bends before it began the long climb into the higher mountains.

It was on the second bend that he caught up with the truck. He tucked his nose in behind it and flipped the horn. If he could bluff the driver into thinking his mate was driving, he would let him overtake – then he would block the road ahead with his own car. Obediently, the truck pulled in to the right on the next short straight section and The Hawk started to bore through. He was only halfway along the length of the truck when the driver spotted him in the rear-view mirror and wrenched his wheel over to the left. The heavy vehicle swung out and the Interpol man had to almost stand on his brakes to avoid being crushed against the sheer face of the pass. On and on thundered the truck, with the sports car tailing it. The Hawk felt a reluctant admiration for the man's driving as he swung the huge truck around the bends, baulking his attempts to pass. Suddenly, he made a mistake. On the next hairpin he took the truck a fraction too wide. The Hawk's foot slammed down on the accelerator . . . there was just room for the little sports car between the truck and a sheer drop of several hundred feet. Desperately, the driver tried to retrieve his error and force the little car off the road. He was too late – The Hawk's judgment was perfect. He cut past with only inches to spare!

Superintendent Bill Downs, accompanied by two Customs Officers, crossed the vehicle yard of Allman Garages and approached the tall, well dressed man who stood watching the Stella refrigerator truck manoeuvre into its parking space.

"Mr Allman?" he asked, politely.

"Yes," said the man. "What can I do for you?" The door of the driver's cab opened and The Hawk jumped down.

"Remember me?" His eyes were hard. "Weber of Zurich – the one you *didn't* murder!" He nodded to Downs. "Take him, Bill!" He watched unemotionally as handcuffs were slipped on the dumbstruck man. He turned to the Customs men. "Strip the inside of the truck and you'll find the contraband stacked between the refrigeration pipes. Pretty smart – we might have gone on looking among the fruit importers instead of the garage where the trucks parked. A twenty-four hour stop gave them plenty of time to unload at leisure." He smiled at Allman. "Fortunately, your driver obliged me with the telephone number!"

KALGAN, JUNGLE BOY

by George Forrest

Kalgan lived among the wild animals in the jungle but when a small white boy wanted to join him, he was accused of kidnapping him and this led Kalgan into a great deal of trouble.

Hssst! Tiki, someone is watching us!"

With a sudden whisper, Kalgan, a bronzed figure clad in a leopard-skin, grew tense and watchful. Tiki, his parrot, fluttered warningly into the air.

The African jungles were silent; a low breeze stirred the tall grass. The antelope steaks Kalgan had been roasting swung forgotten above the camp-fire. But Maza, Kalgan's fully grown lion cub, stiffened and gave an uneasy growl.

"Man!" Kalgan breathed.

His senses told him this. For Kalgan had been reared in the jungles, and his instincts were those of the wild. His one wish was to be a champion athlete, a boxer, and anything else. Beside the hunting-knife that hung at his waist dangled some old boxing gloves a passing trader had given him. He stroked them now as he stood very still.

Friend or foe? Who was the watcher? Maza, the lion, bared its teeth.

"Wah, we find out, Maza!" Kalgan decided, his eyes sparkling. Perhaps it is some warrior who can do battle with me? I have not used my ju-ju gloves for weeks."

Excitement set his blood racing. His keen gaze again scanned the tall grasses and trees. At one spot, fifty yards to the left, the grasses moved a different way to the wind.

"Ugh, a poor hunter! He cannot keep still," Kalgan chuckled. "A white man – we have little to fear. I, Kalgan, must show him how to stalk."

Mischief was in Kalgan's broad smile. Here was sport, and perhaps a battle as well! He tossed his tawny mane of hair from his eyes and reached up to seize the trailing vine from a tree. To the bewildered watcher it seemed next that Kalgan vanished completely. No sound, no visible movement; the watcher could now only see empty space by the flickering camp-fire. Like a flash the jungle boxer whirled into the treetops and began circling to get near the grass where the mysterious watcher crouched.

Soundlessly Kalgan dropped down to earth, then moved cautiously through the tall grasses. No tell-tale rustle served to give him away. He came on the crouching watcher from behind.

"Awarreeeeeeeee!" Kalgan whooped–and sprang on to the figure. Then he jerked back, open-mouthed with surprise.

"Gosh!" gasped the startled "spy" sprawling head-over-heels. "Oh crumbs!"

Kalgan found himself staring at an indignant and freckle-faced schoolboy–a sturdy youngster in khaki shorts and shirt, and with a pair of boxing gloves slung at his waist.

"Gosh!" the spy exclaimed again, staring at Kalgan admiringly. He whistled, his eyes open wide. "Hallo! I'm Jimmy. And you're Kalgan–I've been looking for you. I've heard all about you from the tribesmen at . . ." Jimmy broke off. "I've come to join you in the jungle," he added.

Kalgan blinked. He was too startled to say very much. A keen glance at Jimmy's tattered and stained clothes showed that he'd spent several days in the open.

"You see, I've run away," Jimmy grinned.

He watched Kalgan a little uneasily.

"Wah!" Kalgan's face lit up with pride. He threw back his head and laughed heartily. "Jimmy, I like you," he said.

"Gosh, then–then I can stay with you?" Jimmy burst out.

Kalgan nodded, his own expression as boyish as Jimmy's. He asked no questions, for to him it was all very simple. This white boy, a boy after Kalgan's own heart, had heard of him and wanted to live the sort of life that he did.

"You wish to be warrior!" Kalgan chuckled. "It is good. I, Kalgan, want to be the greatest in the world. Come!"

He strode lithely back to the camp. As they entered the clearing Maza rose quickly to greet them.

"K-Kalgan!" Jimmy bit back a cry for help. He paled a little, but refused to flinch when the lion came right up to him. "H-he's a beauty!" he exclaimed rather shakily.

Kalgan, who'd been looking on closely, nodded in delighted approval. Jimmy's pluck pleased him.

"Him Maza. He like you," he grinned. "Wah, Kalgan make a great warrior of you!" He sat down before the rather burned antelope steaks, drew his hunting-knife, and tossed it across.

"Eat!" he commanded.

The excited Jimmy cut a portion of meat with the knife. Coolly he stroked Maza's head. Tiki, the parrot, settled down on his shoulder.

Kalgan watched his new partner, and felt happier than he'd been for some while. But as he looked at the new boxing gloves Jimmy carried, a sudden thought entered his head.

Perhaps Jimmy knew some great warriors—warriors who would fight with the gloves! Kalgan leaned forward and asked him.

"You see, Jimmy, I seek to do battle," he added. "In the jungle it is hard for warriors like us to get fights. Do you know of any mighty white warrior?"

"Oh! I–er—" Jimmy went very red. He was about to say something, but changed his mind all at once. "No one like you, Kalgan!" he blurted.

"Ugh!" Kalgan shrugged disappointedly.

He reached across to take his hunting-knife back.

But at that moment he saw something else—something that had fallen from his new partner's pocket. It was a photograph, an open-air snap of a husky boxer crouched in a fighting pose! It had been taken before a background of tropical shrubs.

Kalgan frowned puzzledly, yet gave no sign of what he had seen. Jimmy, however, suddenly noticing the snap, grabbed it up and thrust it back in his pocket.

Who was the boxer? Kalgan was mystified and very curious. Why had Jimmy been afraid to explain? Could the white warrior be Jimmy's enemy?

"That's it–Jimmy afraid," Kalgan breathed. "Jimmy's enemy is my enemy, too! I think I go and seek this white warrior!"

His eyes sparkled, for the "magic picture" had told a great deal. The tropical shrubs shown in the background were jungle shrubs, but with a very queer leaf. There was only one place Kalgan knew of where they grew.

"M'lassa! So this white warrior lives near the village of M'lassa," he murmured. "Wah, I seek him–but without Jimmy knowing. Kalgan will do battle with this boxer!"

The meal was finished. Excitedly Kalgan sprang to his feet. He was itching to get into action.

"Jimmy, you see great battle soon!" he burst out. "Come, we have a journey to make!"

A little while later a native canoe was forging along one of the African rivers. Crocodiles lazily edged from its path; a big hippo watched it short-temperedly. Jimmy, bubbling over with questions, sat facing Kalgan, who paddled the canoe swiftly along.

"I not answer questions. This is a surprise," Kalgan chuckled. "I have promised you–you see Kalgan fight."

"But where? When?" the eager Jimmy exclaimed.

Little did he guess Kalgan's plan.

In two days the journey was made. There were many halts. The delighted Kalgan taught his new partner jungle lore, and in return was shown how to use a catapult. They tethered the canoe by a low, muddy bank. The river was a dangerous and little-used route to M'lassa!

Jimmy, who had noticed nothing familiar as yet, stared to where the wide river forged across steamy, dark jungle. A sinister-looking, shadowy island rose from the muddy waters up-stream.

"Gosh, Kalgan, that looks exciting!" he blurted. "I'd like to take the canoe across over there."

"Ugh, it is Spirit Island! Bad ju-ju, Jimmy!" Kalgan said grimly. "You not understand–no one ever go there."

He was superstitious, and had heard strange tales of the island. Even the fiercest tribes gave it a wide berth. It was said that whoever went there was never heard of again!

"Sounds good. It'd make a great hiding-place," Jimmy chuckled. "Phew, it does look a bit eerie, though!"

"Kalgan no coward–but Kalgan no go there," Kalgan shrugged.

They left the canoe and began to make for M'lassa. They were almost there when Jimmy looked around and gave a gasp of dismay.

"Kalgan, this–this is M'lassa!" He grabbed Kalgan's arm. "Please, we've got to go back!"

"Kalgan understand. You have enemy here," Kalgan said quietly. "Perhaps enemy hurt you?" he asked. His narrowed eyes gleamed. "Wah, I find this warrior and—"

The words were never completed, for from the village clearing three white men suddenly strode into view. They wore grim, rather worried expressions, and behind them were a number of natives. And the powerfully built man at the head of the party was the boxer that had been shown in Jimmy's photograph!

"Oh!"

Jimmy wheeled round and ran for dear life. The men saw him. There were wild shouts. Yelling, they dived in pursuit. The crowd of natives suddenly surged forward.

"The warrior! Don't worry, Jimmy. Kalgan not let him catch you–or hurt you again!" Kalgan thundered.

"Awarreeeeee!" he whooped, and sprang forward to meet the men.

He would save Jimmy and gain a fight, too!

"Back, jackals! You chase Kalgan's friend!"

Startled natives paused in their tracks as Kalgan whirled to meet them, eyes blazing. His war-cry rose, a challenge on the air.

Two powerful tribesmen charged forward, but Kalgan's muscular arm hurled them aside. With a lightning move he reached out and seized the trunk of a coconut palm tree.

His bronzed muscles swelled as Kalgan braced himself and, with a superb show of strength, bent the palm back by brute force. He laughed mockingly as he suddenly released it.

The young palm flew back to its former position, acting like some great catapult. As startled monkeys flashed from the foliage of the tree a shower of coconuts catapulted at the pursuers, making them scatter out of the way for safety.

"Awarreeeeeee! My friend teach me that!" Kalgan whooped. "He have catapult – he say it great weapon." But his face grew grim as the three white men still came hurrying on.

Was Jimmy safe? Had Jimmy had time to get away? Kalgan's thoughts were still for his young friend. But equally grimly the boxer of the photograph advanced. He was Cliff Mason, a young but extremely promising heavyweight.

"So it was you! You lured Jimmy away!" Cliff Mason rasped. "Get out of my way! I'm going after him to bring him back!"

"You lie! He came to me!" Kalgan thundered. "You his enemy! Ugh, I avenge him, you coward!"

To Kalgan it all seemed quite obvious. Jimmy, badly treated by this powerful white warrior, had come to Kalgan for safety.

"I said I'm coming!" Cliff Mason gritted.

He suddenly whirled forward with startling speed.

"We'll get Jimmy, Cliff!" another man shouted.

Kalgan, although longing for battle, turned his head to get one fleeting glance. He had to make sure Jimmy was safe. Too late, he glimpsed Cliff Mason upon him.

The young heavyweight took one step. He threw a right that was as fast as the darting tongue of a serpent. It caught Kalgan high on the head. Wham! The jungle seemed to revolve in a circle around Kalgan. The next he knew he was picking himself up from the ground. The white warrior, his two friends, and the tribesmen were pelting along a jungle path, following the direction Jimmy had taken.

"Kalgan fail. He not fail again!" vowed Kalgan.

He was furious with himself, bitterly disappointed, and angry. He must finish the battle with Cliff Mason–and win!

"But Jimmy–I forget Jimmy!" he panted. "Fool! Kalgan fail his friend, too!"

Jimmy's pursuers were now hot in pursuit. With a thrill of dismay, Kalgan realised his young friend might be caught. And he, alone, could not keep back a crowd. But jungle life had made Kalgan think fast. This natural speed now came to his aid. Whirling, he cupped his hands to his lips and uttered a queer, thrilling cry:

"Aaooeeeeeeeee!"

"Awarreeeeeeeee!"

The effect of that cry no white man would have ever believed. Jimmy's pursuers paused in horror at what happened next. The trees above them seemed to grow thick with monkeys; a wild chattering rose on the air.

"Great Scott! Duck!" Cliff Mason yelled warningly.

A coconut whirled down, to barely miss him, from above. Shrieking and squealing in fury, small apes and monkeys hurled down everything in their reach at the party. The pursuing natives took panic and fled.

"Jungle-man's ju-ju!" they gasped. Superstitious fear made them shudder. Jimmy, running wildly for all he was worth, glanced back and chuckled in delight. Kalgan's eerie cries still rang on the air.

"Good old Kalgan! I'll have to get him to teach me that!" Jimmy panted. "Gosh, that's if I can stay with him that long! I told Cliff I'd live a jungle boy's life."

He streaked on towards the river again. But Kalgan was now moving as well.

"Awarreeeeeee!" Kalgan sang out in triumph, and swung through the treetops to where the dismayed white men stood. He dropped down and hit the ground, running.

"You again! You let Jimmy get away!" Cliff Mason spun towards him, tight-lipped. His fists clenched. "You don't care if he dies in the jungle. You let a kid risk his life with all those wild beasts."

"I—" Kalgan's furious reply died on his lips.

He suddenly realised the perils that Cliff Mason meant—perils that the jungle boxer had grown used to. But there was something else, too. For Cliff Mason did not look or sound like a bad man. There was a genuine concern in his voice. Kalgan started as Cliff Mason went on.

"Jimmy happens to be my young brother," the heavyweight gritted. What's more, he was happy with us —until he heard these wild tales about you. Now he's crazy about becoming a jungle boy."

Fists bunched, Cliff Mason took a threatening step forward. But Kalgan's face had gone very white.

So he'd been wrong, the jungle boxer thought with dismay. He was aghast at the mistake he had made.

Kalgan recalled the punch from Cliff Mason that had floored him. It hurt his pride—but the battle must wait. At all cost Jimmy had to come first. Where was he? Was he still safe?

"Put your fists up! Afraid?" flamed Cliff Mason. He brushed aside the restraining hands of his friends. "Jimmy's escaped us – but I'll settle with you!" "Later!" Kalgan whirled on his heel. "Jimmy! I find Jimmy!" he panted. "But you pay for those words later on!"

The following instant he was swinging through the trees. He must find Jimmy Mason again, see what his young friend had to say. And he was anxious for Jimmy's safety.

Now leaping and bounding, the jungle boxer whirled along overgrown paths. He followed Jimmy's tracks, which led towards the river.

"Jimmy! Jimmy! Kalgan seeks you!" he called.

He reached the muddy bank of the river and stared with horror at the place where he had moored the canoe. The canoe was no longer there! A watching crocodile edged across from the mud.

His bronzed body tensed, Kalgan stared up-stream towards the dark shadows of the sinister, overgrown Spirit Island. The truth dawned on him, and he stood very still.

"It'd make a great hiding-place!" Jimmy had laughed.

Kalgan suddenly knew where Jimmy had gone.

"The island–he's gone to hide on Spirit Island." Superstitious fear drained the blood from his lips. "Jimmy go there so white men don't catch him. Island bad ju-ju. But Jimmy not afraid."

Kalgan shuddered at the unknown terrors the island might hold. But Jimmy had gone there; the thought forced him to act.

"Kalgan bring him back!" Kalgan breathed grimly. "Wah, then I fight the white warrior who speak bitter words!

"Awarreeeeeeeeee!" he thundered defiantly. "No man shall say Kalgan afraid."

In a flat, racing dive Kalgan plunged into the river. He was going to Spirit Island!

Jimmy Mason came first, then his fight with Cliff Mason!

Using a magnificent yet natural crawl, Kalgan swam swiftly through the sour-smelling waters. Tiki, his parrot, suddenly fluttered down from above.

"Wah, Tiki, so you are not afraid, either!" It was a relief to Kalgan not to be quite alone. "It is good. We seek Jimmy together."

In a whirl of spray, he reached the dark bank and bounded out, his knife in his teeth. Fear caught him again as he became aware of the uncanny silence. The shadows of Spirit Island looked forbidding.

"Tiki, the air is evil."

Kalgan gripped his knife and sought to conquer his fear. Where was Jimmy?

"Jimmy! Jimmy!" he called, his heart pounding.

Then it happened–a cry that shattered the spell. A frightened, despairing voice answered back.

"Help, Kalgan! Come quickly!" came that pulse-quickening appeal.

That did it! A thousand devils couldn't have stopped Kalgan now. All the ju-ju in the world didn't matter!

"Kalgan come!"

The jungle boxer whirled forward. Swinging from creepers and vines, Kalgan traced the sound. He burst into a round, trampled clearing.

In a flash he took in the queer scene. Every detail imprinted itself in his mind.

Jimmy, white-faced, but gallantly clutching his catapult, stood before what had evidently been a shrine at some time, a semi-circle of weather-cracked stones. Rotted "gods", carved in wood, looked down eerily.

But it was not to the stones Kalgan looked. His gaze was fixed on a pale massive animal at the other side of the clearing. It was the lumbering shape of a white, pig-eyed rhinoceros –a freak monster of that bad–tempered breed!

Of course, it was a ju-ju monster; Kalgan knew that at once. No normal rhino ever grew that colour or size. But any rhinoceros was always left severely alone. For their vicious and uncertain temper made even the most fearless of beasts wary of crossing their path.

"The ju-ju!" Kalgan gasped. "This is his island–he owns it all."

He now understood why the island was always avoided.

The freak rhino sensed Kalgan, but its eyes never left Jimmy. He had disturbed it feeding, and that was enough. With an ear-splitting bellow, it charged.

Several tons of short-sighted fury launched themselves at the boy, who even at that moment had pluck enough to fire his catapult. Jimmy, who had successfully dodged once before, knew that this charge meant the end for him. But—

"Awaarreeeeeeeeeeee!" came a wild battle-cry.

Kalgan, moving with eye–dazzling speed, swung forward from the low bough of a tree. Feet-first, he hurtled through space, to land astride the charging brute's back.

The rhino changed direction–changed enough for Jimmy to dodge death by a foot. A squeal of maddened fury tore the echoes.

"The ju-ju! Of course, I die now!"

Kalgan muttered.

He was surprised to discover that spirit magic had not struck him dead. He decided to live as long as he could.

"Run, Jimmy–to the river!" he shouted. "Find the canoe–get away!"

"But—" The reluctant Jimmy realised he must obey.

The raging rhino had forgotten about the boy now. All its fury was directed towards the man on his back–two muscular hands had clamped on to one of the beast's ears.

Squealing and bellowing the giant rhino crashed deliberately against stones and trees – did everything to hurl Kalgan off. Trees splintered and crashed down to the undergrowth. But always Kalgan's legs and body were out of the way. He rode the brute with the nimble skill of a circus monkey riding a dog.

The queer shrine in the clearing was ruined. The rhino, stunned by the very force of its deliberate collisions, suddenly decided to roll on to its side.

"Wah!" Kalgan whooped.

In a backward somersault, he flashed through the air. The rhino, crashing down in its fury, glimpsed a bronzed body swinging into the trees.

"Kalgan wins! He beats the ju-ju!" cheered Kalgan.

He sped to the river, where Jimmy already had his canoe safely afloat.

"Gosh, you–you beat it, Kalgan!" Jimmy blurted out shakily. "You saved me, and—"

He looked down uneasily before Kalgan's stern glance.

"Jimmy, you run away from your brother and friends. It is not good."

Kalgan tried not to smile.

"You won't send me back?" Jimmy burst out. "You–you promised me, Kalgan. You've promised to make me a great warrior like you. Kalgan, you can't send me back!"

The plea touched Kalgan – he suddenly felt lonely. But he knew that for Jimmy the jungle life was not right. And still he could not go back on his word!

"Jimmy" – Kalgan made up his mind as a sudden thought entered his head – "we are both warriors – there is a warrior's way out."

"What way?" Jimmy Mason burst out.

"I fight your brother to win you," Kalgan answered. It was an effort to force the words out. "If I beat your brother you stay with me. But if I lose, then you must return."

"You won't lose, Kalgan–you won't!" Jimmy Mason's eyes shone with hope. "You're the greatest fighter in all the world, Kalgan! I shall stay with you and—"

"The fight decide that," Kalgan said slowly.

It was an hour or so later that Kalgan, accompanied only by Tiki, the parrot, strode into the village of M'lassa and delivered the strange challenge to Cliff Mason.

"I get it – Jimmy's the prize!" Cliff Mason snapped. "You've asked for it. I'll fight you all right!"

The gloves were donned, and Cliff's pals volunteered to act as seconds. The battle started in a training ring at the rear of a house. Tiki, the parrot, fluttered round, shrieking encouragement.

Cliff Mason was fast and undoubtedly good; his ring-craft baffled Kalgan, but Kalgan had uncanny speed.

Smothering and weathering all the punishment Cliff Mason could give, he fought back with a ferocity nothing could weaken. The first two rounds were Mason's, but from Round No. 3 onwards the fight slowly turned in Kalgan's favour.

Again the jungle boxer bored in, strength and speed triumphing over trained skill. He battered Mason back to the ropes; game, but beaten, Cliff Mason fought back.

The fight was Kalgan's; all he needed was one solid finishing punch.

He had "softened up" Mason, left him ready for the kill. Suddenly, surprisingly, Kalgan seemed to slow up.

Cliff Mason, beaten, weary, and despairing for his brother, watched the jungle boxer through weary eyes. He saw Kalgan's guard suddenly drop. With wild hope, Cliff Mason stepped in. He threw the last punch he had left.

Clop! Kalgan walked right into it. Flame-specked darkness exploded before him.

"Jimmy! I've won Jimmy!" Cliff Mason gulped.

His friends crowded around him. At last Kalgan came to his feet. Quietly he shook hands with Cliff Mason, congratulated him, and told him where Jimmy was waiting. Slowly, very slowly, he walked back through the jungle. His face was sad, his heart heavy as lead.

"Kalgan lose!" he told himself bitterly. "I do it for Jimmy, because I know—" Kalgan broke off.

He turned, to see Cliff Mason running after him.

"Kalgan, I— thanks a lot." Cliff Mason smiled through battered lips. "I'm no fool – you had me beat all the way. I think I know what that punch cost you."

He reddened, and held out his hand. A delighted, happy smile lit up Kalgan's face. The warrior understood! It made things different. He gripped the hand very hard.

"I'll look after Jimmy," Cliff Mason said softly. "Some day I'll tell him the truth–tell him how you let me beat you."

"Wah!"

With a merry whoop, Kalgan swung into the treetops. Tiki, the parrot, met him. Maza, the lion, roared welcomingly from nearby.

"Jungle cruel – no good for Jimmy!" Kalgan exclaimed, knowing that he'd done right. "Now Kalgan go back to his friends!"

THE WORLD OF GIANT
BUTTERFLIES

Captain Condor of the Space Marines landed on a planet inhabited by a people like giant butterflies. But he found that an earth-man was trying to capture them and take them back to earth and that was something that Condor would not allow.

"Captain, this is one of the most fascinating planets we've come across in a long time," declared Sergeant Willis, of the Space Marines, as he steered the two-seater helicopter scout car over a vast expanse of lush green jungle. Captain Condor, who commanded a Space Patrol survey ship, nodded in agreement.

"People think our job is all glamour," he agreed. "They don't realise how often we're disappointed, that most of the planets we visit are either dried up and dead, frozen and dark, covered with seas of molten lava, or wrapped in atmospheres of poisonous gases."

"We've hit the jackpot this time," Willis nodded.

Condor's survey ship had landed on Cygnes III forty-eight hours before, to find the planet a wonderland teeming with new and strange life-forms. Already the ship's teams of biologists, zoologists, botanists, and geologists were busy with recording equipment, gathering information.

"The important thing now is to get our preliminary survey finished quickly to get the planet registered and put under the protection of the Space Patrol, before any get-rich-quick crooks hear of it and start to ruin it," said Condor.

Willis skimmed the helicar past a soaring, jungle-clad cliff-face. The cliff was pitted with openings, all precisely circular as if they had been designed by a mathematician. Suddenly the whole cliff-face appeared to blossom into flashing rainbow colours. Out from the openings came a whirling swarm of beings like giant, gaudily coloured butterflies. They swirled in many-hued flocks around the survey craft.

Condor's crew had dubbed them "the butterfly people", although so far not much had been learned about them. They were intensely inquisitive beings, and showed great curiosity in the behaviour of the survey team, but at the same time they were cautious and timid, and never allowed the Earthmen to come near enough to examine them closely.

"What a sight!" exclaimed Willis. "Do you reckon they're intelligent, Captain?"

Condor was busy with a colour-camera.

"They must be. They obviously built these cliff dwellings. I think they'll turn out to be at least as intelligent as human beings, once we gain their confidence and get to know them," he said.

The wheeling formations of butterfly people broke up as Willis started the helicar descending into a green river valley where the survey ship was based. When Condor alighted, and started towards the hut which he was using as a temporary headquarters, a strange creature darted out of the grass and scuttled towards him on a dozen stubby legs. It was one of a species that the men had dubbed "curlybears".

All curlybears were covered in tufts of fur, the fur was vividly coloured, and no two appeared exactly alike. They grew up to about five feet long, and their legs were so short that they appeared to undulate over the ground. Of all the many creatures which had been found on the planet so far the curlybears were the only ones which showed no fear of the explorers. They were excitable, playful, mischievous.

This one bounded alongside Condor, rubbed itself against him, then reared up on two pairs of hind legs, put another pair of feet on his chest, and tried to rub noses with him. Condor picked up a stick and threw it. The curlybear uttered a peculiarly gruff barking sound, rather like a sea-lion, and galloped excitedly after the stick.

Sergeant Willis had gone to the radio hut to see if there were any messages. Now he came running.

"There's been a news-leak about this place. Cy Ledger's ship just landed, about five miles from here," he reported.

Condor's face darkened. Cy Ledger represented the type of space riff-raff he most detested. His speciality was to scour the planets for bizarre forms of life which he could sell to freak shows, menageries and fair grounds.

There was no telling how much misery Cy Ledger had caused dealing in alien creatures, shipping them half-way across the galaxy to be put in cages or to be trained as performing freaks. Interstellar law forbade dealing in alien creatures above a certain level of intelligence, but Ledger was crafty, and knew all the tricks for evading the law.

"We'll go and see what he's up to," scowled Condor. "I always said I'd nail him one of these days. If he tries anything here—"

Condor, the sergeant, and two marines took a hover-car to the spot where Ledger's collecting ship had landed. The first thing they saw was a curlybear, trapped glumly in a barred cage.

"Ledger, you're under arrest for violating the alien protection laws," Condor announced with satisfaction. "I'm impounding your ship. Willis, take Ledger back and lock him up. You other two, remain on his ship to make sure it doesn't take off."

"This is victimisation!" howled Ledger. "You know the law. This planet isn't protected yet. I've a perfect right—"

"Intelligent life is protected everywhere," Condor retorted.

"I know that," grinned Ledger craftily. "Now these butterfly people, I bet I could get a hundred thousand apiece for those, but I'm not touching them."

"Curlybears are intelligent, too," Condor insisted.

"You can't prove that," challenged Ledger. "I demand you get my lawyer."

"Don't worry—you'll have your lawyer," promised Condor.

"Captain, shall I turn the curlybear loose?" asked Willis.

"No. For the time being we need him in the cage, as evidence," Condor said.

It took about twelve hours for Ledger's lawyer to arrive in a patrol ship. With him came a worried, fussy Space Patrol official named Potter, who drew Condor aside.

"I hope you know what you're doing," he muttered. "You've been heard to say more than once that you'd nail Ledger one day. Headquarters is worried. If he brings a case against us for wrongful arrest—"

"Come and see the evidence for yourself," invited Condor. "I intend demonstrating that curlybears are intelligent."

The curlybear was coiled in the bottom of the cage. It looked as if it was asleep, or ill. The bright shimmering colours had gone out of its fur, which was beginning to look like dry, matted grass.

"The creature looks sick!" exclaimed Potter in alarm.

"It was all right while I was taking care of it," protested Ledger. "I understand these things. It's my trade. If it's ill, it's Condor's fault."

The lawyer was beginning to look pleased.

"We shall bring counter-charges, Captain Condor. Causing damage to my client's property. Cruelty to an alien creature—'

"Condor, get your ship's doctor here," cried Potter. "If this creature dies, and it's proved to be your fault, there will be a scandal."

When the ship's doctor arrived, Potter appealed to him wildly.

"This creature's sick. Do something for it," he begged.

"I'm a doctor, not a vet!"

"There must be something you can try. It's oxygen breathing. Put it in an oxygen tent."

The tent didn't help. The curlybear looked in a bad way. Its fur was moulting in handfuls. It was now curly, round, with its head to its tail, looking like a great, leathery doughnut.

"There's hardly any sign of a heart-beat," announced the doctor.

"Well, Condor, do you still insist on arresting my client?" asked Ledger's lawyer with a smirk. "This is going to make a nasty story if it comes to court—a Space Patrol officer, protector of the rights of aliens, allowing one to die miserably in captivity."

"Who says it's dead?" demanded Condor.

The doctor shot him an unhappy look.

"I'm afraid—"

Condor raised his arm and pointed.

A flock of brightly coloured butterfly people came whirling in over the tree-tops.

They came closer, drifting round on gay, gently beating wings.

42

From the coiled, dried-up looking creature on the ground came a sudden noise like a pistol shot.

"It's splitting open!" yelled Potter.

With a rainbow flash of colour two of the butterfly people alighted softly.

The leathery ring which had been the curlybear was breaking in half. From within came a brilliant gleam of blue and scarlet. A pair of dazzling wings emerged.

The two butterfly people extended tentacle-like limbs to help the struggling creature inside, and another of their own kind emerged from within. All three suddenly rose into the air, and the whole flock whirled in excitement.

Everybody, except Condor, was looking thunderstruck.

He was smiling.

"You should have guessed," he said. "The curlybears and the butterfly people are two forms of the same creature. The curlybears are the young ones, which explains why we found them so playful and amusing. They are like giant caterpillars, and they have to go through a chrysalis stage before they become adult."

Potter sighed with relief and turned to Ledger's lawyer.

"Your client attempted to steal the infant young of an intelligent species. That's a crime on any planet!"

"But I didn't know—" protested Ledger.

"Ignorance is no excuse," snapped his lawyer. "I've got you out of a lot of scrapes, Cy Ledger, but there's nothing I can do to pull you out of this one."

Condor turned to Potter.

"If you're going back to headquarters you can take Ledger with you, and get him out of our way. We've an important job to do here, learning about the butterfly people."

Now, turn to page 109 for another exciting Captain Condor story.

THE PERIL IN THE POOL

Barry Barnes loved his dolphins with all his heart for he had trained them all himself. That was why a new handler was jealous and tried to murder him. But it was Dolly, the dolphin, who came to the rescue and showed her affection for Barry in her own very special way.

Barry Barnes frowned as he heard the angry bark of the dolphins. His pace quickened as he strode towards the circular oceanarium in the early morning light. He reached the open-air pool where his trained dolphins circled, their flukes flailing the blue-green water. Then he saw the new handler, 'Slim' Fitch, with a basket of fish. Fitch was teasing the dolphins by tempting them to jump for a fish, then jerking his hand back at the last moment.

Barry's young face darkened like a thundercloud as he saw Dolly, his favourite, almost crash into the concrete rim of the pool in an attempt to seize her breakfast. His hand tightened on Fitch's shoulder and spun him round. "Stop that!" he snapped.

He took the basket and fed the dolphins himself. Slim Fitch stood glowering at him, his mouth set in a mean line. "Think you're somebody, don't you?" Fitch jeered. "Let me tell you . . ."

Barry cut in sharply. "No, let me tell you. Dolphins are intelligent animals, and they don't respond at all to punishment – that's why our training is based on a reward system."

"Is that so?" Fitch sneered. "Bet I could train 'em quicker and better my way."

"Maybe you could, and maybe you couldn't. One thing's certain though – you'll never do it your way while I'm around."

Slim Fitch pulled off his sweater. Stripped to swimming trunks, he dived into the pool. "Just watch me," he yelled, and grabbed the large plastic hoop Barry had trained his dolphins to jump through.

"Come out of it," Barry shouted, exasperated. It had taken him weeks of patience to perfect this act and he didn't want Fitch spoiling it now.

But Fitch thought he knew best. He swam in among the sleek dolphins, grabbed Dolly by a flipper and tried to force her through the hoop. Alarmed for her delicate skin, Dolly struggled to break free, lashing the water in a frenzy. Other dolphins planed through the pool, circling Fitch and Dolly, long jaws opened to reveal sharp teeth.

"Get out of the water!" Barry ordered curtly.

But Fitch suddenly lost his nerve as he saw the dolphins turn towards him. He mistook their play for hostility, dropped the hoop and grabbed up a stout wooden beam that lay on the concrete rim of the pool. He struck Dolly viciously across the head and she sank unconscious into the blue-green depths.

Immediately, the other dolphins gave vent to shrill distress calls and dived after her. Barry watched anxiously, hesitating to interfere. He knew she would drown unless she were brought promptly to the surface, for a dolphin cannot breathe underwater . . .

But the rest of the dolphins swam beneath Dolly and bore her back to the surface. They held her head above water until she regained consciousness.

Barry, in a towering rage, pulled Fitch out of the pool. "You're sacked," he shouted. "Now get out of here before I lose my temper!"

Muttering under his breath, Slim Fitch slunk away. Barry remained by the pool, watching Dolly intently. He was worried for her. She appeared to be swimming tilted over to one side, not quite upright. He separated her from the school and guided her into an inspection tank where he could keep an eye on her during the day. The dolphins gave three public performances, when they went through their repertory of tricks: leaping for fish, singing in chorus, and chasing a football.

Between each performance, Barry visited Dolly and made a fuss of her. She was fully recovered and seemed to be pining for her friends, so he let her back into the pool after the final show.

Late that night, when the lights went out over the oceanarium, Barry walked down to the pool again.

Dolly was swimming happily and whistled back immediately he signalled her. Her sleek, seven-foot body slid through the water to his side.

"Good girl," Barry said soothingly, and bent to stroke her. Playfully she took his hand in her beak and splashed water over him with her flipper. Barry felt relief; she was going to be all right. He knelt on the concrete rim of the pool, completely engrossed in the dolphin . . .

Slim Fitch came out of the darkness behind Barry, moving silently as a shadow. He gripped a cosh in his hand and his mean face was twisted in viciousness. He had returned to take his revenge.

He padded up behind Barry, arm raised to strike. At the last moment, Barry heard a scuffing sound and half-turned. He cried out, "Fitch!"

The cosh came down with stunning force and Barry toppled backwards into the pool and sank out of sight. Fitch watched with a gloating expression, but there was no sign of Barry coming to the surface. "Good riddance," he muttered and, darting a look round to make sure he was unobserved, hurried away.

Barry struggled as he sank. Fitch's blow seemed to have paralysed him. He couldn't swim and his lungs were bursting. He sank deeper into the dark depths, swallowed water – and blacked out.

Dolly saw her trainer sink under the water and circled him. He gave no sign of recognition and instinctively she knew something was wrong. She cleared her blowhole and gave the distress cry. The other dolphins gathered round Dolly . . . irritated, she shouldered them away. *She* was all right. She dived under the sinking, unconscious form and tried to lift it herself. Another dolphin joined her. And another. Between them, they bore Barry to the surface. Patiently, they held his head in the air till he recovered.

Barry Barnes came to suddenly, wondering what had happened. He spat out water and gulped in air. Then he remembered Fitch, and the blow . . . and realised his dolphins had saved his life. He swam to the concrete rim and hauled himself out of the pool. He went away and returned with a bucket of fish.

"Good girl, Dolly," he murmured. "That trick's worth something extra!"

As he walked away to phone the police, he thought: Slim Fitch was going to get something he wasn't expecting, too.

And Dolly was getting her revenge – by proxy. As this idea struck him, Barry laughed . . .

KAWA, THE CAMEL CHAMP

Kawa was the fastest camel in the whole of Africa and Selim his master was very proud of him. One day, Kawa helped to solve the mystery of a secret cave and earned the gratitude of the Sheikh.

Kawa, the camel, strutted proudly with the smooth, gliding movement of his kind, down the parched, sun-drenched main street of the Middle Eastern town of Petalia. Selim, his young Arab rider, perched on the top of his hump, leant forward and scrubbed the top of Kawa's head with the end of his stick.

"I am glad I got you specially groomed today, O Kawa," he said, "for we have been sent for by the Sheikh himself. He will see that I am keeping you in perfect trim for the Petalia camel race next week."

In reply, Kawa gave a shrill whistle in his throat. It was almost as if he understood every word that his master said.

Well might Selim be very proud of Kawa, for Kawa was a very special camel indeed. Unlike most camels, which were khaki in colour, and sometimes shaggy-coated and scruffy, Kawa was absolutely snow white, from his very muzzle to the tip of his long tail. Not only that, but he was very lithe – a racing camel, the pride and joy of the Sheikh el Sharaf, who owned him. Selim was one of the camel–drivers employed by the Sheikh, and it was his special job to look after Kawa.

Presently, Kawa swept in through the palace gateway and loped across a spacious courtyard, heading for a wide, impressive flight of stone steps, which lead to the entrance of the palace building itself.

Selim prodded Kawa with his stick, giving him the signal to fold his legs under him, and go down. Selim would go into the palace on foot. Camels weren't allowed to enter the Sheikh's magnificent residence!

But Kawa had other ideas. He didn't see why he should be left out, and not see the Sheikh. Kawa knew the Sheikh thought a lot of him and would be pleased to see him. Therefore he took no notice of Selim's signal and marched straight up the steps.

A giant guard in a splendid uniform and wearing a fez came dashing along the veranda to intercept the camel.

"Ho there!" he roared, looking up at Selim. "Have you taken leave of your senses? How dare a dog of a camel-driver take his beast into the palace of the Sheikh!"

"'Tis Kawa's idea, not mine!" retorted Selim. "You try to stop him, Hassim."

Hassim tried to bar Kawa's way. Kawa promptly gave him a disdainful look, whipped his neck round, seized the tassel of the guard's fez between his teeth and, with a swift jerk, tossed it down the palace steps.

Then, while Hassim dived to retrieve his headgear, Kawa barged through the doors and into the palace itself. Down the far end of a cool, stone-built hall, the Sheikh sat cross-legged on a pile of cushions on a platform. A man with a hawk-like face was making a low bow in front of the Sheikh. He was Ali Feisal, rich merchant from a neighbouring state.

Kawa didn't know that, and he couldn't have cared less if he had. All he saw was a human being standing between himself and the provider of all his camel food – the Sheikh himself.

Kawa thrust forward his long, swan-like neck, bared his yellow teeth, took the merchant by the back of his dhoti, and lifted him gently out of the way. For a moment Ali Feisal hung in mid-air, arms and legs waving like a crab in the beak of a seagull, and then he was deposited lightly on the stone floor.

"By the beard of my father!" screeched Ali Feisal. "Never have I been so insulted in my life. I'll kill that carrion camel—"

Next moment, whipping out his scimitar, the merchant sprang at Kawa, meaning to sever the camel's head with one blow.

But Kawa was no ordinary camel. He knew how to look after

himself. He jerked his neck out of the path of the hissing scimitar, shot out his head, and butted Ali Feisal in the stomach. Ali Feisal took three stiff-legged strides backward and then tripped over the edge of an ornamental pond. Splash! He sat down heavily in the water, and came up gasping with rage, while the fountain gently sprayed him from above.

Kawa took no further notice of Ali Feisal, but in turn bowed to the Sheikh, going down low, all four legs tucked under him. Selim took the opportunity to scramble down from Kawa's hump and also bow low alongside him.

Ali Feisal dragged himself from the pool and shook his fist angrily.

"A curse be on the white camel of the Sheikh el Sharaf!" he screeched. "I, Ali Feisal, shall not rest until I have had my revenge!"

And with those words the wealthy merchant stalked from the palace.

Meanwhile, the Sheikh was holding his sides and rocking with mirth.

"Ho, ho, ho!" he roared. "That's the best thing I've seen for years! Never did like that vulture, Ali Feisal. He is too grasping for money."

Then the Sheikh paused, smiling at Selim.

"I will overlook the fact that a camel has forced its way into my palace – for I have a special mission for you and Kawa, O Selim."

Kawa did not understand the instructions that the Sheikh then gave to his rider, Selim. It seemed, however, according to the Sheikh, that several camels had recently been reported missing from the el Sharaf herd. They were transport camels, and so Kawa did not have anything to do with them. But they were valuable, nonetheless. The Sheikh wanted Selim to ride out into the desert and see if he could find out how the camels were being rustled away.

"They usually disappear when they are left unattended in the Wadi el Dufra area," concluded the Sheikh. "I want you to take Kawa out on a training run in that direction at dawn tomorrow and see what you can discover."

And so, at first light the next morning, Kawa found himself skimming across the desert sand in the direction of Wadi el Dufra.

Kawa was revelling in the training run. He ran as fast as possible, neck craned forward. He didn't care that Selim's eyes were darting from side to side, ever on the alert for a clue to the camel rustlers who were at work in the area. All he was interested in was running hard, getting in training for the time when he would have to pit his running powers against the finest camels in the land, in the Petalia camel race.

Suddenly, in the growing light, Kawa was aware of a line of black dots ahead. Closer it came, and now he could see that it was a camel caravan, heading away from Petalia, well-loaded with merchandise. Presently, a lone camel detached itself from the caravan and came towards them, its rider with a rifle at the ready.

Kawa stared at the newcomer, and then felt his fur bristle. For the newcomer was a racing camel, like himself. And he was snow-white all over, too, with the exception of a dark brown patch over one eye.

"Ho, patched one!" shrilled Kawa in camel language. "Think you can run!"

"Huh! I can run faster than you," retorted Patch. "I come from Mistraba, where we have real camels, not broken down hacks like they have in Petalia. Not a single camel can match my speed!"

"Vain words!" snorted Kawa. "Let us see you prove it. We will race now, so that you can do so."

"So be it!" retorted Patch.

Next moment the two camels were tearing across the desert side by side, their hooves kicking up a miniature sandstorm as they went.

Strive though he did, Patch could not draw away from Kawa. So intent was Kawa on the race for its own sake that he didn't realise that he was being manoeuvred by the other up the gentle slope of an escarpment that ended in an almost sheer drop of thirty feet to the flat plain below.

Patch's rider was deliberately guiding his mount so that it would drive Kawa and Selim over the edge! For there was something about the caravan that he didn't want Selim to see, and he was deliberately out to get rid of the young camel-rider. And he would have succeeded, with any other camel but Kawa . . .

Suddenly, as both camels tore along, parallel to the escarpment edge, Patch turned a baleful glance at Kawa.

"This is where you go over the edge, boaster!" he sneered.

And he bore against Kawa, meaning to give him a shoulder charge.

"So that's the game!" shrilled Kawa indignantly. "You can't run, so you take to cheating!"

Without warning, Kawa came to a sudden halt, rearing up on his hind legs. And it was at that moment that Patch charged sideways.

Swoosh!

Instead of thumping against Kawa's side, Patch hit empty air! Next second, unable to stop himself, he went sailing over the edge of the steep drop. Crash! Thud! He rolled over and over down the slope, in a cloud of dust and small stones, and at last came to an abrupt stop against a rock, thirty feet below. Selim rode Kawa down a path to help the fallen rider, who had been k.o.'d. It was at that moment that Patch tried to stagger to his feet. He immediately collapsed, however, his foreleg badly injured.

Selim was bending over the injured beast seeing what he could do to help it, when a voice behind him made him swing around sharply. He saw a hawk-faced Arab staring down at him with hate-filled eyes. It was Ali Feisal, the leader of the caravan, who had come to investigate!

"So!" snapped the newcomer. "We meet again. And this time your fool white camel has gone too far. He has caused my white camel, which I was to ride in the Petalia camel race, to be injured. We will return at once to your master, the Sheikh el Sharaf. You will soon regret that you ever crossed the path of Ali Feisal!"

Ali Feisal! The man whom Kawa had made look a fool in the Sheikh's palace the previous day! What plan of revenge had the cunning merchant in mind?

Shortly afterwards, Selim, and Ali Feisal and his caravan, returned to the palace. The merchant was furious as he faced the Sheikh.

"I sent out a scout to meet your rider," Feisal stormed, "and what happens? Your camel rides my priceless racing camel over the edge of the wadi. My camel is injured – ruined. I demand compensation!"

"What compensation do you ask?" demanded the Sheikh, frowning. "Of course I will refuse you nothing of similar value to your loss."

"I demand two things!" retorted Ali Feisal. "First, that your camel man Selim be dismissed in disgrace. Second, that yon white camel, Kawa, be given to me to replace the one I lost."

"Very well," nodded the Sheikh. "I cannot refuse. If Selim has acted foolishly, he must bear the consequences. He shall be dismissed, and

Kawa is yours."

Kawa did not understand what all the conversation was about. But he knew that when he was led from Petalia, without Selim on his back, he was being parted from his master. And no Selim meant no race! For Kawa was a one-man camel, he would never let anyone other than Selim ride him.

Kawa was wily, however. He knew that if he tried to show fight now he would be whipped and prodded with spears. He looked at Ali Feisal, who was heading him from the palace courtyard triumphantly, and bared his yellow teeth.

Before very long he'd make the treacherous merchant sorry he had ever tried to part a racing camel from his master!

The next two days were torture to Kawa. He was led from the palace to the caravanserai, or enclosure from which trans-desert caravans started. There he was harnessed and loaded so heavily with goods that he could hardly stagger. It wasn't the load that Kawa minded – it was the fact that he, a white racing camel, was being treated as a transport animal!

Later, Kawa joined Ali Feisal's caravan, which left that night, heading for Mistraba, where Ali Feisal came from. After the caravan had travelled several hours, instead of keeping straight on towards its destination, it turned right, and camped in a small oasis, some way beyond the far end of the Wadi el Dufra. The oasis lay at the entrance of a winding canyon which led into the hills.

Whereas the other camels were allowed to go free for the halt, Kawa was kept tightly tethered and was given no food. Time passed. At last, on the second day, Ali Feisal himself approached Kawa, accompanied by two attendants carrying long spears.

Kawa was untethered. Swiftly the two attendants raised their spears, ready to prod him into submission if he gave trouble. But Kawa was motionless, eyeing Ali mildly, without even the slightest trace of a wicked glint in his eye.

"Ho, he is as docile as a mule that has run a hundred miles!" grinned one of the attendants.

"His spirit is broken," agreed the other. "Work as a transport animal, and no food, has dampened his fire!"

"It is good!" growled Ali Feisal. "Saddle him up. I will teach the proud Kawa that he cannot try any tricks on me. Huh! He shall pay for humiliating me at the Sheikh's palace. I'll ride him till he drops. One false step and he'll feel the lash of my whip."

And Ali Feisal drew the long thong of a riding whip through his fingers meaningly.

Kawa let the hawk-faced Arab mount to his back peacefully. Then, as Ali gave him a vicious prod behind the ear with a sharp stick, he moved off at a steady pace across the sands, heading into the canyon. As far as he knew, the canyon was a cul-de-sac. There was to be no escape by bolting up it. Presently Kawa felt a smart lash across his flank that made him shrill in pain.

"Faster, you lame slow-worm!" came Ali's taunting voice. "I had thought to ride you in the Petalia camel race, but if you can do no better than this I am glad that I shall be riding White Star!"

White Star was Ali Feisal's fastest racing camel, and Selim and Kawa's strongest rival in the coming race. Kawa's eyes glinted. It was time for the showdown!

Next moment he put his long neck forward and began to streak across the desert. The two attendants, following on their brown camels, rifles slung across their saddles, soon began to be left behind.

"That is better!" rasped Ali Feisal, looking down at Kawa. "You can keep this up until you drop."

But Kawa had other ideas. He was determined that it would not be himself who did the dropping! He waited until he was about a hundred yards ahead of the attendants, and then he suddenly began to buck and leap like a Wild West bronco.

"You—you treacherous cur!" screeched Ali Feisal, and began to lash at him with his whip.

Kawa reared in the air, came down on all fours and went on, his neck thrust out to its fullest extent. Ali stopped lashing at him and had to hang on like grim death. Suddenly Kawa splayed out his front legs and came to an abrupt halt!

It was too much for Ali Feisal. Utterly unable to keep his seat, he went somersaulting over Kawa's head, and landed in a heap in the sand.

Kawa's one idea was to escape then. He swerved round the fallen Ali, and went around in a wide circle, meaning to make a dash for the open desert.

But charging to cut off his retreat were the two attendants, who now had their rifles at the ready. And other men from Ali's camp, hearing the commotion, were emerging from their tents, mounting their camels, and spreading out across the entrance to the canyon to head him off.

"Shoot the camel down!" screeched Ali Feisal. "I'll teach him to make a fool of me!"

Crack! Crack! Crack!

The Arab's rifles barked, and bullets began to kick up the dust around Kawa's hoofs. He immediately swerved around away from his pursuers, and began to head deeper into the canyon.

On and on tore Kawa. But as he went further and further, a feeling of panic began to creep over him as the walls of the canyon became close together, and began to loom over him. Behind him, the yells of his pursuers struck fear into him. If he was caught by the evil Ali Feisal again, he knew he could expect no mercy. He would be doomed to spend the rest of his days as an overworked, underfed, transport camel! He rounded a bend. His spirits dropped. There ahead loomed a great wall of sandstone – the head of the canyon. There seemed to be no way out.

"If only Selim were here!" Kawa thought to himself desperately. "He would help me find some way out!"

And then something happened which brought the pounding camel to a sliding halt. From behind a group of rocks at the foot of the canyon wall emerged a group of brownish grey camels. They spread out into a line, coming towards him.

Kawa showed the whites of his eyes, and looked round desperately. Ali Feisal, now mounted on a spare camel, and his men, were already coming around the corner behind him: it looked as if he was trapped!

Kawa stared again at the newcomer. New hope surged through him. For all the camels except one were riderless!

Kawa took a chance and charged towards them. And as he got closer to them, he recognised them! They were camels from the Sheikh el Sharaf's herd!

"Bel-Sheba! Raf–el–Din!" he greeted two of them in camel language. "Is there a way out of here? I am pursued by a fiend of a merchant, and may face death!"

"Better ask this human who is driving us, why we are here," retorted Raf-el-Din. "He crept up on us during the night, and drove us through yonder cave. You may escape that way, if he lets you!"

Already, spurred on by shouts from Ali Feisal, the Arab who was driving Raf-el-Din and Co. was swerving his mount to head Kawa off. At once Kawa thrust his neck out and sprinted like mad for the clump of rocks.

The Arab, who was one of Ali Feisal's band, came at him from the side. Already his hand was reaching out to grasp Kawa's head-rein. It seemed that in another few seconds, Kawa's spell of freedom would be over!

But Kawa was no ordinary camel. He wasn't going to be caught as easily as that! Without checking his pace, he turned his head, thrust out his long neck, and grasped the Arab's flowing sleeve with his teeth. A powerful jerk of his powerful neck muscles, and—

"Aaaaaagh!"

The Arab let out a shrill yell of terror, and went headlong from the back of his mount.

Meanwhile, Kawa went tearing on, heading for the clump of boulders from which the Sheikh's camels had emerged.

He found that the rocks hid the entrance to quite a large cave. Into this he went, and for the next half-hour he padded through the darkness, wondering whether he would ever emerge into daylight again. To Kawa's relief all sounds of pursuit had now died away.

At last a shaft of light appeared ahead. Kawa hurried out of the tunnel-like cave to find himself at the head of the Wadi el Dufra, the area from which so many of the Sheikh's camels had been disappearing of late!

The entrance to the cave was close to a spring which fed the river which ran into Petalia. Here were the Sheikh's great water melon plantations, in which grew the great green fruit, with the pink flesh and the big black pips. It was a place where camels normally rarely went.

Kawa was starving. He had seen the humans eat the melons, and so he went up to one, sank his teeth into its skin, and greedily ate. He didn't like it much, but it helped to quench his thirst. Then he went streaking off towards Petalia, in search of Selim.

Long before the outskirts of the desert town came in sight, he saw a lone, familiar figure with a bundle on a stick over his shoulder marching towards him. It was Selim! Uttering a shrill whistle of delight, Kawa went prancing up to his master.

"Alas, there is nothing to be pleased about, O Kawa," said Selim gravely, after a while. "I have been dismissed from the service of the Sheikh in disgrace. He blames me for having to give you to that rogue Ali Feisal. We must not show our faces in Petalia. If we did I should be imprisoned for stealing you back from Ali – band you would not be allowed to run in the race for the Sheikh, anyway. You now belong to Ali Feisal."

Just then Selim reached up and took something from the fold of Kawa's jowl. He stared at it, bewildered.

"What is this, you rascal?" he demanded. "A melon pip! You have been in the Sheikh's plantation. Whatever for?"

Acting on a hunch, Selim rode Kawa back to the top of Wadi el Dufra. There Kawa led him to the entrance to the cave tunnel, and the footprints of many camels going into it. Then he took him through the cave and showed him Ali Feisal's camp in the canyon beyond.

"So that's the way the camels were stolen!" Selim gasped at last. "H'mm, I cannot go to the Sheikh and tell him about it. He would think I was spinning a yarn. But I have a plan, my speedy one, which means we shall run in the camel race, and bowl out that twister Ali Feisal at one blow. Yet it all depends on you winning that race, Kawa!"

It was the start of the great Petalia camel race! A dozen of the fleetest, finest camels in the land were lined up in the main street of the desert town, ready for the starter's signal. White camels, yellow camels, grey, and brown, all carefully groomed for the great event, all proudly erect and strutting.

Many of these magnificent beasts turned their heads and cast disdainful looks towards the outside flank of the line. For there was a thirteenth camel – a late entry – and what a contrast to the others!

The newcomer was a dirty, brownish grey. His hair was unkempt and shaggy. He held himself with an apologetic air, as if he had no right to be there.

"Complete outsider!" sneered White Star, Ali Feisal's mount.

"What chance can he have?" leered another entry. "And look at his rider – looks like one of the rabble from the poor quarter of the city!"

The rider of the thirteenth camel didn't look much better than his mount. He had a dirty burnous, and a whispy grey beard that hung down his chest. Little did anyone realise that the mystery entrant was none other than Kawa, and his rider, Selim!

Kawa had strongly objected to having thick hair clippings of transport camels stuck all over his glossy white coat, to disguise him, but he had realised that Selim was doing it for some good purpose, and so he had put up with it.

"Have patience and courage, proud one," whispered Selim in his ear. "Very shortly Ali Feisal, stealer of camels, will be unmasked."

Crack! The starter's gun fired.

Instantly the line of camels shot forward in a surging mass. A yell of excitement went up from the watching crowd.

"They're off!"

"Number thirteen is last!"

It was true! Kawa had been left almost standing!

Then off he went, lumbering down the course, catching all the dust of the other competitors as they tore out into the desert.

The route was a straight one – out to a clump of palm trees two miles out into the desert, and then back to the start in the town centre again.

"Hurry!" Selim hissed in Kawa's ear. "Remember all depends on your beating White Star!"

Kawa didn't understand the words, but he caught the urgency of their meaning. He stretched his long neck forward, and began to go like the wind.

Hoofs pounding, he surged onward. One, two, three camels he overtook, and by the time he reached the clump of palms he was up in the middle of the bunch, and still going strong.

Back towards Petalia the field went, White Star well out in front. Ali Feisal had a confident grin on his face. He thought victory was as good as his. The main street of Petalia seemed to race towards Ali as his mount glided towards it, running easily over the sand.

"Well done, White Star!" the merchant cried. "But–but haste on! We are challenged!" And he began to apply his whip viciously to his mount.

Then, as Ali Feisal glanced at the challenger he nearly fell from his saddle! For the camel overtaking him was the thirteenth camel – the scruffy outsider!

Kawa had really got the bit between his teeth. He couldn't resist turning his head and taunting White Star.

"Ho, stupid one!" he shrilled. "So you think you can beat the great Kawa – when when he is so disguised that even his own owner, the Sheikh, can't recognise him!"

White Star turned a baleful eye towards Kawa. His yellow fangs were bared.

"You shall not win!" he hissed, and took a savage bite at Kawa's flank.

Kawa swerved to avoid the clashing teeth. But White Star's fangs gnashed together on the matted hair with which Kawa was disguised. Next moment, a large strip of the brownish grey stuff was tugged away, leaving a vivid patch of white for all the watchers to see.

A great shout went up. For now Selim had tugged off his beard. And Kawa could feel him ripping off the rest of his disguise. It now suited Selim that everyone should know who he was – and that the camel he was riding was Kawa.

Kawa was delighted. Now everyone would know that he, the greatest racing camel of them all, was taking part in the great Petalia race!

"Now I'll show 'em!" he thought, and immediately increased his pace.

White Star did all he could to stave off Kawa's challenge as his unscrupulous rider lashed at him with his whip.

But there was no holding Kawa now. Steadily he began to pull ahead, saw out of the corner of his eye his rival's evil, straining head dropping further and further behind. Seconds later, three lengths ahead of Ali Feisal and White Star, he crossed the winning line.

Almost immediately he was aware of Selim shouting in his ear.

"On, Kawa! Do not stop! The Sheikh and his men are pursuing us! So is Ali Feisal! They would fling me into prison, and give you back to yon rogue. You must keep ahead until we reach the secret cave and show the Sheikh that Ali has been stealing his camels!"

Though weary after the gruelling race, Kawa kept going. He didn't realise what it was all about, but he knew that for his master's sake he had to keep running. Soon Kawa entered the Wadi el Dufra. Now the shouts of the Sheikh's men were getting louder every moment, as Kawa began to flag.

Through the Wadi went the camels. They swept past the melon plantation and into the cave–like tunnel which led through to the canyon. Some minutes later, panting and wheezing, Kawa entered into the canyon at the other end. At last a group of browsing camels appeared ahead. Nearby were the tents of Ali Feisal's camp.

By this time the Sheikh, on another fast camel, had caught up with Selim. He glanced from Ali Feisal to Selim, and then to Raf-el-Din and the transport camels that had been rustled away from his herd.

"Those are my camels!" he roared. "What are they doing in your camp, Ali Feisal? Aha! I see it all, now. You are responsible for the rustling of my camels! I will have you thrown into prison for this treachery!"

Ali Feisal realised that he was beaten, and quickly confessed that he had indeed been using the secret cave as a means of stealing the Sheikh's camels. Over-confident, he had left his camp standing near the entrance to the canyon. He had planned to rejoin the caravan after the race!

"And the plan would have succeeded if it hadn't been for you, O Kawa," Selim told his mount.

Kawa had won the greatest race of his life!

And when the Sheikh, back at the palace, hung the Gold Star of Petalia around the victorious camel's neck, Kawa's hump almost visibly swelled with pride!

BUCKAROO BILL

by Edward Home-Gall

Buckaroo Bill, the Cowboy Champ of Double Diamond Ranch, took on the massive bully, Tough-Guy Tamson, and taught him a lesson or two about who was the better man.

"O. K., sheriff, I'll tame Tough-Guy Tamson for you. Where'll I find him, right now?"

The speaker was Buckaroo Bill Hardy. Joe Gardner, Sheriff of Whispering Creek, looked up from where he sat at his office desk, into the glinting eyes of the bronzed-faced cowboy. A worried expression was on his face.

"But, see here, Buckaroo Bill, I ain't so sure I ought-a let you try!" he said slowly. "Tough-Guy Tamson is a dangerous man. You're big an' tough yourself, Bucka, but Tough-Guy is a good bit bigger than you."

Buckaroo Bill Hardy, the Cowboy Champ of the Double-Diamond Ranch, laughed quietly.

"The bigger they are, sheriff," he drawled, "the harder they drop, I guess! But if this big ape is goin' around makin' himself a nuisance, then why don't you jail him for disturbing the peace?"

The sheriff shrugged.

"Because Tough-Guy ain't broken no real law yet," he grunted in reply.

"But he's vowed that he will, if any o' us start tryin' to jailhouse him."

Tough-Guy Tamson was a red-haired giant who had signed on as a cowpuncher for the Red Star Ranch at Dixie Springs. The whole outfit hated him because of his fiery–tempered, bullying nature, but they couldn't sack him because he did the work of any two other cowpokes on the range.

"Tough-Guy's chief trouble, I guess," went on Sheriff Joe Gardner to Buckaroo, "is that he's bossed it about for so long wherever he's gone that his strength has gone to his head. But I figger that, at heart, he can't be a bad hombre."

At that moment a series of gunshots rang out from midway down Whispering Creek's one-and-only main street. They were accompanied by a raucous roar of laughter.

Going over to the open office window, Buckaroo and the sheriff peered out and saw a red-haired, six-foot-six giant standing in the open bat-wing doors of the Hot Spot Saloon. His huge back was to the street, and two smoking six-guns were in his fists.

"That's Tough-Guy Tamson!" exclaimed Buckaroo Bill. "Been gettin' himself hooched-up with Dutch courage at the bar, eh?"

"That's just whar you're wrong, Bucka," replied the sheriff. "Tough-Guy Tamson don't drink – an' he lets everyone know it, by shootin' glasses out of inoffensive citizens' and peace–abidin' cowpokes' hands."

"Seems to me that all that Tough-Guy Tamson needs, for his own good, an' for the good of the whole community, is to be taken down a peg or two," grinned Buckaroo. "I'm promisin' nothin', sheriff, but I'll see what I can do for you. I've tamed tougher hosses than that hombre, so maybe I'll be able to do somethin' about tamin' him."

"Watch your step, Bucka," frowned the sheriff.

Buckaroo strode from the sheriff's office, with the grin still upon his bronzed face as he stepped out into the dusty street.

"Come on, pards," he said softly. "Looks like we've got a tough job to tackle."

Those words were spoken to Red Flame, his wonder-horse, and Wolf, the war-veteran alsatian Buckaroo Bill had found wandering in the mountains.

The alsatian, with the bronco's reins held lightly between its powerful teeth, led Red Flame down the road in Buckaroo Bill's wake.

It was wagging its bushy tail slowly from side to side, as if it knew that its young master was leading them straight into trouble.

The shooting outside the Hot Spot Saloon had ended now. A group of sullen-faced cowboys with some of Buckaroo Bill's pards of the Double-Diamond outfit among them, were clustered at each end of its long veranda, angrily watching Tough-Guy Tamson. Tough-Guy was in the centre of the veranda. He was standing upon one leg, with the foot of his other leg resting upon the back of a kneeling cowboy, whom Buckaroo instantly recognised as a bar-lounger named Shirker Quirke.

Kneeling alongside Quirke was a slimly built young greenhorn, Pat Bristoe, of the Red Star outfit. Pat was stripped to the waist, nervously polishing the bully's jackboot with his own shirt.

In one hand Tough-Guy Tamson grasped one of his six-guns; in the other he held a wire-haired terrier!

"Say, Tamson," shouted one of the cowboys, "lay off tormenting that kid, or that dog!"

"Or what?" jeered the big-limbed bully. "Mind your own business, or maybe I'll make it your turn next."

Buckaroo Bill was now barely five yards from the centre of the veranda. The cowboys tensed as they now saw him for the first time – and recognised him as the Cowboy Champ of the Mangana territory. Signalling his horse and his dog to halt, Buckaroo Bill climbed slowly up the veranda steps.

Tough-Guy Tamson hadn't seen him yet.

"Thar's mud on the toe of that boot, polecat!" Tough-Guy snapped to the kneeling tenderfoot who was polishing his boots. "Lick it off with your tongue – unless you want me to shoot this dog, so as you can use its tail for a brush!"

Alarmed for the safety of his pet, Pat Bristoe hesitated for a moment, and then lowered his mouth towards the offending smear of mud on the bully's boot.

"I shouldn't, Pat!" drawled Buckaroo Bill. "It's not the outside of that boot that needs cleanin'; it's the inside!"

Tough-Guy Tamson jerked his red head with a snort of fury. Silence gripped the veranda. Buckaroo Bill and Tough-Guy were now standing face to face, staring at each other challengingly.

Tough was the first to break the silence.

"Maybe you'd prefer to do the lickin' yourself, Buckaroo Bill?" he rapped.

"It looks like I'll have to do another sort of licking," drawled Buckaroo, "in order to clean up this township. You can scram, Pat Bristoe, this bullyin' ham won't shoot your dog. He's not that much of a no-good!"

Tough-Guy Tamson's other victim, Shirker Quirke, was a slimy toad at the best of times, and Buckaroo Bill didn't care what happened to him – but he didn't mean to stand by and see a decent youngster like Pat Bristoe being humiliated.

The tenderfoot, shooting a glance of deep gratitude at the Cowboy Champ, backed swiftly away.

Tough-Guy Tamson saw red.

"So you want to take his place, eh?" he bellowed. "O. K., then, Buckaroo Bill – start dancin'!"

The muzzle of his six–gun flashed down towards Buckaroo's feet, barking savagely. Bullets thudded like hammer blows into the wooden floor of the veranda, making a menacing display of black holes between his two jack-boots.

But Buckaroo didn't budge!

At last, releasing the little terrier from his grasp, Tough-Guy whipped out his second six–gun.

"Get dancin'," he roared, "or my next slug will drill a hole through your foot!"

The cowboys watched their Cowboy Champ breathlessly. Would Buckaroo Bill start to dance, or had he the nerve to go on defying Tough-Guy Tamson, at the risk of being crippled for life?

Still Buckaroo Bill stood his ground. The only movement of his body had been a faint signal, with one hand, to his two four-legged pards, Red Flame and Wolf!

Tough-Guy Tamson's face was going black with rage. His fingers tightened savagely upon the butt of one of his six-guns.

"Right, Buckaroo Bill," he snarled through gritted teeth. "You've asked for it!"

And then, a split second before his crooked finger could pull the trigger, a grey streak flashed through the air at him.

It was Wolf! The alsatian's bared teeth were flashing straight towards the tough's throat. As the bully staggered back, Red Flame moved up behind him. Buckaroo Bill had trained his two four-legged pals how to act if anyone pointed a gun at him—and they were acting now.

Red Flame's teeth closed with a snap upon the back of the bully's highly-coloured scarf. Then she gave a lightning toss of her fiery mane, and Tough-Guy Tamson, despite his huge weight, was jerked bodily from his feet, to pitch headlong from the veranda and sprawl full-length in the dusty street. His guns spun from his grasp.

Buckaroo Bill's gaze flashed towards a well-filled horse-trough standing alongside the saloon.

"Thanks, pards," he said to Red Flame and Wolf. "Now I guess that big ham needs coolin' down."

The watching cowboys, hooting with laughter, formed a ring around the horse-trough. They could see what was coming.

And so, too, could Tough-Guy Tamson.

Buckaroo drew his guns, pointing them at the bully of the Red Star outfit.

He laughed quietly.

"Just now, polecat, you saw fit to entertain me with an exhibition of how slick you can be with a pair of rods," he drawled. "Now maybe you'd like to see how I can shape with a brace o' six-guns? I figger you're a hombre that goes around lookin' for trouble too much – an' maybe it's that red hair of yours which makes you do that. Maybe you'd be best without some of it?"

The gun in Buckaroo's right hand barked viciously. A bullet, grazing the top of Tough-Guy's head, cut off a wiry curl of red hair and sent it leaping into the air. Then Buckaroo Bill's left-hand gun spoke – and another lock of red hair leapt from the top of the bully's head.

Tough-Guy Tamson's face went green with sudden terror.

"Quit it, dang you!" he howled. "No guy can shoot thet straight an' keep it up! You'll plug me!"

"I'll admit there's a risk of that!" smiled Buckaroo Bill. "But if I do, the boys here'll give you a decent funeral. If you don't want me to do any more shootin', you'd best bolt for cover – like any other skunk."

Tough-Guy looked wildly around.

"How about that horse-trough?" grinned Buckaroo. "Turn your back to it and roll into it, like as if you was gettin' into bed. Or perhaps you'd like to lose some more hair, and —"

There was no need for him to finish the sentence. Tough-Guy had had enough!

Backing hastily towards the water-trough, Tough-Guy rolled over backwards into it with a mighty splash and disappeared from view. A shout went up.

A dozen cowboys, whooping with joy over Buckaroo Bill's victory, bounded forward. Seizing hold of the trough, they rolled it upside-down.

Tough-Guy's huge body was wedged firmly inside it. A wild howl of laughter came from all sides as he struggled up on to his hands and knees with the trough covering him, so that he looked like an overgrown tortoise.

"Now get moving out of town," shouted Sheriff Joe Gardner, who had witnessed everything. "Buckaroo Bill's made you the laughin'-stock of Whispering Creek – an' that ought to tame you, if anythin' will."

"Buckaroo Bill ain't tamed nothin'!" came Tough-Guy Tamson's muffled roar from beneath the horse–trough. "I'll get even with him for this if it's the last thing I ever do! Then I'll make him fight me, man to man!"

"That'll suit me fine!" retorted Buckaroo. "You can name your day for that meeting, hombre. But I guess I'll need to do a bit o' trainin' for the fight; how about havin' it today week – right here?"

"I'll be back!" came Tough-Guy's angry voice from beneath the trough. "And you'd best make out your will before the fight, 'cos it'll be too late to do it when it's over!"

Buckaroo tapped the bottom of the trough with the butt of one of his six-guns.

"How's this for a magnificent specimen of the Texas Tortoise?" he laughed.

The watching cowboys guffawed with mirth.

"Get movin'," Sheriff Gardner shouted to Tough-Guy. "I'll give you ten minutes to get out o' town!"

Unable to escape from the trough, Tough-Guy made his way down the dusty street on his hands and knees.

Nearly the whole population of Whispering Creek collected at the end of the dusty street to watch what they believed must be the taming of Tough-Guy Tamson. The little Wild West town re-echoed to roars of laughter as cowboys and townsfolk watched the big-limbed bully crawling, like a giant tortoise, in and out of a cluster of rocks until he was at last able to find two between which he could wedge the trough, so that he could extract himself from inside it.

Rising to his feet, leaving the trough wedged between the rocks, he shook one huge fist at the laughing crowd. Then, turning his back sullenly upon them, he set out in a rolling gait across the prairie; he was too proud to ask for his horse, which he had left tethered in the stable–yard at the back of the Hot Spot Saloon.

"I figger we've punished him enough," grinned Buckaroo Bill. "I'll get his hoss an' send it after him!"

As Buckaroo entered the stable–yard he saw that there was someone crouching behind the hind legs of Tough-Guy's horse. He gave an angry exclamation as he suddenly caught the glint of a knife in the crouching man's hand – with its sharp edge moving towards one of the unsuspecting animal's legs.

The man was obviously out to hamstring Tough-Guy's horse, so that it could never run again! Buckaroo Bill's six-gun flashed out from its holster and barked viciously.

His bullet hit the knife a fraction of a second before it could complete its foul work, and sent it spinning from the tobacco-stained fingers of the man who had been about to sever the delicate tendon at the back of the horse's leg.

The man looked round with a guilty start. It was Shirker Quirke! Buckaroo Bill strode up to Shirker, his face white with rage. With a sidelong sweep of his arm he sent him sprawling to the ground.

"You slimy toad!" the Cowboy Champ cried angrily. "Hamstring Tough-Guy Tamson's hoss, would you?"

"Well, why not?" snarled Shirker. "Look what he done to me outside the saloon! Do him good to get blistered feet, walkin' back twenty miles to his ranch!"

Buckaroo glared down contemptuously at the cringing barlounger.

"If you were a man, you'd know better'n to try to take it out of a guy by crippling his hoss," he said angrily. "If I tell the boys about this they'll half-kill you."

"You won't tell 'em, Bucka?" whined Shirker.

"I dunno," grunted Buckaroo. "I'll think it over!"

Tough-Guy Tamson showed no gratitude at having his horse sent out to him by Buckaroo. Catching it as it trotted down the trail towards him, he mounted and, without once looking back towards Whispering Creek, rode away towards the near-by foothills.

Buckaroo Bill now found himself the hero of the little township. But, hating being made a fuss of, he promptly gave the population something else to think about by supplying them with a thrilling exhibition of bronco-busting!

A pal from a near-by ranch had bought a horse which nobody could ride – and Buckaroo Bill, the best rough-rider in the Mangana territory, settled down to another job of taming a rebel.

Upon the same stretch of open prairie just outside the town, which had been the scene of Tough-Guy Tamson's humiliating departure, Buckaroo entertained a thrilled crowd of cowboys to an exhibition of bronco-busting worthy of an all-star rodeo.

For twenty minutes the four-legged rebel beneath him tried every devilish trick to unship him from its back. Then, at last, the panting bronco began to give up the onesided fight, and admit that it had met its master.

Just as the bronco was making one last despairing, stiff-legged attempt to unseat him, the crisp report of a rifle rang out from among the foothills into which Tough-Guy Tamson had recently ridden.

Buckaroo Bill heard a bullet thud home into the horse beneath him, and the next thing he knew was that he was pitching headlong towards the ground, with the horse rolling over on top of him.

For a moment it felt to him as if his ribs were being crushed in – and then the agony ceased as he became unconscious.

From all sides horrified cowboys rushed to his aid. Risking injuries to themselves from the threshing legs of the dying horse, they dragged him clear.

Whose hand had fired that murderous shot from the foothills? It looked as if Tough-Guy Tamson had wasted no time in keeping his threat of vengeance against Buckaroo Bill!

Buckaroo Bill Hardy opened his eyes to find himself stretched upon a bunk in Sheriff Joe Gardner's office, with his lanky pal of the Double-Diamond outfit, Giraffe Jackson, bending anxiously over him.

"How are you feelin', Bucka?" Giraffe asked sympathetically. "The doc says you've no bones broken, an' you'll be all right after a few days' rest."

Gritting his teeth, Buckaroo swung himself up from the bunk.

"If there's no broken bones, then why do I need a few days' rest?" he grunted. "It's mighty quiet here, pard; where is everyone?"

"The sheriff an' the whole town's out huntin' that jasper who aimed to plug you, an' shot the bronco instead," answered Giraffe. "I figger they'll get him – and I wouldn't like to be wearin' his boots when they bring him back to town. They're in the right mood for a lynching! That lowdown polecat has gone a step too far this time!"

"Meanin' who, pard?" Buckaroo snapped.

"Why, Tough-Guy Tamson, o' course!" grunted Giraffe. "He's the hombre they're after!"

"Then they're after the wrong man!" cried Buckaroo. "I handied Tough-Guy's horse, didn't I? There wasn't a rifle in the saddle-boot when I sent it off after him. Where'd Tough-Guy get a rifle from among the foothills? They don't grow on trees!"

Suddenly Buckaroo Bill looked out of the window, and then leapt to his feet.

"Say, Giraffe," he gasped, "how long've I bin unconscious?"

" 'Bout two or three hours, I guess," answered Giraffe. "Why?"

"They've caught Tough-Guy – an' they're bringing him in!" cried Buckaroo. "I reckon we've gotter act mighty fast, or the wrong man is goin' to get lynched! Try an' get into Shirker Quirke's shack down the street without him seein' you, and see if you can find a rifle there that's been fired recently."

"What's that slimy toad Shirker got to do with someone tryin' to shoot you?" asked Giraffe in a surprised voice.

"I caught him tryin' to hamstring Tough-Guy's hoss, out of spite," answered Buckaroo, "an' I reckon he's scared that I'll spread it around. If that bullet had got me, it would have been mighty useful for

71

Quirke, in two ways – it would have kept me quiet about what I know about him, an' it would hev got Tough-Guy Tamson lynched for the shootin'! I'll go out and meet this lynching party, an' stall for time till you show up!"

By the time that Buckaroo reached the returning mob of angry cowboys, they had halted Tough-Guy Tamson under an old oak-tree on the edge of the town.

Sheriff Joe Gardner was not in the party, and it was clear that the bully's angry captors meant to take full advantage of this by taking the law into their own hands. Someone slung a noose over a low bough of the oak-tree.

"I've a right to a fair trial!" growled Tough-Guy Tamson fiercely. "I tell you I didn't fire thet shot at Buckaroo Bill or at the horse!"

"Maybe he should have a trial?" rapped out Buckaroo.

At the sound of his voice, Tough-Guy Tamson looked savagely in Buckaroo Bill's direction.

"So you figger you've got this frame-up of yours so water-tight that your jury would find me guilty, eh?" he roared. "Mebbe it is one of your own pards that fired that rifle, to put a noose around my neck! You've thought up a mighty smart way of gettin' out of fightin' me next week!"

Buckaroo Bill leapt up on to the trunk of a fallen tree.

"Listen to me, fellers!" he bellowed. "I ain't havin' any hombre leavin' this world thinkin' that I'm scared to fight him. Just to prove this polecat is lyin', I'm goin' to fight him before you lynch him!"

The Cowboy Champ's words created a stir – and would have created a bigger one if it had been known that he was offering to fight Tough-Guy in order to save his life.

A clearance in the cattle-yard at the back of the town was chosen for the scene of the fight.

The two stripped off their shirts and boots, and shaped up to each other, surrounded by an audience of excited cowboys and curious steers and bulls.

Although Buckaroo Bill was big and well proportioned, he was dwarfed by his giant opponent.

Suddenly Tough-Guy Tamson pounced, giving a gorilla-like roar of rage.

"I've a right to a fair trial!"

A shout of dismay thundered up from all sides.

Buckaroo Bill, in trying to dodge away from his opponent's massive arms, had slipped. He recovered himself quickly, but not quick enough to escape from being caught inside the bully's bear-like arms.

"Now I'm goin' to crush the life out o' you!" roared Tough-Guy.

The arms closed around Buckaroo, the muscles tightening. The agony, after the crushing weight of a horse falling on top of him, was almost more than he could bear.

He decided to try a ju-jitsu trick!

Suddenly going limp, he reeled backwards two quick paces, and then threw himself towards the ground, dragging his overbalancing opponent after him. The bully somersaulted above Buckaroo's head, and then crashed to the ground, with a force that three-parts winded him.

In a flash Buckaroo Bill was up on his feet. The cattle-pens echoed to an amazed cheer of delight from the cowboys.

And then, above the cheering, rang out a frantic cry in young Pat Bristoe's voice.

"Look out, Bucka! Run for your life!"

Buckaroo swung round. Tough though he was, and used to handling cattle, his breath caught in his throat.

Upon one side of the yard there was an extra stout, iron-barred pen, reserved for only the most savage of bulls. Its present occupant, a colossal long-horn, was the biggest and most ferocious bull that had been passed through Whispering Creek.

And now the padlock was lying on the ground beside the open gate of the pen, and the monster bull was charging out towards Buckaroo Bill and Tough-Guy Tamson.

Quickly Buckaroo decided on a plan of action. Leaping to meet the bull, he hurled himself, in a javelin–like dive, straight for its head.

His two hands closed accurately around each of its wide-spread horns. And then, like a gymnast on a vaulting-horse, he pressed up on his arms and shot his legs, pressed tightly together, up between them.

The weight of his flying body jerked the bull's huge head round. Its forelegs became crossed and, as Buckaroo released his hold and shot feet-first away to safety, it crashed heavily to the ground.

Dozens of cowboys flocked towards it, and seconds later many experienced hands were pinning the madly struggling brute down.

And then everyone noticed that there was another fight going on upon one side of the pen from which the bull had escaped.

Giraffe Jackson and Shirker Quirke were rolling over and over there in a cloud of dust. At their side there was a rifle!

Shirker was dragged to his feet, looking scared and white.

"Don't lynch me!" he whined. "When I loosened that bull, Tough-Guy Tamson looked like crushing Buckaroo to death. I did it to save Buckaroo Bill!"

Giraffe snorted indignantly.

"Don't listen to his lies!" he snorted. "Thet's his rifle, an' one shot's been fired through it – the one he fired at Buckaroo Bill! Maybe he'd like to claim thet he fired thet shot at Bucka to save him from bein' thrown by that poor brute of a bronco he'd just broken in?"

Fortunately, Sheriff Joe Gardner arrived upon the scene at that moment, just in time to march Shirker Quirke off to the jail-house and save him from a lynching.

And then Tough-Guy Tamson's huge right hand descended upon Buckaroo Bill's shoulder, in a powerful but friendly grip.

"I'd like to shake with you, Buckaroo – if you'll let me!" he said thickly. "I figger you've repaid me for tryin' to make you dance with bullets by saving my life twice – once from a rope an' once from that bull. Maybe I'm bigger'n you in brawn, Bucka – but you've got me beat in brain, pluck an' skill. I reckon you can tell yourself, an' all Whispering Creek, that you've tamed Tough-Guy Tamson. You won't find me slingin' my weight about any more, after today."

Buckaroo Bill's right hand shot out even quicker than when he was drawing one of his six-guns!

THE MONSTER OF THE POOL

by Wilfred McNeilly

Willie McCorcoran had always longed to catch the giant lobster in the pool and one day, after a fierce struggle, he succeeded. But the end of the fight was not quite what Willie expected!

Willie John McCorcoran gazed into the deep, green water of the pool in the rocks.

Willie John wanted a cycle to help him with his morning paper round. And at the foot of the pool there lay a cycle.

It was a living cycle, with great nippers twelve inches long, and a speckled, blue-black shell. Red feelers sprouted from its head, weaving ceaselessly through the water.

In fact, it was a lobster – the biggest Willie John had ever seen. It obviously weighed a good eight pounds. And at five shillings a pound, that made forty shillings – which was the exact price Jimmy Joe O'Hara was asking for his old bike.

"I'll get you yet," Willie John shouted down at the lobster.

But the words were a hollow boast. For he had been trying for a full week to catch Old Blueback. He had tried a well-baited lobster pot. But Old Blueback had ignored it. He had tried to snare it with a loop of wire on the end of a long cane. But one touch of the wire, and the lobster had flashed for cover, swimming backwards as if jet–propelled. He had even tried to spear it with two needle-pointed nails lashed to the end of the same cane.

Old Blueback had let the makeshift harpoon come within inches and had then quietly flicked himself back into the crevice in the rocks that was his lair.

Back at home in his grandfather's cottage, Willie John questioned the old man about lobsters. For his grandfather had been a famous lobsterman in his day, the most famous in Glengurlie, which was a little fishing village in Northern Ireland.

"A rabbit used to be good bait when I was at the fishing. But you'd have a hard job to find a rabbit these days. And, then again, you could try a mirror," the old man advised.

"A mirror? Sure, you're joking!"

"I am not! There's many a time we've tried a mirror when no other bait would do. Whether it was the glint of it that drew them, or the sight of their own ugly faces I wouldn't be knowing. But it worked!"

Not sure if the old man joked or not, Willie John tried a fragment of mirror the next day as bait in the lobster pot. Excitedly, he saw the great lobster leave its crevice and crawl about the pot. But it did not go inside. For two more days the boy tried the piece of mirror. Still Old Blueback remained free. And still the cycle stayed unbought.

Then one morning Willie John made a mistake in his paper round. He forgot the peppery Captain Burke. But the old sea captain did not forget him when they met at the paper shop.

"It's always the same," the old man snorted. "If you want to be sure of a thing you have to get it yourself."

The words stuck in the boy's mind. When he went back to the pool again he knew what he must do. Willie John was wearing his bathing trunks now. Carefully, he lowered himself into the water without disturbing it. He drove smoothly downward, arms and legs beating an easy rhythm. Would the lobster wait? Would his presence frighten it?

The monster of the pool did not seem to sense the boy's approach until the last split-second. Willie John's hand was stretching out to grasp the broad back when it moved.

One powerful flick of the tail sent it shooting backward into its lair.

But Old Blueback had not gone completely to ground. Its tail was in the crevice but not its whole body. It crouched there with long feelers stretching outward.

The first hint of danger would drive it back swiftly into the dark safety of its lair. But it was not yet sure that Willie John *was* danger.

The tip of a feeler brushed lightly across the boy's face, and instinctively he snatched at it. For a moment he held – and tugged.

Old Blueback was jerked towards him – and again Willie John grabbed. But so did the lobster. Its big, knobbly right claw gripped the boy's left wrist just as Willie John snatched at its back.

Willie John had caught the lobster. And the lobster had caught Willie John!

There was a strength in the shellfish that the boy could never have expected. In its own element, fighting for its life, the lobster seemed to have the strength of a man. Willie John felt himself being pulled bodily towards the crevice. And once the lobster got its body in, once it wedged itself in the crevice, Willie John would be doomed. He would have no hope at all of jerking himself free.

Now, too, his breath was almost exhausted. He had been under for almost a minute. Frantically, he kicked out – trying to drag himself and the lobster upward.

His flying foot sent a shower of small stones from the bottom flashing through the water. Some passed over the lobster, struck it from behind.

Thinking this a new attack, the lobster freed the grip of its massive claw and spun about in the water.

And though his lungs cried out for air, Willie John did not try for the surface at once. Again he grabbed at the lobster. This time he had it from behind, his hands closing on the hard shell just behind the joint of the nippers.

Now Old Blueback was helpless. The claws could not reach backward to seize the hands that held him.

Willie John headed for the surface with his prize still held in his outstretched hands.

Old Blueback had looked big in the water. Out on the rocks, in the bright light of day he looked even bigger.

The boy was turning for home when he glanced at the pool. It glared back at him in the sunlight with a strange emptiness. For a moment, Willie John stood undecided, battling with himself. On impulse, he acted.

"Get you back home!" he yelled. He hurled his burden from him savagely, wanting to get the action over before he changed his mind.

Old Blueback hit the water with a splash, and the boy moved forward to watch the great lobster sink to safety. But, even as he moved, his eye was caught by something else . . . something that sparkled in the sand by the edge of the pool. His breath escaped in a low whistle of surprise as he stooped to pick it up. Willie John knew little about jewellery – but he guessed that the diamond ring that sparkled in the sand would be worth a better bike than ever Old Blueback would have paid for.

How had it got there? Had it lain buried for years until, coming ashore with his prize, he had scuffed it to the surface? Or had it come up from the bottom of the pool – perhaps caught up in the lobster's claws, and loosened in the struggle? Willie John would never know the answer. But, all the same, he yelled his thanks at the great, blueblack shape that reigned once more in the green, silent waters of the pool.

THE VANISHING POLICEMEN

by Mark Grimshaw

When three London policemen were kidnapped, Scotland Yard called in the great private detective, Colwyn Dane, to solve the mystery, but the case proved to be one of the most baffling that he had ever handled.

"Gosh! That's the third copper who's been kidnapped since last night!" exclaimed Slick Chester.

With his famous chief, Colwyn Dane, Slick was in the consulting-room at The Turrets, the ace detective's North London home. Dane had just been speaking to Scotland Yard on the phone, and there was a thoughtful frown on his keen, clean-cut face, as he returned the receiver to its hooks.

"That's right, Slick," he agreed. "Three policemen have been kidnapped within the past twelve hours or so. Two have since been released, unharmed – but neither was able to give a clue to his kidnappers. The third case happened only half an hour ago."

"But what's the big idea?" frowned Slick. "Kidnapping a copper! It seems crazy to me. I suppose the policemen weren't robbed, guv'nor?" he asked, a sudden thought striking him.

Dane shook his head.

"On the contrary, when the two kidnapped men were returned, each was the richer by two pounds," said the ace 'tec. "A couple of pound notes had been placed in each man's pocket!"

Slick shook his head, puzzled. It got crazier and crazier. Why should anybody pay two pounds to kidnap a policeman and then release him again straight away?

"It certainly is a mystery," went on Dane. "But this may mean something. All the men concerned come from the Overly Lane Police Station, and the three of them were on duty yesterday at the same time. So we're going along to Overly Lane now. I'm determined to get to the bottom of this mystery!"

Ten minutes later, in Dane's powerful sports car, the 'tecs were on their way to the East End, where the Overly Lane Police Station was situated. Leaving the car outside, they made their way to the charge-room, where they found a puzzled-looking sergeant.

"What's the trouble, sergeant?" Dane asked him.

"It's P.–C. 57–the chap who was kidnapped this morning, sir," said the sergeant. "He's come back–like the others. He says he was taking a short cut through a back street, when a cloth or something was thrown over his head. It must have been soaked in dope, because P.–C. 57 doesn't remember another thing till he opened his eyes and found himself lying on the railway embankment, sir. And there was a couple of quid in his tunic pocket, sir, just the same as the other two kidnapped men had!"

"Has anything else unusual happened, sergeant?" questioned Dane, after a few moments' thought.

"No, sir," replied the station sergeant. "Leastways, there was one little thing," he corrected himself. "Last night, one of the windows at the back here was forced. I suppose you would call it unusual to break into a police station, sir?"

"I certainly would," nodded the ace 'tec. "Anything missing?"

"Not a thing, sir. And nothing was disturbed. It was a proper mystery. If you ask me, sir," said the sergeant confidentially, "somebody is playing a joke on us. Kidnapping policemen and breaking into the station–it doesn't make sense–does it? And–hey, what's that?"

It was a loud explosion, accompanied by a crash of splintering glass, that cut short his words.

"That's the window of the inspector's room!" gasped the sergeant. "He's out. We'd better go and see what's happened!"

Every policeman in the building had got the same idea, and there was a milling crowd in the passage when Dane and Slick, with the sergeant at their heels, reached the door of the inspector's room. Turning the handle, Dane flung the door open. The room was full of smoke, and on the floor were the remains of an exploded firework. The window had been blown outward, and only a jagged fringe of glass remained in the frame. Dane darted to the window. It overlooked the street. Nobody was around, but fifty yards away was a corner.

"He could have dodged round there," said Dane to the sergeant. "Who? Why, the person who threw the firework, of course!"

"Firework!" snorted the sergeant. "That proves what I said, sir. Somebody is playing jokes on us. Here, you – and you!" The sergeant spun round, pointing at two of the constables. "Get after him!" he roared.

The sergeant left the room – then came running back. He grabbed Dane by the arm.

"There's something else happened, sir," panted the sergeant. "A man has escaped from the cells. He got away while everybody was here at the front of the building!"

With a grim look on his face, Dane followed the sergeant to the empty cell.

"It was locked all right, sir, when the constable in charge came rushing to the inspector's office," explained the sergeant, as Dane examined the lock. "The door was open when he returned."

"It was opened by a skeleton key," declared Dane. "The prisoner couldn't have reached the lock. So he was helped from outside. That, I imagine, was the reason for the firework thrown through the inspector's window. It was intended to draw everyone to the front of the building, while the prisoner was freed."

The sergeant's face fell.

"Who was the prisoner?" asked Dane.

"A young Chinaman named Brunning, sir," replied the sergeant. "He's never been in our hands before. He was arrested yesterday—"

"By one of the three kidnapped constables?" asked Dane.

"No, sir. It was by a man who's gone on leave," corrected the sergeant.

While he went off to start a search for the escaped prisoner, Dane made a scrutiny of the empty cell. Suddenly the ace 'tec prised a small object from a crevice behind the wash-bowl. Slick saw that it was a tiny enamelled badge, on which were two writhing dragons breathing flame.

"It's the badge of a powerful Chinese Secret Society," stated Dane.

"You mean it belonged to Brunning's rescuers?" put in Slick. "No, it can't be that. They wouldn't have put it there, would they?"

"No. But the prisoner himself might have done," replied Dane. "Why? He hid it because he didn't want the police to discover that he was a member of the secret society. As far as I know, the secret society isn't operating in London. But I'm going to make sure. You've heard of Lo Sung?"

"He's the old Chinaman who keeps a junk-shop in Limehouse," nodded Slick. "But you won't get anything out of him, guv'nor—except a pack of lies. He's the crookedest—"

"But he knows more than anybody else about what's happening in the Chinese underworld," broke in Dane. "I think he'll help us!"

Slick had his doubts. But he was soon driving Dane from the police station.

Parking their car some distance from Lo Sung's shabby shop, the 'tecs made their way there on foot. Lo Sung himself was behind the counter. He was a wispy Chinaman, with a wrinkled face and shifty eyes. Having explained their mission, Dane slid the secret society's badge, which he'd f o u n d in the police station cell, on to the counter. Lo Sung's slant e y e s narrowed. Then he shook his head.

"No savvy!" he declared.

"I told you so, guv'nor," said Slick, as they left the junk-shop. "You didn't get a thing out of him, did you?"

"Not so far," admitted Dane. "But I think he's going to tell me all I want to know. In here!"

The 'tecs dodged into an entry, and the wondering Slick saw that Dane had fitted a tiny earphone to his ear. From it an almost invisible wire ran back to the shop they had just left.

"There's a microphone at the other end," Dane told him. "I stuck it on the counter, so that it will pick up any sounds in the shop. I've got a hunch that Lo Sung is going to start talking before long."

As Dane listened, he heard a faint scraping sound over the wire. He knew that Lo Sung was dialling a number at the shop's telephone. Then, after a short pause, there came Lo Sung's voice. For some minutes Dane listened. There was a grim look on his face when finally he turned to Slick.

"That's what I expected," he said. "Lo Sung rang up the chief of the society to put him wise that I'm on their track."

"So you heard him say where the boss of the gang hangs out?" put in Slick.

"I wasn't quite as lucky as that," replied the ace 'tec. "But I know the society has its headquarters at a Chinese laundry. I could tell that from the background noises. And I know the code-marks that laundry uses. A couple of Chinese boys were checking Lo Sung's washing at the shop. That should be enough to trace the laundry, I think. And, after that, we shan't be long before we're at grips with the Dragon!"

"Dragon?" echoed Slick.

"He's the head man of the secret society," explained Dane. "And, from the way Lo Sung spoke, he's a pretty ruthless blighter. We're up against something big, Slick!" the ace 'tec added, as he stuffed the tiny earphone into his pocket. "But I'm going to solve the mystery of the kidnapped policemen!"

"We'll set about finding out w h e r e the Dragon's Chinese laundry is," went on Colwyn Dane. "It must be somewhere in this district. But first we've got to get ourselves a disguise."

They soon reached the bomb site where they had parked their car. Dane took the wheel. They'd only gone a few streets when he pulled up at a theatrical costumier's shop.

"This is where we get our disguises, Slick," he grinned. "But first I'll put the car away in the garage just along the street."

That done, Dane and Slick entered the costumier's. When they left, in the late afternoon, they were disguised as a couple of seamen, and Dane had in his pocket a list of all the Chinese laundries in the neighbourhood.

One of them was the laundry where the Dragon and his secret society had their lair!

The disguised 'tecs soon reached the first Chinese laundry on the list. The spectacled Chinaman behind the counter had an evil face and a sinister squint. Was this the place? Slick wondered. Dane pushed a freshly laundered neckerchief across the counter. In it was a long, jagged rent.

"Look, you swab!" he bellowed at the Chinese assistant. "My mate told me to bring this back. What do you mean by sending out a lubberly job like this? It wasn't torn when he sent it in for washing!"

The spectacled Chinaman peered at the neckerchief. Then he shook his head.

"You come allee w'ong place, mistel," he lisped. "Scarf no sent flom this laundly."

Dane appeared unconvinced.

"How do you make that out?" he demanded.

"This laundly not use that mark, mistel," the man replied, pointing to some letters inked in a corner of the neckerchief. "That belong Charlie's Chinese Laundly in Rowside Lane. You takee scarf there."

"You bet I will," said Dane, as he and Slick left the shop.

Outside, Dane chuckled softly.

"So it's Charlie's Laundry we want," he said. "That's where we'll find the Dragon—and maybe Brunning, the chap who was rescued from the police station."

Slick was thoughtful as they turned towards Rowside Lane. How did Dane know that the marked neckerchief came from the laundry where the Dragon had his headquarters?

"Of course!" gasped Slick, when they reached Rowside Lane. "You put the mark on the neckerchief, guv'nor. It's the same as the one you heard over the microphone. It's the mark of the Dragon's laundry hide-out!"

Dane chuckled again. His stunt to discover which laundry the Dragon was using had worked!

"Now to give the Dragon a surprise!" he exclaimed.

It was quite dark now, and Charlie's laundry was brightly lit. It seemed harmless and above board; but Dane had spotted a slant-eyed man at the back of the shop, whose gimlet eyes scrutinised every customer.

"We shan't get past him in a hurry," Dane told Slick. "And I guess the yard entrance is under close watch, too. The Dragon's lair is well guarded. We've got to get in somehow, though."

For ten minutes the disguised 'tecs watched from the street. Twice, in that time, vans turned into the yard next to the laundry.

"There's more vans expected," Dane whispered to Slick, "or they'd have closed the gates. That gives us a chance. Come on!"

Fifty yards away, a low railway bridge spanned the street. Followed by the wondering Slick, Dane climbed up to the track and darted along it until he was directly above the street. Then he swung himself over the bridge's parapet, and a moment later the pair of them were clinging by their hands to a narrow ledge above the roadway.

A van clattered under the bridge. It was a laundry van! As it passed beneath them, Dane whispered some instructions to Slick. Loosing their grip, they dropped together, landing with scarcely a sound on the roof of the van.

They were lying flat along the roof when the van turned into the yard by Charlie's laundry.

This time, the gates were closed behind the van. But the 'tecs had got inside the yard unseen—and that was all that mattered to Dane.

Would he manage to get to grips with the Dragon? Was he going to solve the mystery of the policemen who had been kidnapped and then let loose?

Twenty minutes later the disguised 'tecs were still sprawled on the roof. The van had been unloaded, and its driver had gone off somewhere. Only a watchman walked about, locking doors and putting out the lights. Finally, he entered a small lean-to across the yard.

"We're going to see what he's up to," whispered Dane, when five minutes passed and he did not reappear.

Sliding from the van roof, the 'tecs hurried to the lean-to and peered inside. There wasn't a sign of the watchman. What could have happened to him? There was no window or other door, and the shed was empty save for a few large, shabby hampers.

Dane examined the hampers in turn. All were empty. Then he spotted a dark cotton thread adhering to one basket. It was the same colour as the loose jacket the watchman had worn, and he remembered noticing a freshly repaired rent on the man's sleeve.

"It looks as if he was in the habit of coming this way," mused Dane. "Why did he tear his sleeve on this particular hamper?"

The ace 'tec peered closer. Suddenly he swung a leg over the side and told Slick to follow. Crouching in the hamper, he lowered the lid on them and then pushed at a spot on the floor. Instantly, the hamper, with them inside it, started to descend smoothly and silently.

Slick drew a deep breath. So that was it! The innocent-looking hamper was really a secret lift, which the watchman had used before them!

Was it carrying them down to the Dragon's lair?

With hardly a bump the hamper came to rest. Cautiously Dane raised the lid. He saw a long passage, dimly lit by swaying lanterns. Nobody was in sight, and not a sound came to the 'tecs' ears as they swung themselves from the basket lift. There was an acrid smell, however, that made Slick wrinkle his nose in disgust.

"Opium!" he whispered. "Looks as if that's the secret society's racket! But I don't see what that has got to do with the kidnapped policemen!"

Dane didn't reply. His hand had dipped to the pocket of his reefer jacket, where it closed over the butt of a gun. Then, with every sense on the alert, he led the way along the passage, with Slick following. The passage twisted and turned. Then a curtain-hung door, from beyond which came the sound of voices, blocked their way. Drawing the curtain aside, Dane found the door slightly ajar. Through it, he saw a narrow slice of a room, the walls of which were hung with silken curtains showing fire-breathing dragons.

On a gilded throne sat the most sinister-looking Oriental he had ever seen in his life. The Chinaman's face and head were quite bare of hair, his lips were just a cruel line, and his eyes were unfathomable pools of evil.

Was that the Dragon himself? Dane wondered. Was he the hidden power that was somehow linked with the mystery of the kidnapped policemen?

Those evil eyes suddenly switched to the door. The lips parted in a grating, snarling laugh.

"Enter, Mr. Dane!" came a mocking command. "The Dragon awaits you!"

At the same moment Dane heard a rush of feet behind him, and he knew that further attempt at concealment was just waste of time. He and Slick were in a trap. The Dragon's hirelings were obviously closing in on them. But Dane wasn't giving in. From his pocket he whipped out his gun and levelled it at the leering, sinister figure.

"Stay where you are!" he shouted to the men at his back. "Come any nearer, and I'll shoot the Dragon! I've got him covered!"

But the Chinamen came on.

Turning, Slick saw them. They were an evil-looking bunch, with glinting knives in their hands. At their head was the watchman they had seen in the laundry yard.

Nearer – nearer! Dane gritted his teeth. He'd got to show them he meant business. Crack! He'd fired at the Dragon's legs. At any rate, he'd force the secret society's leader to call off his men. But nothing like that happened. The Dragon still smiled–the same evil, inscrutable smile! Dane fired again. Crack! Crack! Crack! Still the Dragon smiled, apparently untouched by the bullets.

Dane thought fast. He'd never missed like that in his life! Was the Dragon proof against guns? There was no time for speculation at a moment like this. A yellow arm streaked over Dane's shoulder, grabbed the smoking gun, and he was knocked off his feet.

With half a dozen Chinamen on top of him, the ace 'tec fought desperately; but the odds were overwhelming, and, with Slick already a prisoner, he was dragged through the curtained doorway.

Then he saw the reason for his wasted bullets. He had been firing at an image cunningly thrown on to a screen by means of mirrors! The actual throne was on the opposite side of the room, where he could not possibly have seen it from the doorway.

From it the Dragon leered at him viciously.

"Forgive the illusion, Mr. Dane," the Dragon purred. "I was expecting you. There is, you observe, a warning light on the wall here that glows red when an unauthorised person uses our secret lift and fails to press a certain electric button. As I had already heard that you were inquiring about our society, I was ready for any disguise. Moreover, I was hoping you'd come to my humble abode. Why?" His voice changed to a deadly hiss. "Hearken, and you shall hear. The person whom the police dogs arrested last night–whom you know as Brunning – was my excellent nephew—"

"So you were behind his escape from the police station?" snapped Dane.

"That is so," agreed the Dragon. "Would you have me leave my nephew in the unclean hands of the foreign devils?"

Dane did some fast thinking. He was beginning to see partly why the policemen had been kidnapped. The Dragon thought that they had been responsible for his nephew's arrest, only to discover later that he was mistaken.

"Tell me!" hissed the Dragon, leaning forward with blazing eyes. "Who was the dog that arrested my nephew and took him to the police station? Tell me his name, and I assure you that after we have caught him he will be released again. No harm shall come to him. He will be set free – like the other policemen – and money will be given to him."

Dane's lips set tightly.

"Speak!" screamed the Chinese gang-boss. "Tell me, or—" He broke off, as a newcomer entered the room and whispered something.

"It is well!" went on the Dragon, his eyes flaming with triumph as he turned to Dane. "My nephew has remembered the number of the policeman who arrested him. We shall kidnap that policeman, and then let him go, knowing nothing about our illustrious society. But you and your accomplice have learnt too much about us – you must die! However, that can wait until I return. Take them away!" the Dragon roared at his hirelings. "Your lives shall be forfeited if they escape!"

To Slick's surprise, Dane submitted tamely as they were hustled from the room by the Chinese thugs. But the "tameness" was only an act. Dane was alert for any chance of a breakaway, and the chance came when they were making their way, with raised arms, along a narrow catwalk beside a rushing rainwater sewer.

Suddenly Dane swung back his leg. His heel crashed painfully into the shins of the Chinaman immediately behind him.

And that was when Dane went into action. Down came his arms, and Chinamen went spinning as he lashed out to left and right. Then, grabbing Slick around the waist, he took a flying leap into the sewer.

The swirling rain-waters closed over their heads, and Dane allowed himself to be carried along by the powerful current. Lack of breath forced them to the surface – but only for a moment. Then they were swimming under-water again.

Suddenly their further progress was barred by a rusty grating.

It took Dane only a few minutes to smash a way through it. They were carried on to the wide waters of the river, from which they

"Who was the dog that arrested my nephew . . . ?"

clambered after swimming for half a mile or so.

"We're going to the East End garage where we've left the car," said Dane. "And we've got to move fast, or the Dragon will beat us yet!"

Move fast they did.

Within half an hour the 'tecs had changed into their own clothes at the theatrical costumier's. Then they drove their car from the nearby garage, after Dane had spent some time on the phone there. They struck northwards, heading for a famous fishing village. When at last they pulled up in front of the village inn, the church clock was striking eleven.

"Why did we come here, guv'nor?" asked Slick.

"We've come to see somebody staying here. Somebody who started a fishing holiday last night!"

"Who's that, guv'nor?"

"The policeman who arrested the Dragon's nephew," replied Dane. "I learned he was here when I rang up the police station on the phone at the garage. And—"

The ace 'tec broke off suddenly. They had entered the inn. From somewhere above came a brief shout. Next moment, telling Slick to follow, Dane was leaping up the stairs, three steps at a time; and in his hand was a gun he had brought from the car.

Reaching the landing, he hurled himself at a door, beneath which showed a crack of light. It was a bedroom, and the 'tecs saw a startling scene as they burst inside.

Pinned to the bed was a struggling man in shirt and police-uniform trousers. A slant-eyed yellow man was holding a knife at his throat, and two more were forcing him down.

A fourth Chinaman, whom the 'tecs recognised as the Dragon himself, was searching the policeman's tunic.

With a cry of triumph the Dragon pulled out a cheap propelling pencil.

Then Dane butted in.

"Up with your hands – all of you!" he barked, moving the gun fanwise. "All right, Slick," he went on, as the Chinese crooks stared at him in amazement. "Frisk them!"

Helped by the constable, who had heaved himself from the bed, Slick carried out his famous chief's instructions. By that time the innkeeper and two other men had arrived, and the Chinamen were speedily made prisoners.

Dane held out the propelling pencil.

"Where did you get this, constable?" he asked.

"Off a man named Brunning, who I arrested yesterday, sir," replied the policeman. "I know it should have been handed in with the rest of the things from his pockets, but I forgot all about it, and brought it on holiday with me."

"A good thing you did," smiled Dane. "If you hadn't, it would have gone when the police station was broken into last night by one of the Dragon's men!"

Slick gasped.

"Gosh! So it was the pencil that the Dragon was after?" he exploded. "His gang kidnapped the policemen who were on patrol in the district where his nephew was arrested because he thought one of them might have it. But I don't see what he wanted a tin pencil for."

"Oh, don't you?" asked Dane.

As he spoke he twisted the pencil in his fingers. It came apart, and from the metal tube he shook a tightly-rolled paper.

"It's a message for the Dragon about smuggling a cargo of drugs," he went on, when he had examined the paper. "That's why the Dragon was keen to get it. He knew that with this paper the police could and would smash his dope racket. And that's just what's going to happen now!"

Colwyn Dane solves yet another exciting mystery on page 183.

THE DOG THAT KNEW TOO MUCH

by Harry Belfield

When "Square-Deal" Sullivan rescued an old man from the river in the Canadian backwoods, the man gave him a strange message about his dog. Little did Square-Deal guess that this chance remark would lead him into great danger and that the dog would solve a mystery for him.

"Gosh!" That was a shout for help, or my name's not Square-Deal Sullivan!"

Rod Sullivan, nicknamed Square–Deal and the youngest lumberjack at the Twisted Pine Logging Camp, paused at his work to listen. He was alone in the big woods, felling a giant tree, and for a while the only sound he heard was the roar of the nearby river. Then, faintly, above the noise of rushing water, a hoarse, despairing cry came to his ears.

Square-Deal didn't wait a moment longer. Crashing through the forest undergrowth, he came out on the river-bank.

One glance was enough for him. In midstream was a frail birch-bark canoe, with an elderly man seated in it. The man had lost his paddle, and the canoe was completely out of control. To make matters worse, several huge logs, spinning in the current, were sweeping down on it.

Square-Deal sprang into action. A mighty leap carried him to the nearest log.

Under his sudden weight the log bucked viciously, and he only just managed to save himself from a tumble by using his long-handled axe as a balancing pole. As he steadied himself he jumped on to a second log, and from that to a third. Each leap carried him closer to the runaway canoe. Square-Deal made another frantic jump and landed on a fourth log. It swayed so violently that he was forced to straddle it and work his way along it.

As he was almost at the end of the log he reached out with his axe.

"Got it!" he breathed as the gleaming axe-head hooked over the gunwale of the canoe.

But he had spoken too soon. A sudden eddy swept the canoe away from him.

Square-Deal gasped with dismay. He realised that, instead of hooking the canoe, the sharp axe-blade had sliced through the flimsy hull and water was pouring through a gaping rent in the canoe's side. The canoe's passenger let out a yell as his craft began to sink.

"I can't swim!" he cried hoarsely.

Square-Deal didn't mean to let a stroke of bad luck thwart his rescue attempt. Hurling himself from the log he plunged into the river and struck out for the sinking canoe. He was not a moment too soon. Already the canoe was down to its gunwale. It sank lower every second, and the old man began to struggle in the water.

Square-Deal cut his way through the water with a powerful crawl stroke, but just before he reached the spot the old man sank out of sight. Like a flash, Square-Deal duck-dived down through the muddy water.

One of the logs rushed by him, carried fast on the powerful current. Square-Deal jerked himself aside to avoid it, but he was too late – the huge log grazed his shoulder, numbing his arm to the elbow.

Square-Deal gritted his teeth. Although he was in real trouble, the thought of giving up his rescue attempt never even entered his head. Groping around in the gloom of the river water, his fingers touched a woollen jacket.

Quickly he grasped the jacket and heaved with all his might. The man came up slowly. He was unconscious and hung, a dead weight, in Square-Deal's grasp.

The young lumberjack struck out for the bank, dragging his burden behind him. With one arm almost useless from the shock of the blow he had received, Square-Deal found it a hard struggle to battle his way against the current.

When at last he reached the rocky bank and pulled the old man up on to safe ground, Square-Deal was all in. Even so, his first thought was for the man he had rescued from the canoe.

Square-Deal had recognised him as an old prospector named Charlie, who lived in a tiny shack not far from Twisted Pine, with only a dog for company.

To his relief the old fellow was still alive, though there was an ugly bruise on his forehead where the drifting log had struck him a glancing blow.

As Square-Deal bent over him Charlie mumbled something.

"Griff knows . . ."

Square-Deal was puzzled. Griff was the name of Charlie's dog. What would a dog know? It couldn't speak, so how could it tell Square-Deal anything? Before he could ask any questions, Charlie spoke again in a hoarse whisper.

"Look after Griff!" he pleaded.

"I'll do that," Square-Deal promised. "You can count on me, Charlie. You don't need to worry. I'll take care of Griff. But what's this about him knowing something? What does Griff know?"

Charlie, however, was too ill to reply. In vain Square-Deal tried to revive him. Finally he gathered the unconscious prospector in his arms and carried him back to the logging camp.

"He needs a doctor bad," he told the clerk. "You'd best get through to the hospital on the radio. They'll send out an ambulance plane for him. Meantime, I've got a promise to keep. I'll see you later!"

Square-Deal headed straight to Charlie's lonely shack in the forest. As he strode along he tried to figure out what it was that Griff could know. But it was as big a mystery as ever when he came in sight of the cabin.

"Maybe Griff will put me wise somehow," he told himself as he lifted the latch.

He stepped inside. Then, just inside the room, he came to a sudden halt. Normally Charlie's shack was as clean and bright as a new pin, but now it looked as if it had been struck by a tornado.

"Maybe Griff could have slipped his collar," Square-Deal mused, "but if he had he'd still be in the cabin – the window's closed and the door was latched, so he couldn't have got out—"

As a sudden thought struck him, Square-Deal went out through the door of the cabin and began to hunt around on the ground outside. The young lumberman had the tracking skill of an Indian, and in a few minutes the slight traces left on the ground told him that someone had entered the hut since the time Charlie had left it. From the signs Square-Deal found, it seemed clear that the man had been wearing spiked lumberjack's boots and that he had dragged the dog out of the hut behind him!

"So Griff was taken away!" gritted Square-Deal. "Maybe Charlie was expecting trouble when he told me to look after his dog. Well, I'm not letting Charlie down. I'm going to find the feller who took his dog away, and get Griff back!"

Square-Deal carried on with his search of the shack. But the place had been thoroughly ransacked already, and he learned nothing further. At last he gave up and concentrated on the tracks around the door. Even they proved of little help, for they stopped a dozen yards from the shack.

"It looks as if it's not going to be easy to find that dog," muttered the young lumberjack.

Then a sudden idea struck him. His face was more cheerful as he returned to the Twisted Pine Lumber Camp. He'd thought of a way to find out the identity of Griff's kidnapper! And that was the first step towards keeping his promise to Charlie!

When he reached the camp, the odd-job man was scrubbing out the long shed where the lumberjacks had their meals.

"I'll never get it done before the fellers come in for their supper," grumbled the odd-job man.

"I'll lend a hand," volunteered Square-Deal.

Soon he was on his knees, smearing soap on the floor. The odd-job man watched approvingly. Though he didn't realise it, it was all part of Square-Deal's scheme to identify Griff's kidnapper! Presently there was a chorus of shouts outside. The hungry lumberjacks were returning from the big woods. Laughing and yelling, they charged towards the hut where Square-Deal was still scrubbing the floor.

Leading by a yard, one husky lumberjack dived through the doorway. As he did so he stepped right on a bar of soap that Square-Deal had left in his path. His feet shot away from under him, and he landed on his back with a wallop that shook the cabin. Two other burly lumbermen were too close behind him to check themselves in time. They piled on top of him. Other men skidded helplessly into the hut. Soon there was a heap of floundering, yelling lumberjacks in the doorway.

"Sorry, boys!" cried Square-Deal, leaping to his feet. "Looks as if I left too much soap down!"

A pair of waving legs showed from among the heaving pile. Square-Deal glimpsed boots shod with long spikes, and on the spikes of one boot was wedged a cake of soap.

"Get me outa here!" called a voice from the bottom of the pile.

It was the foreman – a fellow named Jake Fallon, a giant of a man. His leg thrashed the air in front of Square-Deal's face – and Square-Deal suddenly jumped into action, grabbed the waving leg and heaved with all his might.

Jake Fallon came out of the heap of struggling men and tumbled to the floor.

None too gently Square-Deal set him on his feet.

"Shut up, Jake!" said Square-Deal as the foreman started to storm at him. "Maybe I left that cake of soap around on purpose – see?"

"Why?" snorted the foreman.

"Because I was lookin' for a certain guy," returned Square-Deal. "The only thing I knew about this feller I was lookin' for was that he'd got certain spikes missing from the sole of his boots. I learned that from studying the tracks he left at Charlie's shack."

"What's this got to do with me?" demanded the foreman.

"Just this, Jake!" snapped Square-Deal. "Your boots are missing the same spikes as the tracks I found. Maybe you'd like to tell me why you took Charlie's dog away?"

An uneasy gleam showed in the foreman's narrowed eyes.

"I don't know what you're talking about," he blustered. "I don't know nothing about any dog, and I ain't been near Charlie's cabin for a month or more. But I'm givin' you a word of warnin', Sullivan," he hissed. "Keep outa my way, or mebbe you'll get hurt 'worse'n Charlie."

Square-Deal turned away without another word.

He knew that the foreman was lying – and would only tell more lies to cover himself. Square-Deal hadn't a hope of learning anything about Griff from Jake Fallon, but he reckoned he had figured out another way to trace the dog and to keep his promise to Charlie.

During supper in the lumberman's hut, the talk was mainly of Charlie who had been flown to the nearest hospital without recovering consciousness. Square-Deal told the story of his rescue of the old prospector, but he took good care not to mention Charlie's mysterious words uttered before he lost consciousness: "Griff knows!"

As he spoke, Square-Deal watched Jake Fallon carefully. But whatever the burly foreman knew about Griff's disappearance from Charlie's hut, he kept quiet about it and gave nothing away. By the time he climbed into his bunk that night he had still neither done nor said anything which might make Square-Deal more suspicious.

A couple of hours passed. The only sound that could be heard in the lumberjacks' bunkhouse was the heavy breathing of the sleeping men, dog-tired after a hard day's work in the woods.

But Square-Deal was wide awake – and listening intently. Suddenly he heard a floorboard creak. It came from close to the bunk where Jake Fallon slept. There was another creak, then a sound of stealthy movement.

"Fallon's got out of bed," Square-Deal muttered to himself. "He seems to be making his way to the door."

Next moment, Square-Deal heard the squeak of a hinge, and the bunkhouse door opened. The foreman slipped outside. Square-Deal was determined to find out where he had gone. He got up from his bunk, dressed hurriedly, and a minute later he followed Fallon through the bunkhouse door.

It was a dark, moonless night, but Square-Deal could just make out the shadowy figure of Fallon entering the thick woods which bordered the lumber camp. Quickly Square-Deal set off after the foreman. It was as black as pitch in the forest, but the occasional crackle of a stick under Fallon's foot served to guide Square-Deal. Soon he realised that Fallon was heading in the direction of Charlie's shack.

Suddenly Square-Deal stopped short. He heard a curious muffled sound. It took him some moments to realise that it was the barking of a dog.

"It's my bet that the dog is Griff!" muttered Square-Deal. "And from the sound of his bark he's in real trouble. I've got to find him!"

Square-Deal spotted a clearing in the forest only a few steps ahead. As he reached it the rising moon glimmered between the trees. Its light revealed the shadowy mouth of a cave in a sandy ridge.

Now Square-Deal realised why Griff's bark had sounded muffled – the dog was imprisoned in the cave! And Fallon must have gone there, too, judging from the noise the dog was making.

Soundlessly, Square-Deal groped his way through the darkness of the tunnel. A gleam of torchlight showed ahead of him, and suddenly he heard another angry growl from the dog.

"Griff doesn't seem to like Fallon," chuckled Square-Deal. "And I can't say I blame him!"

But, next second, Square-Deal's words ended in an indignant gasp as he heard the sudden crack of a whip, followed by a yelp from Griff. Square-Deal bounded forward. Three strides brought him to where the tunnel widened into a cave. There, in the dim light of a torch, he saw Griff chained to a stake which had been firmly driven into the ground. Swinging a heavy whip above the dog stood Jake Fallon.

"I'll show you who's boss, you mangy brute!" the foreman shouted wildly. "Then you're gonna lead me to your master's secret!"

As the lash hissed downwards, Square-Deal leapt at Jake Fallon and slammed a terrific punch at his chin. Fallon stumbled sideways, and Square-Deal wrenched the whip from his grasp, tossing it into a corner of the cave.

"You won't be needing that, Fallon!" he snapped angrily. "You reckoned you'd make Griff lead you to his master's secret, and when he wouldn't do it you thought you could beat him into showing you! Well, I'm gonna stop you!"

Fallon had been badly shaken by Square-Deal's sudden appearance in the cave, but he had soon recovered himself.

"I warned you to stay out of my way, Sullivan!" he roared. "You wouldn't take my advice so now I'm gonna fix you! Take that, for a start!"

Fallon swung a savage blow at Square-Deal's head. The young lumberjack ducked it in the nick of time, and the punch slid harmlessly over his head. In a flash Square-Deal jerked himself aside and, catching the foreman off-balance, slammed a straight left to his jaw. The blow rocked Fallon back on to his heels, but it did no real damage, except to add to the foreman's fury.

"I'll make you sorry for that!" he screeched as he closed with Square-Deal.

Next moment the two lumbermen were fighting hammer and tongs, trading punch for punch. Fallon was a good deal heavier than Square-Deal and had a much greater reach, but Square-Deal was far more agile than his opponent.

As the foreman closed in to attack him, his arms flailing wildly, Square-Deal realised that he would have to wear out his opponent by keeping out of the way of his whirling arms until he was tired. Only then could he afford to sail in and finish the fight on more or less equal terms.

But at the moment the treacherous lumberman was far from exhausted.

Square-Deal saw a sledgehammer punch coming straight for him, and hurled himself out of reach. Fallon aimed a punch with his other fist. For a second it seemed that Square-Deal was in real trouble, but he dodged the blow cleverly.

Suddenly Fallon unleashed a terrific attack, determined to finish the fight quickly. Square-Deal jumped to right and left as if he was an acrobat, successfully avoiding every punch that the foreman threw at him.

Jake Fallon was becoming more and more furious every moment.

"I'll fix you, Sullivan!" he bellowed viciously.

Square-Deal moved faster. He was harder to hit than a shadow. Now Fallon was beginning to tire. His punches lacked the sting of the earlier ones.

Square-Deal sailed in with a burst of hard punching. Fallon retreated, trying to cover up. But the move brought him within reach of Griff, who, since the fight had started, had been leaping about excitedly, eager to join in the scrap, but stopped short by his chain! His sharp, white teeth snapped against Fallon's leg, tearing a piece from his trousers.

Fallon stumbled sideways, lost his balance and measured his length on the floor. Griff barked excitedly, as if encouraging Square-Deal to sail in and finish the fight!

But Square-Deal did nothing of the sort. Instead, he drew back and allowed Fallon to struggle to his feet. Even in a fierce fight he lived up to his nickname and gave his opponent a square deal!

Fallon climbed up unsteadily. His eyes narrowed with hatred as he rushed again at Square-Deal and lashed out with one foot.

The lumberman's boot caught Square-Deal on the ankle before he could jump out of reach. He staggered towards the wall of the cave. At the same instant Fallon drove another kick at him, caught him off balance and sent him crashing to the floor. Square-Deal's head hit the cave wall a glancing blow, and he was out to the wide.

"That'll teach you to keep your nose outa other guys' business," snarled the foreman. "And now I'll deal with you," he added, whirling on Griff. "Come on! You're gonna show me where your master's hidden his secret."

It was an hour later when Square-Deal opened his eyes and realised that he was alone in the cave.

He was furious that he had allowed himself to be k.o.'d. by Fallon and was determined to keep his promise to Charlie, the old prospector.

His main concern was to learn what had happened to Griff. Quickly he studied the tracks left in the soft soil. He soon learned that Fallon had dragged Griff away by his chain. In fact, Griff had gone so unwillingly with the foreman that he had left a clear trail for Square-Deal to follow. It led through the woods and up to the cabin where Charlie lived.

Square-Deal approached the shack warily. A moving light showed through the window, and he realised that the rascally foreman must still be there.

Suddenly the door opened. Through it came Griff, tugging at his chain, the other end of which was held by Fallon. The dog made for the little patch of ground that Charlie had cultivated and proceeded to scratch in it vigorously. Then with a triumphant yelp he pulled a large bone from the hole he had made!

All Griff had done was to lead Fallon to the spot where he had hidden a bone! Suddenly there was an elated shout from Fallon. Square-Deal's hopes fell as the foreman stooped and dragged a small sacking-wrapped bundle from the hole.

Square-Deal realised the truth of the words he had heard Charlie utter after his rescue from the river – Griff had "known" because Charlie had buried something important in the very spot where Griff had buried a bone!

But the young lumberjack wasted no more time on speculation. In half a dozen leaping strides he came up behind the foreman. Fallon whirled and tried to drag something from his pocket. But this time Square-Deal was taking no chances. His fist slammed Fallon's jaw, and as Fallon tottered Square-Deal let loose another sledgehammer punch.

"That makes up for the way you treated Griff," he gritted, as the foreman hit the ground with a crash, dropping the package he had taken from the hole.

Square-Deal scooped up the slim bundle Fallon had dropped, tore off the covering of sackcloth and exposed a folded paper. The moonlight was strong enough for him to see that it was a roughly-drawn map.

"Gosh! It's a map showing where Charlie had struck gold," he muttered excitedly. "I'm taking care of it till he comes out of hospital, Fallon. And I'm looking after Griff, too!"

When Charlie came out of hospital, none the worse for his ducking in the river, Square-Deal and Griff met him at the door.

As Square-Deal had reckoned, the map was a guide to the position of a lucky strike that Charlie had made – and the strike proved lucky for Square-Deal, too, for after hearing his story the old prospector insisted on Square-Deal becoming his partner in the Twisted Pine Gold Mine.

IVORY CHALLENGE

Rex Stanton was out trying to capture an ivory poacher in Africa when he was ambushed by him. He was knocked unconscious and left bound helpless across an animal trail. There was nothing he could do when a leopard found him and then a wild elephant . . .

Rex Stanton opened his eyes to brilliant, blinding sunlight. His head throbbed. Through a mist he saw the vivid green fronds of the jungle.

A deep voice spoke. "See, B'wana, the Game Ranger wakes!"

Another man laughed. It was Jeff Baseley . . .

Stanton had been tracking Baseley, sure in his own mind that the unscrupulous white hunter was behind the ivory poaching in his reserve. But Stanton had been careless – and his final memory was of a stunning blow on the head. He struggled to rise, but something held him. He craned his neck to find out what it was. He discovered that he lay spread-eagled on his back, wrists and ankles lashed to wooden stakes driven deep into the ground. Baseley's gloating face swam into focus.

"You were too bright for your own good, Ranger. As soon as I found you on my trail, I knew I had to do something about you . . .

"Know where you're lying, Stanton? You're staked out across an animal run leading down to a salt lick!"

A sweat bead trickled into the corner of Stanton's eye. Animals, like human beings, needed salt. The wild beasts of the jungle would come with the onset of darkness, using their run – and find him.

Baseley whistled a fragment of tune.

"We're leaving you now, Ranger. Wonder what'll get to you first? Could be ants . . . or even a rhino. Afterwards we'll return to remove your cords and the stakes. That way, it will look like an accident!"

It was a diabolical plan, and no-one would ever suspect Baseley.

"Come on, M'Polo, let's go."

Stanton heard them fade into the bush, and then silence fell over the jungle. He was alone, staked across the trail under a blazing sun. Flies settled on his face. He struggled ineffectually with his cords. Then something moved close by. A mamba! His blood ran cold as the venomous snake began to cross his body. He held his breath, not daring to stir . . .

As he froze, pictures from the past flashed across his mind. He relived the flooding of the Kariba Dam.

There had been an elephant, Tusker, marooned on an island in the lake with her calf. The calf would not take to the water, and Tusker would not leave the calf. He had netted the calf and floated it off on a raft, but still Tusker refused to enter the water. She was an unusual elephant with an ivory blaze on her forehead.

He had borrowed a tape-recorder and broadcast the sound of a herd from the mainland, the sound of elephants calling to each other. And Tusker had answered. She had slid into the water and swum to safety. His last memory was of Tusker herding her calf into the jungle . . .

The mamba passed on its way. Stanton relaxed again, almost sobbing with relief.

Then he heard gunshots farther down the trail. Baseley was not content to wait. He was stampeding wild animals towards him. The brush crackled, and a staccato cough sounded close to his ear . . . *leopard!*

He saw the big cat as it opened its jaws, snarling angrily.

A paw slashed at Stanton's ribs, drew blood. Helpless, he waited for certain death. He had no chance at all. Suddenly the ground shook. The leopard turned to face a newcomer. It crouched over him, spitting. Then he heard the trumpeting of a wild elephant.

It checked at the sight of the cat. It swayed above Stanton, a monstrous bulk, and there was an ivory blaze between the flapping grey ears.

"Tusker," he croaked. Tusker!"

The big cat turned and snarled at him. Stanton shouted louder, *"Tusker!"*

The elephant lumbered forward, button-eyes fixed on him. She lowered her head and gleaming tusks stabbed at the leopard. She trumpeted a challenge.

The cat sprang for the mountain of leathery hide. Tusker lifted her forefeet and her massive feet thudded to the earth inches from Stanton's head. She coiled her trunk about the cat's tawny body, lifted it high in the air and dashed it to the ground. The leopard was dead in an instant.

Tusker's trunk descended again, but gently now. She snatched at the wooden stakes, uprooted them.

Stanton, free, climbed to his feet. "Thanks, Tusker," he said. "Thanks, old girl."

Slowly, the elephant moved off into the jungle. Stanton watched her go, a lump in his throat. No-one would ever believe him, but he knew Tusker had recognized him. He knew a favour had been returned.

Grimly, he settled to wait for Baseley to come for him. This was one arrest he would be glad to make.

THE PLANET OF MYSTERY

Blackie Gordon was a space pirate who had murdered helpless people on the planet, Valla, but trouble was in store for him when Captain Condor of the Space Marines suddenly arrived one day.

"I've planned and schemed for this. It's taken years but it's been worth it. The chance of a lifetime, and we've grabbed it. We'll wallow in luxury for the rest of our days."

Blackie Gordon, a dark, heavily-bearded, piratical-looking man surveyed the smouldering, ray-gunned ruin of what had a short time before been a peaceful town. He smiled with satisfaction. His hard eyes showed no pity for the sprawled bodies of the natives he and his four companions had just murdered.

Here, on this planet Valla, violence was almost unknown. Blackie and his companions had butchered a helpless, defenceless community, and were now stripping the place of loot and loading it into their space yacht.

Native works of art, constructed in rare minerals and precious stones, were famous throughout the galaxy, but as the Vallans were a simple people, with no interest in trade or profit, samples of their work were scarce outside their own planet, and much coveted by collectors. The loot Blackie's men were now cramming into their spacecraft was going to fetch a fabulous fortune back on Earth.

"I wish we hadn't let one or two of them get away to raise the alarm," muttered one of the men uneasily. "This planet is under the protection of the Interstellar Survey Service, and Captain Condor arrived yesterday on a routine inspection."

Chuck Bray, the most youthful member of the vicious gang, laughed scornfully at his companion's fears.

"But we're not waiting here for Condor to find us, are we Blackie?" he asked.

"Too right we're not," agreed Blackie. "As soon as we've got as much as we can carry we're blasting off."

"Are you sure we're not already overloaded?" asked the uneasy one.

Chuck, who had been stacking the loot inside as the others brought it to him, disappeared into the airlock, calling over his shoulder.

"I'll just check."

The airlock clanged shut. From within the ship came the ominous rumble of a startermotor.

"Chuck!" yelled Blackie.

A mocking laugh sounded in his helmet radio.

"Sorry, Blackie. But the ship *would* be overloaded with you four aboard. I'm going to have to leave you behind. So long."

"Chuck – you wouldn't—"

"It's like you're so fond of saying, Blackie. The chance of a lifetime. I'd be a fool to settle for a one-fifth share when I can have it all for myself."

The ship was taking off. Blackie snatched up a ray-gun and fired wildly. A cloud of white vapour billowed out near the jet-tubes and for a moment the space yacht seemed to falter in its upward climb. Then it accelerated swiftly and became a vanishing dot which rode a vapour trail stretching away out into space.

"The rat! He's marooned us!" gasped one of the men.

"Double-crossed!" grated Blackie. "But I'll get even. One day I'll catch up with him. I don't care how long it takes. And when I do—"

"What about Condor? We'd better start running for it."

"There's nowhere to run," Blackie said bitterly. He was right.

A short time later a patrol boat landed. From it stepped Captain Condor, accompanied by Sergeant Willis, of the Space Marines.

Blackie was waiting alone to greet them. At first he tried to bluff it out.

"Captain, am I glad to see you! I'd been wondering how to get in

110

touch with the authorities. We were exploring, you see, when we came on this terrible mess. I guess some bunch of crooks—"

"Cut it out, Blackie Gordon," Condor said coldly. "We monitored your radio conversation with Chuck, just before he took off. We know everything. You're under arrest."

"I'm not taking the whole rap," snapped Blackie. "Chuck is as guilty as any of us."

"We know where to pick him up. He didn't get far. You damaged his tubes when you fired at him. He crash-landed on Negus."

"Thanks for telling me. I'm going after him and you're going to help me," grinned Blackie. "Look behind you, Captain."

Condor turned. Blackie's men had come out of hiding. Four ray-guns were aimed at Condor and Willis!

"I'd kill you now, but for one thing," Blackie said coldly. "None of us knows how to handle a service ship like yours. We need you two to navigate."

"Don't try it," warned Condor. "You'll only be storing up more trouble for yourself."

"This was the chance of a lifetime," insisted Blackie. "I'm not letting it get away from me."

A peculiar smile played round Condor's lips.

"All right, Blackie. We'll take you there. But you're going to wish we hadn't!"

Negus was a small, uninhabited planet, orbiting close to its parent sun. But small though it was, it had a land area of several thousand square miles, and searching it for an object as tiny as a crashed space-yacht, even with the help of electronic scanners, wasn't easy. They circled the planet a number of times before Willis spotted the wreck. It was bedded in the sand in the jungle-fringed shore of a wide and empty ocean.

Condor realised then why it had been so hard to find. Chuck had crashed on the planet's night side. They had had to wait until the spot came round to the sunlit side before they could see it.

The scout ship touched down on the shore. As Blackie moved eagerly to the airlock door Condor turned to him.

"Blackie, I'm warning you for your own good. You're a wholesale murderer. But you'd do better to turn back and take your punishment than go out there looking for Chuck."

Blackie sneered.

"I've got a lifetime ahead of me. Do you think I want to spend it in some institute for the scientific correction of criminals? I'm planning to live every minute of it in the lap of luxury, once I've settled with Chuck."

He approached the wrecked ship, gun in hand, shouting.

"Come on out, Chuck!"

But the wreck was empty. There was no sign of Chuck, or the loot. Then he noticed footprints in the sand, leading into the jungle.

"He's had time to hide it somewhere. Come on!"

The lush vegetation was fresh and springlike. The densely packed shrubs and undergrowth was in budding leaf. Once clear of the shore the heat became sweltering and oppressive. Blackie opened his helmet, then unzipped his heavy suit. His followers copied him, but as Willis moved to do the same, Condor stopped him with a warning gesture.

They came to a clearing. Blackie saw something move, and yelled.

Willis caught his breath at the sight which met them.

An old, old man, with a dirty beard reaching almost to his waist, was trying to hide from them by crawling on all fours. He was clad only in a shirt that had been torn to tatters by brambles. Blackie pounced on him, grabbing him by his skeleton-like arm.

"Where's the man from that ship? What did he do with the stuff?"

The ancient being stared at him with puzzled eyes. Blackie grabbed his dirty beard, twisting it savagely. The old man mumbled meaninglessly.

"Quit it, Blackie," urged one of the men. "He can't understand you."

"No? Take a look. That's Chuck's shirt he's wearing. And Chuck's wrist—watch!" stormed Blackie.

He would have beaten his victim mercilessly if Condor hadn't intervened.

"You're wasting your time, Blackie," he warned.

The crook snarled and turned away.

"The stuff's here somewhere. I'll find it," he vowed.

All around them the vegetation was now in blossom. Some of it was even bearing fruit. An hour later leaves withered and began to drop.

The ground was thick with fallen fruit. Fresh new growth pushed its way up through a mat of decay.

They stumbled on. Time and again Willis was tempted to open his suffocating helmet, but Condor stopped him. At last they came to another clearing. It contained a number of dome-shaped, prefabricated plastic huts, half-buried under decayed vegetation.

Blackie looked suspiciously at Condor.

"What sort of people live around here?" he demanded.

"None," Condor answered. "A survey party did investigate this planet. But for special reasons they didn't stay long."

Blackie ignored the warning behind the words. But his face was beginning to look worn and lined. His eyes were growing anxious, puzzled. He began to search the huts. Suddenly he let out a yell of triumph.

"It's here. All of it. Stacked in this hut. That means Chuck must be around somewhere. He'll come back to it. We'll wait!"

The hours passed. The surrounding vegetation made new growth, blossomed, fruited and withered many times. The men were all beginning to look strangely drawn and haggard.

"I'm tired," Blackie confessed. "We'll kip until morning. There's no hurry. The rest of you take it in turns to watch Condor."

He threw himself on the ground. When he woke his bones ached. Night had passed and dawn was breaking.

In the dim light he could see that Condor and Willis, despite the discomfort, had slept in their space suits. He shifted his gaze, then sat up with a gasp. A totally unfamiliar figure, an old man with a tangled beard, sat slumped at the entrance to the hut. He looked round. Two more wrinkled, white–bearded figures were sleeping near him.

He yelled.

"Condor!" he shouted. "Who are these old freaks? Where are my men."

Condor unzipped a pocket on his space suit and brought out a mirror.

"Take a look at yourself, Blackie," he said.

Blackie recoiled in terror. His beard was black no longer. It was white and tangled. His strong, cruel face, was gaunt and withered with age.

"No!" he cried.

"I tried to warn you. You wouldn't listen," Condor said. "Surely you noticed how quickly the vegetation here matures and withers? This planet's sun gives off radiations which speed-up the life-cycle. That's why our survey team didn't stay long. Negus is useless to humans. Every few minutes a man ages a year – unless he's protected against the radiation."

Blackie shuddered.

"That old man – the one wearing Chuck's shirt—"

"Was Chuck," nodded Condor. "There's nothing we can do for him, but we may just be able to save the rest of you from dying of old age if you surrender yourselves to me right away and we get you off this planet fast."

Blackie clawed for his discarded space suit. He was so feeble that Willis had to help him with it.

"You should have listened to me, and taken your punishment, Blackie," Condor said. "You've punished yourself, far worse. You murdered a lot of innocent people to gain for yourself a lifetime of luxury. It's gone, Blackie. You've lived it, in one single night on this planet!"

Have you read The World of Giant Butterflies on page 39?
It is another adventure about Captain Condor in outer space.

"You've punished yourself far worse . . ."

THE RIDDLE OF THE MISSING SOCCER STAR

by Hal Chiltington

What did happen when Tommy Drew, the soccer star, crashed his car and yet mysteriously disappeared from underneath it? This was the problem that faced the great detective, Maxwell Keene, in one of the greatest mysteries of his career.

"Gosh! It should be a game worth watching guv'nor," exclaimed Sparks Cogan, the young assistant of the famous private detective, Maxwell Keene. "I hope Tommy Drew plays on top form. If he does he should get two or three goals!"

Sparks was driving his famous chief along a lonely country road. They were on their way to watch a vital League football match between Minver United and Hammond Swifts, whose star centre-forward, Tommy Drew, had been hitting the headlines lately.

Because Tommy was an old pal of Sparks Cogan, the detective had given themselves plenty of time to get to the ground. Sparks hoped to be able to meet Tommy for a few minutes before the match.

Suddenly a loud blare sounded right on their tail. Next moment an open red sports car streaked past them. Its single occupant was a well-built chap with a shock of tousled hair. He gave the 'tecs a cheery wave as he overtook them.

"That's Tommy Drew!" cried Sparks. "He must be in a hurry to get to the ground. Anyhow, we'll see him there!"

The red car disappeared round a distant bend of the road ahead. Seconds later a crash came faintly to the 'tecs' ears from somewhere around the same bend. Keene's jaw jutted.

"Sounds as if your pal has run into trouble," he snapped. "Step on it, Sparks!"

Sparks did not need to be told twice. Suddenly anxious that his old friend had met with a fearful accident, he put his foot down. The big car surged forward.

As soon as they rounded the bend, they saw in one glance what had happened. Tommy Drew's red sports car had run off the road and overturned in the ditch. Its wheels were still spinning, but there was not a sign of the star footballer.

"He could still be underneath, guv'nor," gritted Sparks. "And the car may catch fire at any moment! We've got to do something to save him!"

Keene had already realised that peril. Before his car had stopped rolling, he whipped the door open, heaved himself to his feet and took a flying leap on to the grass verge at the roadside. He landed on all fours within a yard of the overturned car and reached it in a single bound. Its door had jammed, and the reek of spilled petrol came to his nostrils as he wrenched at the handle.

Precious seconds were wasted before the door opened. The petrol smell was stronger when at last he peered inside. At any moment now there might be an explosion, and the car would go up in flames!

"Keep away, Sparks!" he called to his young assistant. "I'll see to Drew!"

Then he had a shock.

Nobody was in the car.

He looked again. No, he hadn't made a mistake! There was no sign of Tommy Drew. There was no time for a third look. With a terrific roar a column of flame leapt up from beneath the bonnet.

Keene was forced to jump backwards from the terrific heat. Sparks jumped from the car and ran towards the blazing vehicle.

"Quick, guv'nor!" he cried. "We've got to do something to get Tommy out of that blaze!"

"No!" rapped Keene. "Keep back! You can't do anything for Tommy! For the simple reason – he isn't in that car!"

"Wha-at!" exclaimed Sparks, pulling up in amazement. "Not in it? But that's impossible. Only a few moments ago we saw him driving it at full tilt round the corner—"

"Nevertheless," broke in Keene quietly, "when I looked into that car just now, there wasn't a soul in it. And I had a good long inspection to make sure."

"Then—then—what on earth's happened to Tommy?" gasped Sparks.

"Your guess is as good as mine," retorted Keene. "I scent a strange mystery here. Let's have a look round to make sure he hasn't been flung clear."

But though the 'tecs searched the hedges and ditches all around the blazing car, they couldn't find a trace of the missing footballer. Next, Keene turned his attention to the road along which they had come.

There, on the tarmac, were marks which showed where the red car had gone into a terrific skid. What could have caused that skid? Keene wondered.

Then the 'tec noticed that where the skid started a large tree grew at the roadside, with spreading branches overhanging the road. That gave him an idea.

While Sparks watched wonderingly, he darted to the tree, climbed its gnarled trunk and worked his way along a bough. Now he was above the very spot where the skid had started.

His sharp eyes spotted some marks on the bark—marks that could have been made by someone climbing the tree. For some time he searched around. Then he swung himself down from the tree and rejoined his young assistant.

"Find any clues, guv'nor?" demanded Sparks breathlessly.

"Enough to tell me that Tommy Drew has been kidnapped!" was Keene's startling reply.

"Kidnapped!" echoed Sparks. "How on earth do you know that?"

"By marks I saw up in that tree. There were grooves and pieces of hemp from a rope sticking to the bark which tell me that the kidnappers, who were crouched up in that tree, lassoed Tommy as he drove past underneath and pulled him up out of his car," replied Keene. "Now let's have a look round to see if we can see any signs that'll tell us which way the kidnappers went."

It did not take long for the 'tec to pick up a trail which led off into some nearby woods. But any hope of overtaking the crooks vanished when they slithered down into a sunken road and saw the tyre-tracks of a car that had been recently parked there.

"Drew was dumped in the car, and it was driven off at speed," said Keene, after a careful scrutiny of the road. "They've been gone five minutes or so, so there's not a hope of overtaking them. But here's something that may help to find your pal."

As he spoke, Keene picked up a shining key from the grass, where the waiting car had stood.

"It's slightly warm! That means it must have come from somebody's pocket!" went on the 'tec. "One of the kidnappers could have dropped it. And there are initials stamped on it. H. S.! Does that mean anything to you?"

Sparks looked thoughtful.

"Could be Hammond Swifts – Tommy's team," he said.

"Exactly," agreed Maxwell Keene. "It looks as if one of the kidnappers was connected with the Swifts. I've got a hunch we'll find out who kidnapped him when we get to the Swifts' ground. There may be a chance we can rescue him in time for the match this afternoon."

"By gosh, you're right, guv'nor!" cried Sparks. "But there's no time to waste. Come on—let's get moving. We haven't much time!"

Fired with the urgency of finding the kidnapped Soccer star before the match was to start, Sparks made the 'tecs' car scorch the road on the way to the Hammond Swifts' ground.

Once there, Maxwell Keene made his way to the office of one of the directors, and told him of his startling suspicion–that one of his team's best players had been nobbled on the way to the ground!

The director was all for informing the police at once.

"No – don't do that – yet!" pleaded Maxwell Keene. "I've a suspicion the kidnappers may not be far from this ground, and if you do that you may put them on their guard. If I haven't found Tommy Drew by the time the match is due to start then you can call in the police."

Outside the office Maxwell Keene pulled the key he had found from his pocket.

"This could tell us something," he mused. "It could even lead us right to Tommy – if only I knew what door it fitted. Right, Sparks! That's a job for you," he added, handing him the key. "Go and have a bash at it! But don't tell anyone why you're making inquiries. I'll be making inquiries elsewhere. I'll meet you at our seats in the stand in twenty minutes' time."

"O. K., guv'nor!"

Sparks dashed away with the key, determined not to fall down on the job. He'd already decided on his plans, and it was to a door marked MANAGER that he made his way.

"Come in!" called a hard voice, as he knocked.

Sparks went inside. Inside, a big man with a pair of gimlet eyes and a mouth like a rat-trap, sat at a desk. Sparks knew him at once. His name was Ratlin, and he was the manager of the Swifts.

He gave Sparks a searching glance.

"Well, what's the trouble?" he demanded.

"There isn't any trouble, Mr. Ratlin," returned the boy 'tec. "I just wondered if you could help me. Ever seen a key like this before, sir?" he asked, sliding the key on to the desk.

The manager's eyes slitted as he turned the key over, examining it closely. He pondered a long time before he spoke.

"Why, sure!" he said at last. "Looks to me like it belongs to one of the store-rooms. I can't be certain which. But I haven't got time to check on it myself. Just wait a minute while I send for one of my groundsmen."

Ratlin thumbed a bell-push on his desk. A few moments later there came a knock at the door and a lean, hard-faced man in cloth cap and denims came into the room.

"You sent for me, sir?" he inquired.

"Ah, yes, Jameson," said the manager. "This young man has brought a key here and thinks it may be one of ours. Take it, and check up on it, will you?" He turned to Sparks. "You can go with him. It'll save time. If it doesn't fit any of our locks, you can keep it."

Sparks glanced at Jameson. The man was staring hard at the key—and then he glanced at Mr. Ratlin. A look seemed to pass between them. Was it his imagination, or did either or both these men know more about the key than they pretended?

"This way, please!" Jameson's voice cut across his thoughts. "We'll go down the store-room corridor and see if the key fits any of the doors there."

Jameson led Sparks along a deserted corridor from which opened several doors. They tried the key in each. In the first the key wouldn't fit, the second would not budge, in the third the key turned easily.

The door swung open.

"That's the one!" gasped Sparks. "May I have a look inside?" he added, hoping to find further clues that would solve the mystery of the missing footballer.

"Sure!" said Jameson. "Step right in!"

Sparks stepped unsuspectingly across the threshold. Then things happened in a hurry.

Swoosh! A sack was flung over Sparks' head. Before he could cry out a man's arm whipped over his shoulder and tightened around his throat in a strangle-hold. He was yanked backward. At the same instant a knee dug into the small of his back, and his feet went flying into the air.

He was powerless to struggle. The inside of the sack was soaked with some potent drug, and already his senses were slipping away from him.

As if from afar he heard Jameson's hard laugh.

"Take him away, Mike," the assistant groundsman was saying. "Put him with the other. I'm going to make sure he does no more snooping."

Sparks heard no more. His last thought, before unconsciousness claimed him, was that he had fallen down on the job.

If only he could have got word through to his chief that the groundsman was a crook!

Suppose Maxwell Keene fell into the same trap!

Meantime, the 'tec had finished his inquiries and was waiting for Sparks' return. There was only ten minutes to kick-off now.

So far Keene's inquiries had led him nowhere. His one hope was that Sparks had had more success. But as the minutes ticked away, and the teams trotted out for the kickabout in front of goal, there was still no sign of his young assistant. What had happened to him? Keene was getting worried. At last he decided to make some inquiries, and the first person he thought about was – Ratlin!

Ratlin was writing at the desk when Keene reached the office.

"Yes, I've seen him," he admitted when the 'tec had explained his business. "He was here about half an hour ago. Wanted me to identify a key. But I was too busy to attend to him then, and he went off with one of my groundsmen, Jameson. I haven't seen him since."

Keene's eyes slitted. So Sparks had left the office! Why hadn't he returned to the stand? It began to look as if Sparks, like Tommy Drew, had vanished into thin air!

"Could I have the key back?" asked Keene suddenly.

"Certainly," said Ratlin, and once more sent for Jameson. The man handed over the key and then left the room.

The 'tec took the key. He gave it a quick glance and was about to drop it into his pocket when suddenly he stiffened. Then he left the office without another word.

Alone outside, however, he took the key from his pocket and gave it a closer scrutiny. In the main it was indistinguishable from the key he had given into Sparks' keeping. But the ace 'tec had formed the habit of noticing small, and apparently unimportant details. There was one thing missing from the key now.

Originally there had been a small scratch on the metal. It was no longer there! Keene's eyes slitted.

It wasn't the same key!

For some reason, either the manager or the groundsman had substituted a different key. Why?

"It's my hunch that either Ratlin or Jameson is mixed up in this somewhere," he muttered. "It's hardly likely to be Ratlin. A manager is hardly likely to kidnap one of his own players. Then – I've got to test Jameson first. See if he's up to some funny game. And that football gives me an idea how to do it."

Maxwell Keene had spotted an old football lying in a corner. He picked it up, produced a piece of chalk from his pocket and wrote upon the leather:

"LOOK OUT – THE COPS KNOW!"

Then he carried the ball down to the end of the stand, where he knew the groundsmen's hut was situated.

He chuckled as he looked into the window of the hut. For there was only one man there – Jameson!

"Now for it!" grunted Keene, ran forward and took a powerful drop-kick at the ball.

It was a goal-getter all the way. The ball disappeared through the window. For several seconds nothing more happened. Then there was a startled shout in Jameson's voice. A moment later, ball in hand, he appeared at the window, searching the courtyard with quick uneasy glances.

Keene, however, took good care to stay out of sight, and he saw nobody around. He was clearly jittery as he stepped back into the room.

"I thought as much," chuckled the ace detective. "That's got him guessing. Now will he act the way I want?"

So far things had gone according to plan, but Maxwell Keene was taking no chances. Swiftly he went into action. Dodging from cover to cover, he reached the window in a matter of moments. Cautiously he raised his head above the sill and looked into the room.

Jameson was no longer there! What was more, the single door was bolted on the inside. Clearly he had not left that way.

Where had he gone? And why?

Keene meant to know the answer. In next to no time he had opened the window and scrambled into the room. Like a bloodhound on the scent, he searched around. Suddenly he spotted some marks on the floor. The 'tec realised they were footprints which Jameson had made on his way from the window. They led to a large wall cupboard. It was locked – but the footprints seemed to disappear into the door.

Using a pocket-tool of his own invention he had the cupboard open in a twinkling. Inside was only a pile of dusty papers!

But Keene wasn't deceived. More marks on the floor caught his eagle eye, and he quested round the cupboard, thrusting here and there.

Suddenly there was a click. Then the back of the cupboard slid aside, revealing a black cavity beyond, with steps leading downward.

Keene did not hesitate a moment. Silently he groped his way down the steps, thrilling as he heard the murmur of voices. A light showed in the blackness ahead. A moment later he was in a dimly-lit tunnel, with a door standing slightly ajar at its end.

Keene slid towards the door. He had to watch his step now! A single creak would have betrayed him. But he reached the door without mishap and risked a quick glance into the cellar beyond.

Four men were there. Three of them were tough-looking types. The fourth was Jameson.

"Somebody wised me off," Jameson was saying. "The police know about this dump."

"So what, boss?"

"We've got to get out of here," Jameson went on. "And the quicker the better. What's more, the dicks haven't got to find anything if they come nosin' round. So – jump to it! Fetch Tommy Drew and the other guy along, Mike."

Two prisoners, roped and gagged, were dragged into the cellar. The watching Keene drew a deep breath. One was Sparks, the other the Swifts' centre-forward. His stunt had worked! He had found the missing soccer star!

Keene waited no longer. From his pocket he whipped out a gun and, moving it fanwise, stepped from the doorway.

"Stick your hands up – all of you!" he ordered. "That's better," he added as the crisp command was obeyed. "Now get hold of this, Jameson. That somebody who wised you off was – me! Why did I do it? Because I guessed you would panic and lead me here."

Fear showed in Jameson's eyes.

"I suspected you because of the keys," the detective went on. "You see, I'd figured out why you made a switch. You were scared the key we found would be traced to you. My guess is that it was the key to the phoney cupboard in your office, and the police were the last people you wanted to nose in on what was going on down here."

Keeping the crooks covered, Keene swiftly set Sparks and Tommy Drew free. They in turn used their bonds to tie up the beaten men. Then Keene led the way into the next cellar.

There stood a large lorry. Keene pulled back the flap of the tarpaulin at the back and peered inside. The vehicle contained a big load of cigarettes, worth thousands of pounds!

"I guessed as much!" nodded the 'tec. "This chap Jameson, quite a new groundsman, was using one of these cellars as a hiding-place for lorry loads of stuff his gang was stealing, knowing the police would be unlikely to search a football ground."

"You're right, Mr. Keene," agreed Tommy Drew. "But I got suspicious when I saw a lorry come into the back of the stand when I was training late last evening. I was going to make more investigations and then go to the police. But the gang nabbed me on the way to the match this morning. They'd have bumped me off if you hadn't stepped in. I don't know how to thank you."

"You can thank me and Sparks by playing a real blinder of a game in the match this afternoon," returned Keene. "If you're to be in time for the kick-off you've got to hurry!"

Tommy just made it in time for the kick-off, and showed his gratitude to the 'tecs by scoring two goals for his team. The fans roared their heads off with delight – but none of them knew that, had it not been for Maxwell Keene and Sparks, their idol wouldn't have turned out at all.

Tommy was certainly on top form that day. His first goal came after fifteen minutes of play. Gathering a loose ball, he made a brilliant solo run down the field, ran rings round the defending backs and cracked the ball past the startled goalie.

"Phew, it's a good job you rescued Tommy, guv'nor," Sparks breathed to his boss. "I don't know what the Swifts would've done without him!"

Tommy's second goal came in the second half, and it was one of the finest solo efforts ever seen on that ground.

Maxwell Keene clasped the young centre-forward by the hand as he left the field.

"Well done, Tommy!" he cried. "You played a great game. I'm pleased you won!"

But Jameson and his confederates weren't pleased. They were in the hands of the police – and booked for a long spell in goal!

MANSION OF DOOM

Dirk Boland was a private investigator who never lost a case, but even he did not expect the series of adventures that befell him when he was called to an eerie mansion to solve a murder.

"Please, Mr. Boland, you've *got* to help me!" Facing private investigator Dirk Boland across a cluttered desk in his untidy, unswept office was a nervous young man who had introduced himself as Edmund Grabe.

Dirk Boland was used to clients coming in with stories which led him to all kinds of violent assignments, but this man's story was to lead to a fantastic adventure.

The investigator leaned back in his chair and put his feet up on the desk, dislodging a pile of papers which fell unnoticed to the floor.

"Let me get this straight," he said. "Your grandfather has just died and left some money. And you are scared to go to the reading of his will. Right?"

Edmund Grabe nodded. "Correct, Mr. Boland."

"But why?"

Grabe shifted uncomfortably. "Mr. Boland, I think my grandfather was murdered!"

At these words, Boland took his feet off the desk and sat up straight, suddenly alert. Edmund Grabe leaned forward, eager now that he had got the private eye's full attention.

"There are a number of reasons," he said, "and they all add up to the same thing. Not only was my grandfather murdered, but he *knew* he was going to be murdered. Just before he died, he kept saying peculiar things . . . like: 'Step carefully in future, Edmund.' Or: 'I won't be with you very long.' Yet he was in perfect health!"

Grabe swallowed, then continued. "First, let me put you in the picture. My grandfather was Colonel Horatio Grabe. When he retired from the army he went into business and made a tidy fortune, almost half-a-million pounds. Last week he was killed in an air crash."

Boland flicked his fingers. "Of course! I recall the name, now. I read about the accident in the papers–he crashed while piloting his own private plane."

"That crash was no accident," Edmund Grabe answered sombrely. "It was only the last of a series of 'accidents' which he miraculously escaped–like being run over by a hit-and-run car, or tripped up on a railway station into the path of an oncoming express. Anyway, my grandfather was a perfect pilot!"

Boland cast his mind back over what he could remember of the disaster. The cause of the crash hadn't been found in the wreckage. Apparently the plane had simply dived into the ground, out of control.

"So you think somebody sabotaged the engine?" he queried.

"I do. And it must be somebody who stands to gain by his death. In other words, one of the surviving relatives who will be mentioned in the will!"

"Hmmm, this gets interesting," Boland remarked. "But even accepting your story–and I don't say I do–what are you afraid of? The reading of a will can't hurt you!"

"That's just it," Grabe replied. "My grandfather left special instructions for the reading of the will–rather peculiar instructions. For one thing, it's not to be read in London but in a weird, rambling old mansion which my grandfather owned. It's high in the Austrian Alps. All the people concerned in the will must stay there for several days before the will is read. This means that I am going to be cooped up for days with a possible killer. Why, one of the relatives–a second cousin of mine–is a gangster! Furthermore, the mansion has the reputation of being haunted!"

Boland chewed his pencil reflectively.

Suddenly he made up his mind. "Okay," he grinned, "I'll come with you to the Austrian Alps. But I only hope you're not wasting my time!"

The ski-lift took them only part of the way up the mountain. Then they had to go by foot.

"Phew!" Dirk Boland said as they made their way up the great slanting snow-fields. "Your grandfather certainly liked to build his houses in remote places."

"It was *his* grandfather who built it," Edmund said with a slight smile. "It's really old. Besides, it's more like a castle than a house."

At length they came to a deep ravine crossed by a narrow bridge. Beyond it, far up the slope, could be seen a glowering, rambling building of grey stone. Boland paused to behold the mansion. Even from this distance there was something moody and foreboding about the sullen structure.

A number of skiers were gliding about the snow slope. As Boland and Grabe crossed the bridge one of them swooped down towards them, swerved to a stop and whipped goggles from his eyes.

It was a bony-faced man with crew-cut, bleachwhite hair. "Hiya, folks," he said in a strong American accent. "Let me introduce myself. I'm Dwight G. Schaeffer–a nephew of the deceased Colonel Grabe. And which of my dear relatives might you two be? I'm afraid I don't know many of them personally."

"I'm Edmund Grabe," Boland's companion said. "And this is a . . . a friend I've brought along."

The American frowned. "I thought we were all supposed to be relatives of the deceased here. I don't recall friends being mentioned."

"Well, I've brought him," Edmund said defiantly. "There's nothing in the instructions that says I can't."

Without replying, Schaeffer turned his back on them and trudged up the slope, the two new arrivals following.

Once in the house, they were greeted by Mr. Jennings, Colonel Grabe's lawyer. A tall, slim dapper man, he accepted Boland's presence without comment.

"When is the will going to be read?" Boland asked.

Jennings smiled mysteriously. "In a few days" he said. "Exactly when is something I can't tell you."

"Why not?" Boland questioned suspiciously. "What's the big secret?"

"Er, I can only say that I have my instructions, and I will obey them to the letter," Mr. Jennings answered amiably.

A short while later it became dark, and they were introduced to the rest of the relatives in the mansion's huge drawing room. There were seven of them in all, including Edmund. Boland inspected them all closely, keenly aware that they were here for only one thing.

They all expected to get a share of the dead Colonel's fortune!

Most of them weren't particularly interesting. There was a young army officer, Captain Colin Campbell. There was also Muriel Newsome, a niece of Grabe's. Boland's attention soon went, however, to a man called Billy Grabe, a nephew of the dead Colonel.

For Billy Grabe was the gangster Edmund had mentioned! Like all the others, he bore a family resemblance. But his face was gloomy and dark, and bore the scars of many fights.

Boland sidled over to him. "Evening Billy," he murmured. "Inspector Kemp says he hasn't seen much of you lately."

Billy looked up, startled. "Strewth!" he gasped. "Are you a cop?"

"Not quite, Bill. In fact, not at all." Boland studied the man. As a matter of fact he hadn't known him previously–but it was ten to one that the mention of one of Scotland Yard's leading lights would mean something to the gangster.

"Listen," Billy said hoarsely, "I know I've been pretty crooked in my time, but it's all over, see. I gave it up."

"But old habits die hard, don't they, Billy?"

"I-I tell yer it's all over," the man stammered. "I've been going straight for years!"

Boland regarded him carefully. Billy sounded sincere–but one never knew. Suddenly there was a crash of thunder outside and lightning flickered through the windows. The storm which had been building all that day was breaking.

Mr. Jennings entered, clearing his throat. "Well," he said in a friendly tone, "now that we're all here, I thought we might look over the mansion! Follow me, please."

Nervously the guests rose and Jennings led them out of the hall and down a dim, stone passage.

"This is the armoury," he said as they came into a big stone chamber with swords and antique guns hanging on the walls.

Lightning flashed outside, casting a weird white light into the hall and creating flickering shadows. The guests drew closer together instinctively. Already the house seemed to be throwing a spell over them.

"Gee, it's spooky!" Dwight Schaeffer whispered above the muttering thunder.

"Nothing to be afraid of," Jennings said briskly. "This way, we'll go down to the wine cellars. This house is simply honeycombed with cellars underneath, you know—it's a real maze!"

Chatting brightly, he led them into another stone passage which sloped down into the ground. The light here was from smoky torches—apparently electricity didn't extend to this part of the house.

Suddenly, the party stopped with one accord. A patch of spectral white light had appeared further down the corridor.

It floated nearer. Muriel Newsome screamed.

The others all uttered gasps of sheer terror. Even Boland had to suppress an urge to run. For the light had resolved itself into—a ghost!

A glowing figure floated up the corridor towards them. The bricks of the passage were plainly visible through the spectre. The apparition was that of a slight old man with gleaming, enraged eyes.

The lips of the ghost were moving, but no sound came. Then Boland noticed that it held up a placard in its hand—a placard bearing an inscription.

"*Justice,*" it read. "*Give me justice.*"

"It's him," screamed Muriel Newsome. "It's the ghost of Colonel Grabe!"

With those words, the group panicked. They all went scrambling up the tunnel as fast as their legs would take them, with only one thought in their minds—to get away from that glowing apparition!

Boland steeled himself, and remained behind. Even Jennings, he noticed, had fled. Steadfastly he forced himself to face the ghost.

"What is it?" he said. "What do you want?"

But the ghost simply faded away.

Thoughtfully Boland walked back up the tunnel. What did all this mean, he wondered? Could he believe his eyes? Had he really seen a ghost? Was such a thing possible?

He gave the matter careful thought.

The thunderstorm was still in full spate when he arrived back in the drawing room. Muriel Newsome was wringing her hands hysterically.

"I can't stay here another minute!" she shrilled. "I've got to leave–I'm going back to London–where it's safe!"

"If you leave this house before the will is read, you forfeit your share of it," Jennings said, apparently recovering his composure. "The Colonel was very clear on that point."

"I don't care!" she retorted. "I don't *want* the money–I'm going!"

"Me, too!" chorused several of the others, including Billy, the ex-gangster. Dwight Schaeffer was white-faced and trembling, but he said nothing.

Just then, over the low rumble of distant thunder came another blast. Dirk Boland whirled. His trained ears told him one thing. That wasn't thunder. It was an explosion–and it came from the direction of the ravine!

He dashed from the room, out the front entrance of the building and into the cold flurrying snow. The wind howled, tearing at him. Steadily he worked his way down the slope, ploughing through mounting snowbanks which the storm was building up. Eventually he reached the ravine.

The bridge was shattered, completely destroyed. Remnants of it hung on either side of the chasm. Down below, was nothing but the deep, black, unscaleable gulf which had swallowed it up.

He trudged his way back to the house and gave them the news.

"It–it must have been struck by lightning!" Dwight Schaeffer stuttered.

"Maybe," Boland said. Privately, he knew differently. He knew the difference between a lightning strike and high explosives. Someone had blown up the bridge–deliberately!

"At any rate," he told them, "one thing is clear. That bridge was our only means of access to the outside world–and it will be at least two weeks before anyone comes to our rescue. Whether we like it or not, *we're marooned here.*"

"Marooned!" echoed one of Colonel Grabe's grandsons in a voice like doom itself. "Marooned in this house–with a ghost!"

Next morning, after an uneasy night spent amid the hooting of the wind and the rattling of the tiles, the guests went outside, glad to be away even for a short while from the terrifying mansion.

The storm was over and it was a sunny morning. The guests peered down the snow slope towards the ravine.

"Look!" Muriel Newsome cried. "Snow bridges have formed over the ravine! We can cross!"

"Don't be fool enough to try!" Dirk Boland rapped out. "That snow won't support your weight—you'd simply go tumbling into the canyon."

Muriel sighed with disappointment.

"Anyway," she said, "let's go skiing. I need something to take my mind off what happened last night!"

"Say, that's a swell idea!" Dwight Schaeffer enthused. "Come on, I'll race you to the shed and we'll get the gear out."

While the rest of the party went to fetch the skiing equipment, Boland was left alone with Jennings.

"Look here, let me make a suggestion," he said. "Why don't you read the will straight away? Surely it can't make any difference now? And it might put an end to the suspense these people are going through."

"Sorry, Mr. Boland," the other said. "I have my instructions. I have no right to change them."

The others returned with the skiing gear. Boland broke off the conversation and tried on a pair of skis. Jennings, it seemed, was the only one who didn't intend to try his luck—indeed, Boland could scarcely imagine that erect, proper figure hurtling down a slope at all.

He propelled himself down the slope, experimentally twisting and turning. Soon all the guests were zooming about the slope. Boland thought it was just a little foolhardy to go skiing with the ravine so close by, but the slope didn't lead directly to it, and all the guests seemed competent skiers, so he decided there was nothing to worry about.

He drew apart from the others and came to a stop further down the slope. Something was on his mind.

Who had blown up the bridge? Even more puzzling, why had they done it? No one had anything to gain by it—in fact, the old Colonel's descendants had everything to gain if some of them left, since the money would be shared out among those who remained.

He glanced up at the mansion, glowering on its ridge, and shuddered. It was almost as if the house itself wanted to keep them there—wanted to torment them.

Suddenly a shrill cry broke into his thoughts. Speeding down the slope, heading straight for the ravine was Muriel Newsome! Boland waited for her to swerve in another direction, but then he realised that she was going far too fast. More than that, she had completely lost her nerve and was out of control!

Desperately Boland urged himself into action and slid down the slope with gathering speed. With horror, he realised that within seconds the girl would be over the edge!

Furiously he pushed himself along, the girl's frightened cries sounding in his ears. Nearer and nearer came the yawning chasm—then the girl hurtled past him. He was a split second too late!

Boland flung himself sideways, flung out his hand and just grabbed the back of Muriel's jacket, pulling her off balance. With a shriek she toppled into the snow.

Then both of them went slithering down the slope! Boland dug his hands into the snow and jammed in his skis, trying to slow them down. At last they came to a stop, only inches away from the edge!

Boland, releasing himself from his skis, pulled Muriel away from the precipice.

"Well, that'll teach you to be more careful!" Boland said, grinning to reassure her. "Don't go so fast next time."

"But—but I was pushed!" she exclaimed.

Boland's jaw dropped.

"Yes! I felt someone push me from behind—and suddenly I was going too fast to stop!"

"Who was it?" Boland demanded.

"I–I don't know."

"Well, come on. Let's get back to the house!"

"It has to be someone in this room!"

Dirk Boland was speaking to the assembled guests. He had just told them of Muriel's narrow escape.

Boland's hard, grey eyes rested on each of them in turn, staring particularly hard at Billy Grabe. The ex-gangster shifted uncomfortably.

"Don't look at me like that," he protested. "All right—I used to be a crook. But I never was a killer!"

Boland thought for a moment. "The point is, did anyone *see* who actually pushed Miss Newsome?"

They all shook their heads. "It—it must be him," someone whispered. "The ghost of Colonel Grabe!"

"Ghosts can't push," Boland retorted. "But listen to this—whoever is responsible for all this, from now on you've got me to reckon with!"

A dreadful cry wailed through the ancient mansion.

Dirk Boland shot from his bed, grabbing the small automatic he kept under his pillow. He checked the time on his watch—it was the early hours of the following morning!

Outside in the corridor he found Jennings, looking really scared for the first time.

"Did . . . Did you hear that?" he gasped.

Boland nodded and pushed forward in the direction of the sound. They went down towards the cellars, through cold, dank passages.

None of the others followed them. Presumably they were keeping to their rooms, terrified.

Then Boland pulled up sharp. Ahead, came a familiar glow!

And into view came the eerily radiant figure of the old Colonel. This time he seemed more substantial—Boland could not see through his body—but there was no mistaking the slightly-built old man.

This time he spoke! A hoarse voice like the rustling of old leaves came from his lips.

"Change the will!" the voice said. "Change my will!"

Jennings uttered a cry of terror. "But—but how, Colonel?" he trembled. "How do you want it changed?"

"I wish to leave all the money to—my nephew, Billy Grabe!"

Boland lunged forward. But the figure receded down the corridor—and then disappeared!

Jennings was shaking. "Oh dear, oh dear!" he muttered. "We shall have to do what he says!"

Boland took hold of the man's arm. "Now look here, Mr. Jennings," he said. "I can see you're frightened out of your wits. But

"Change my will!"

I seem to remember that you weren't nearly so frightened when the ghost appeared for the first time. Why?"

Jennings swallowed. "Because–because you see, Mr. Boland–I knew about the first ghost. It wasn't a ghost at all. It was just a clever trick done by means of a film projector and mirrors. I helped arrange it."

Boland thrust his automatic in his belt. Now he was getting somewhere. "Okay," he said seriously. "Let's have the story."

"Old Colonel Grabe was certain that one of his relatives was trying to kill him for his share of the inheritance money," Jennings explained. "And he decided that if the killer succeeded, then he wanted justice. So he arranged for me to invite all the people mentioned in the will to this house. We fixed up the 'ghost', and also the explosives under the bridge so that no one could get away. His idea was that the guilty one would crack up under strain of being confronted by the ghost of his victim, and give himself away."

"I see!" Boland exclaimed. "I thought there was something strange about the way you were acting!"

Jennings managed to smile. "All this is not really in my line, I'm afraid. But the second ghost–I know nothing about it! It must really be the Colonel!"

"Hmm . . . I'm still not sure I believe in ghosts," Boland said, rubbing his chin. "If you ask me—"

A shout cut him off. Edmund Grabe came dashing down corridor.

"John Jackson and Captain Campbell!" he exclaimed when he saw Boland. "They've both disappeared!"

Muriel Newsome was sobbing when the party gathered together again.

"It's terrible–terrible!" she moaned. "To be spirited away by ghosts like that! Oh, who'll be next?"

Edmund Grabe sidled up to Boland. "What do you think?" he muttered.

Boland sighed. "Well, unless it *is* true about ghosts, somebody has to be behind it," he said.

"Then it must be Billy the gangster," Edmund replied, casting a hard glance at the gloomy ex-crook. "There's no one else I suspect . . ."

He broke off. Dwight Schaeffer was speaking in a loud voice.

"I don't want any of the money! I'm scared to death! I say we should give the money to Billy, and then these spirits will leave us alone. It's obviously what the Colonel wants!"

Billy glowered and said nothing.

Boland cut in. "We're doing nothing just yet. I suggest we all go back to bed and talk about it in the morning."

"But what if—" someone began.

Boland held up his hand. "There's nothing else to be done ladies and gentlemen. In the morning, we can talk further."

At last he had persuaded them to return to their rooms, and walked towards his.

But instead of entering it, he merely opened and closed the door loudly. Then, waiting for the house to settle down , he set off towards the lower part of the building.

Whatever the answer to the mystery was, he was sure that was where he would find it. As he pressed farther into the gloomy maze, lighting his way by means of a dim pocket torch, he saw that the underneath of the house was a warren of passages. It would be possible to hide an army down there!

Stepping carefully, he rounded a corner. A long passage stretched ahead of him. The yellow beam from his torch shone down it—and a figure moved in the shadows at the far end!

Boland broke into a run. He reached the end of the passage and stared down each of the two corridors leading off it, straining his eyes and waving the torch. Suddenly he caught a glimpse of a running figure!

Now he could hear the scuffing sound the figure made as it ran on the bare stone. Boland pelted after it, gaining slightly. In near-darkness, the chase continued through winding passages and up and down worn stone staircases.

And Boland was gradually gaining on the fugitive, forcing him towards the edge of the house. Once, he almost caught up, and heard ragged, fast breathing. Then the shadowy figure bounded up some narrow stairs!

Boland pounded after him. Then he heard a crash of glass, and saw starlight. The fugitive had left the house. He followed, jumping through broken french windows. He was standing on the crisp snow. Glancing around him, he saw his quarry, black against the snow, staggering away from the house.

Suddenly the figure turned and lifted its arm towards Boland. A shot rang out. Boland flung himself to the ground as a bullet whistled past his ear. Then he pulled out his automatic, sent a shot in return, and leaped to his feet to continue the chase, running zig-zag to dodge any sudden bullets.

The man had now reached the pile of skiing equipment which had been left outside the house after Muriel Newsome's "accident". Hastily the figure strapped on a pair of skis, grabbed a couple of sticks and pushed himself off down the slope.

Panting, Boland reached the ski equipment and grabbed a pair of skis. Then he leapt off down the slope in pursuit.

The other man was a good skier, but Boland was better. Rapidly he gained on the fleeing fugitive. His quarry swerved suddenly, unexpectedly—but this suited Boland fine! He turned at the same time, and swept straight on to a sudden swift rise in the ground which bore him swiftly upward. His momentum sent him flying through the air—to land only a few feet behind the other skier!

There was no sound but the hissing of their skis over the snow as the two shadow-like figures sped through the night. Rapidly Boland overhauled his quarry. But then the man turned again, desperately, and flung himself further down the slope.

They were dangerously near the ravine now, but Boland knew he could not give up. Seconds later they were hurtling along the edge of the ravine itself, both of them frantically pushing with their sticks as they sought to increase their speed.

Then the man ahead did an unexpected thing. He slowed down and almost came to a stop. Not realising in time, Boland came on.

With a sudden turn and a flick, the other man dealt him a powerful blow with his ski-stick! The point jabbed towards his face, and Boland over-balanced!

The two tussled for a moment, then the other flung the investigator over the edge!

As he felt himself tumbling through the space, Boland dropped his ski-sticks and reached out desperately. His hands caught on an outcropping of rock just below the edge of the precipice.

Somehow he managed to hang on with one arm while he released his cumbersome skis and sent them tumbling into the abyss. Then he levered himself painfully back over the edge and knelt in the snow, gasping with exhaustion.

The fugitive was no more than a dot stumbling back towards the house. And Boland hadn't even caught a glimpse of his face!

But that didn't matter. With a wry grin he climbed to his feet and set off back towards the Mansion of Doom. Back in his room he went instantly to sleep–with his fingers curled around the butt of his automatic!

Next morning there was more bad news.

"Muriel Newsome and Dwight Schaeffer–both vanished!" Jennings gasped in horror.

They were seated in the breakfast room, a much depleted group now.

"Well, what on earth happens to us now?" Edmund Grabe asked Boland. "It couldn't have been Schaeffer–he's been taken like the rest!" He turned angrily to Billy Grabe. "It must be him behind all this–he must have killed my grandfather!"

The ex-gangster had been sunk in himself ever since they met. He had been eating his breakfast sullenly, moodily.

"It ain't me!" he whined. "I never killed anybody! Honest!"

"Take it easy," Boland said over the excited voices. "It wasn't Billy."

Edmund snorted in disgust. "A fine private investigator you are!" he exclaimed. "You do nothing but sit around all day–and meanwhile four people have disappeared!"

"No sleuth in the world can do anything about ghosts, Mr. Grabe," Jennings the lawyer said solemnly. Apparently he was fully convinced that the ghost who had demanded a change in the will was genuine.

Boland rose to his feet. "When we first arrived here, you took us on a very interesting tour of the house, Mr. Jennings. Now let me take you all on a tour–one which you will find equally interesting!"

Puzzled, they followed as he led them down the same route he had taken the night before. Soon they were among the masses of crumbled masonry and dark tunnels which seemed to press down so heavily.

When they came to the place where he had first seen the figure, he stopped, inspecting the walls. "Ah–I thought so!" he said. "This stone has obviously been moved recently!"

He pushed one of the stones making up the wall. It moved–and with a grating noise a whole section of the wall slid aside!

"A secret passage!"

"The house must be full of them," Boland explained. "And it didn't take our villain long to find one and make use of it!" He stepped forward into the narrow passage, holding his gun ahead of him. The others followed in single file.

About a minute later they came out into a large chamber. And the sight which met their eyes brought gasps of amazement.

Tied up and sitting by the wall were Johnny Jackson, Captain Campbell and Muriel Newsome. But the fourth person who had disappeared–Dwight Schaeffer–was on his feet. He whirled round as they entered.

"You!" he snarled. "Yo-you're dead!"

"Not dead, and not a ghost either, Schaeffer," Boland told him. He pointed to Schaeffer. "There's your culprit, not Billy Grabe, but Dwight G. Schaeffer, who made himself 'disappear' so as to divert suspicion from himself!"

Boland stooped, picking up some jars from the floor. "And here's your 'ghost' –Schaeffer himself, with the aid of make-up and a tin of luminous paint!"

"He's lying!" Schaeffer protested, white-faced. "I–I discovered these people here, just before you came."

Boland laughed. "Sorry, Schaeffer, the game's up! I'll say one thing, though–you've got nerve. Old man Grabe arranged the first 'ghost' himself, hoping that it would make his killer's nerve crack and so reveal him. Instead, it simply gave you an idea for getting *all* the money, instead of just a part of it. You dressed yourself up as the old man and demanded a change in the will, then started kidnapping people so that the others would be frightened into obeying."

"Nonsense!" Schaeffer protested. "If that's so, why did the ghost want to give the money to Billy, not me? *He* must be behind it!"

At these words a groan broke out from Billy Grabe.

"I'll confess, I'll confess!" he moaned.

All except Boland looked at Billy in astonishment.

"I *knew* that it was Schaeffer all the time," Billy said, burying his face in his hands. "Schaeffer knows about a couple of big robberies I did years back–and he said that if I didn't help him, he'd tell the police! He wanted all the money to go to me so that no suspicion would fall on him. Afterwards I was to give him all the money!"

"That's what I thought, Billy," Boland said quietly. "You see, Schaeffer, I knew last night that it wasn't Billy I was after. Billy isn't a very good skier–you are!"

With a snarl, Schaeffer acted. Pushing Billy aside, he rushed up the narrow secret passage before Boland could stop him. The private investigator ran after him. Schaeffer headed for the outside and Boland soon found himself on the snow slope again.

This time there was no time for skis. Schaeffer ran down the slope towards the ravine. Boland couldn't understand what his plan was, but when Schaeffer reached the ravine he suddenly realised.

Boland yelled desperately.

"No, Schaeffer! Don't try to cross by that snow bridge!"

But Schaeffer was heedless of the warning. In panic, he dashed over the fragile arc of snow that had spanned the deep ravine since the start of the snowstorm.

The snow collapsed with a flurry. With a long, aching howl, Schaeffer fell to his doom.

Boland trudged back to the house. He was met by Edmund Grabe.

"So that's the man who killed my grandfather!" he said.

Boland nodded. "We can't prove it, but from what's happened here we know it's true."

He looked up at the grim old mansion. "Yes, Colonel Grabe's shadow was over this house, all right–but not in quite the way you all thought. Now perhaps we can hear the terms of the will and then see about getting back to civilisation!"

THE LAST FIGHT

Sabre, the proud old bull moose, was setting out on his last journey across the crisp Arctic snow. He had been a great leader of the herd in his time but now he knew he was dying. Then, suddenly, the wolves barred his path and he had to fight his last fight of all.

Sabre, the great bull moose, moved across the crisp snow with the jaunty step of an animal many, many years younger. The breath from his broad muzzle clouded white in the chilly air.

Disturbed ptarmigan – a kind of grouse – whirred away from the ground ahead of him; an Arctic fox glided like a furtive shadow into the shelter of the woods. Sabre scarcely gave them a glance. He trod on, urged by an instinct which had turned him from the herd.

He was dying! Sabre, greatest fighter of them all, was obeying the law of the wilds – and setting out on a lonely journey from which he would not return. A journey which must end in his last – and greatest – battle.

He had no fears. He had lived well, fought hard – he had no regrets. Seven feet high, Sabre towered above the ground. He held his head proudly, swinging his great antlers – seventy inches of vicious horn-spread.

Moose, except in Autumn, are normally timid; Sabre had never been timid at all. His great hooves, also part of his armament, broke into a loping, easy gallop. His objective was fixed; he was going to a place he had always remembered – the scene of the first, and greatest battle, as yet, in his life.

It was many years ago that Sabre had fought and defeated Fury, the herd leader. His old eyes glowed at the memory. Again the clash of frenzied antlers and hooves rang in his mind. It had been a battle of giants, with Fury the more experienced and wily. Again and again Sabre had recoiled from the impact of a ruthless and deadly opponent. His loping gallop increased in its tempo, as he relived that triumph now long dead in the past.

Sabre's blood and heart-beats quickened to the thrill of the way he had beaten Fury. He was Sabre the Proud, Sabre the Unbeaten, Sabre – Greatest Fighter of Them All!

The miles wound like a white tape behind him. But there were still, he knew, many miles to go. Now he was climbing. The steep ground should have tired his failing heart, but it did not. He felt even younger and glowed with pride.

The first wolf sighted Sabre. It gave no apparent sign, yet within moments there were other ghostly shapes, each appearing as if from nowhere. Sabre scented and sensed them, and a wild joy surged within him. He began to realise what form his last battle was to take.

He ran faster. Suddenly around him again were the familiar trees and landmarks; the snowy ridge where pure whiteness merged with the grey-white of air. This was the end of the pilgrimage! This, the place where he had fought, outwitted and defeated Fury the Magnificent! The old feeling of triumph flooded back. He was ready, and he knew what would come.

The wolves were soundless. The ferocious shadows, gathering in number, were aware that their numbers were sufficient. This was wisdom, for attacking a Bull Moose even if old, could be hazardous; and life meant as much to a wolf as to anyone else.

The wolves formed a half-circle as Sabre turned at bay. Three rushed together, biting in the swift, snapping fashion peculiar to wolves.

The great head and antlers scythed down, the wide spread of horn killing the foremost wolf. Sabre thundered a cry, then met the full, concerted attack. His antlers sent grey bodies spinning through the air; his pawing hooves descended like death-dealing flails.

The wolves' savagery increased, for the scent of comrades' wounds intoxicated them with blood lust.

Sabre towered above the scene, dominated it completely. He knew his intention, knew how he would dictate the course of this – his last – fight. He remembered the conquest of Fury; the odds had been against him then, but the present was far more satisfying. Wolves were his natural enemy, and the hatred within him would make victory more sweet.

Now they hung from him. His hide, so tough as to be almost impenetrable, supported the weight of many bodies. The four-legged murderers knew that their quarry would soon fall. Triumph rang in their cries, for now Sabre was swaying. He was backing and this showed he was beaten. So the wolves advanced – and it was a miracle how he supported their weight.

Sabre swayed and backed on . . . this was the moment he had been waiting for. He took one more backward step, and the rearguard of the wolves followed in one wave.

The end came. Sabre lurched back into space, lurched over the brink of the sheer descent which fell 300 ft. to the river. It was from this very brink, so many years ago, that Fury the Magnificent had plunged headlong – plunged on helplessly after Sabre had cunningly side-stepped his charge.

This time it was Sabre who whirled down into space. With him went the doomed, horrified attackers; the attackers who were already too late in releasing their holds. The following wolf-pack, obeying instinct, had been hunting a quarry. Some tried to halt at the brink. But the slippery snow, compressed by many feet, allowed no grip.

As for Sabre, he was dead. The great fighting heart had given out at the very instant the cold air rushed about him. He knew nothing, and his spirit had joined that of Fury.

The circle of the great Bull Moose's life was completed, and the river received the end of the story. Forty wolves perished, and Sabre would have rejoiced at the victory. Only Sabre – Sabre the Unbeatable, Greatest Fighter of All – was now dead!

COACHMAN JUDD

When "Cracker" Judd pulled up his stage-coach in Gunsmoke City, he let himself in for a great deal of trouble, for soon he found himself in a desperate fight against bandits – but Judd was a little too clever for them.

"Whoa, my beauties!"

Jim Judd–better known as "Cracker" Judd because of his great skill with his driving whip–shouted the words as he pulled the four horses of his stage-coach to a halt in front of the sheriff's office at Gunsmoke City. Then, pulling out a small sack from underneath his seat, he leapt down to the ground and hurried into the office. He grinned at the burly figure seated behind a rather dilapidated desk.

"Here's your mail, Mike," he told the sheriff. "Right on the dot as usual. So long–be seeing you next trip!"

Suddenly, as Cracker stepped back out into the street, a jeering laugh fell upon his ears. He turned–to see a man who was leaning against a hitching-rack with his thumbs stuck inside his over-ornamented gun-belt.

Cracker recognised the newcomer as Joe Sloan–a man he disliked intensely.

"That's just like you, Judd," Joe Sloan sneered. "Always boasting about being dead on time. Why, if we had a decent coach on the route, a good half-hour could be knocked off the time from River Bend to Gunsmoke City."

Cracker grinned.

"There isn't a driver in the West who could knock half an hour off my time," he said.

The other sneered at him.

"You think you're on a good thing, don't you?" he snapped. "I suppose you think you're going to have your yearly contract renewed today? I suppose you've forgotten how many times you've been held up by the Red Bandit."

Just for a moment Cracker Judd's face lost its smile.

"You're making a slight mistake, Sloan," he rapped. "You mean that the Red Bandit has tried to hold me up many times! He's certainly tried, Sloan, but so far he's only succeeded in getting away with a few dollars' worth of stuff."

Joe Sloan levered himself away from the hitching-rack.

"Anyway, that outfit of yours is too slow. You mark my words, Judd. There's going to be a new and really fast coach on this run before long."

"I'll be ready for it when it comes along," Cracker answered, swinging himself into his driving seat.

Next moment, the stage was racing out of Gunsmoke, heading for the town of Pinetop.

Cracker's eyes were narrowed thoughtfully as he left Gunsmoke. More than anything else in the world he was proud of his stage-coach and of his horses. Cracker hadn't shown it, but Joe Sloan's sneering words had annoyed him.

"So I'm too slow, am I?" he muttered. "Huh! If anybody ever knocks half an hour off the time between River Bend and Gunsmoke I reckon I'm the man who'll do it, though!"

Then Cracker frowned when he remembered Sloan's reference to the Red Bandit. During the past year a gang of bandits, headed by a man who always wore a red mask, had appeared in the district. They had carried out a number of daring robberies but they had never had much luck as far as the stage-coach was concerned. Nobody knew the identity of the Red Bandit, or that of any of his gang.

"Steady, there!"

Cracker yelled the words as a sharp bend in the trail loomed ahead. Next moment the stage slowed slightly—but even so, it went round the corner on two wheels!

A second later, as the coach landed on all its wheels again, the unexpected happened.

Without warning, two masked riders, holding levelled six-guns, appeared on the trail, directly in front of the swaying coach. One of them wore a red mask; the other wore a black mask.

"Pull up if you want to go on living!" rapped the man with the red mask.

Cracker's eyes narrowed.

"The Red Bandit and one of his gang!" he muttered. "Well, they're not stopping me!"

He leant back as though he intended to bring all his weight upon the reins. But as he did so his right hand snatched up his long-leashed driving whip. A split second later the long leash flashed out.

Crack!

The thin end of the whip curled over the red-masked bandit's wrist. Immediately the startled gunman let his gun fall from his grasp. At the same time the bandits' horses, startled, reared on their haunches!

"Yippee!" Cracker Judd yelled.

His whip cracked again—but this time over the heads of his two leading horses. Instantly the stage surged forward, forcing the two masked men to turn their horses aside. When Cracker turned his head a few seconds later, to look back, the two bandits were still fighting to control their frightened mounts.

"Huh! They won't worry me again today," Cracker gritted. "Reckon I'm too near to Pinetop for them to come chasing after me now."

Pinetop was the smallest of the three towns on the stage-coach route. Cracker had no passengers or goods to pick up there, so he didn't even stop. As he careered through the one main street he threw down a small bundle of mail in front of the sheriff's office.

Shortly afterwards, dead on time as usual, he swung his horses into the main street of River Bend. Immediately, he gave an amazed gasp. Standing in front of the sheriff's office was another stage-coach. It looked a brand-new affair and four magnificent horses were harnessed to it.

"H'mm!" Cracker muttered. "Seems that somebody else is after my job. Perhaps Joe Sloan knew about this stage-coach when he shot off his mouth to me."

Pulling up alongside the strange stage-coach, Cracker catapulted out of his driving seat and went into the sheriff's office. Another surprise awaited him there for he found Hank Marlow, the sheriff, in conversation with Joe Sloan.

Cracker Judd thought swiftly. He realised that Sloan must have ridden for River Bend almost immediately after their conversation outside the sheriff's office at Gunsmoke City!

Just for a moment Cracker stared at Sloan. He remembered their conversation. It seemed strange that he should have encountered the Red Bandit so soon after Sloan had mentioned the name.

Then, ignoring Sloan, Cracker crossed to the sheriff's desk.

"Well, Hank," he said, "I reckon it's the day when I sign on the dotted line again. Today's the renewal date for the stage-coach contract, I believe."

Hank Marlow looked up at Cracker.

"It isn't just a case of signing on the dotted line, Cracker," he said. "You see, there's another applicant now for the stage-coach contract."

Cracker frowned.

"Who's applying for the contract?" he demanded.

The sheriff jerked his thumb at the flashily–dressed Joe Sloan.

"He is," he said.

Joe Sloan gave a quiet chuckle.

"If you hadn't been in such a hurry over in Gunsmoke," he said, "I'd have told you there. That's my outfit outside and I reckon it's twice as good a turn-out as your broken-down stage and horses."

Cracker struggled to keep his temper under control.

"I–er–I ain't got the deciding to do," Hank Marlow said hastily. "A meeting of my Highways Committee has been called for this evening, and they'll decide the matter then."

Joe Sloan leered at Cracker.

"Huh! If I were you I'd start looking for a new job!" he said.

An hour later the River Bend Highways Committee congregated in the sheriff's office. There were twelve members altogether.

"O. K. It's up to you to decide the matter of the stage-coach contract!" the sheriff told them. "But as–er–Cracker Judd has served us well I, for one, think he should be given the contract."

However, it was soon obvious that Joe Sloan's new stage-coach and his horses had made a big impression upon a number of the committee members—for when it came to a vote, it was discovered that the meeting was equally divided.

Instantly Cracker stepped forward.

"It seems we're not getting anywhere like this," he stated. "But I know how to settle the problem. Sloan says he can do the journey in better time than me, so I reckon it's up to him to prove it. I therefore suggest that both of us take part in a stage-coach race over the usual route tomorrow. First man home to River Bend gets the contract. What do you think of that?"

There were shouts of enthusiastic approval. Such a sporting competition appealed strongly to the Westerners.

Joe Sloan smiled.

"It suits me," he said confidently.

"Right! Then it's fixed," Cracker replied.

Next morning practically the whole population of River Bend awaited the start of the great race. And as the two coaches stood side by side in front of the sheriff's office, it was Sloan's outfit which impressed the crowds. It looked spick-and-span next to Cracker Judd's ramshackle coach.

For some minutes both drivers stood in readiness alongside their vehicles. Then, as the command to start was given by Hank Marlow, the sheriff, both drivers leapt into their seats, snatched up the reins, released their brakes, and then they were away!

There were wild shouts of encouragement from the crowd as Joe Sloan immediately shot into the lead. Then the two coaches thundered out of the town. Soon they were stirring up so much dust that they could scarcely be seen.

Cracker was seated firmly in his driving seat. He seemed quite content to let his rival draw farther and farther away from him.

"It's the last half of the journey that's going to count," Cracker muttered under his breath. "If Sloan tires out his team before then, so much the better."

The first few miles of the course were easy going and Joe Sloan steadily increased his lead. But Cracker had set the pace he wanted and he intended to keep that pace for a long time to come.

"It seemed that the race was over . . ."

An hour later, both stages were racing through hilly country. Here, both Cracker and Joe Sloan found that great skill was needed in order to keep their coaches clear of the deepest ruts.

"I'll start closing up on Sloan once we're through Horseshoe Pass," Cracker decided suddenly.

He saw Joe Sloan drive his stage up the long slope that led to Horseshoe Pass, and then he saw him disappear through its narrow entrance. Cracker's horses started to climb at their same steady pace. Nearer and nearer the coach came to the narrow opening. And then—something prompted Cracker to look up. For one dreadful moment then he held his breath.

There was a sheer wall of rock high above him and, right at the top of it, a huge boulder was in the act of falling into space—towards the stage–coach trail!

Then, as Cracker caught a glimpse of a figure darting out of sight, his thoughts raced. He realised in a flash that the man had deliberately pushed the boulder over the cliff!

In a matter of seconds an avalanche would come sweeping down to block the entrance to the pass. It seemed that the race was over as far as Cracker Judd was concerned!

Had Cracker hesitated for a moment then, all would have been lost. But no sooner did he see the toppling boulder than he snatched up his long driving whip. Swoosh! It snaked forward, and then cracked like a pistol shot over the heads of his two leading horses!

Next moment, the stage was racing forward at a terrific speed, swinging violently from side to side as it did so.

Boo-oo-oommmm!

There was a thundering sound above Cracker, and for a dreadful moment he thought he had attempted the impossible. Stones clattered down upon the roof of the stage, and then from behind him came a crash that made the ground shudder. The huge boulder had fallen just behind the stage.

Cracker had missed death by a matter of yards!

When he glanced back a great cloud of dust hung over the scene and of the narrow entrance to the pass there was no sign. Cracker's mouth set determinedly as he urged on his horses.

"Somebody was out to stop me winning the race," he gritted, "but who?"

For a few seconds Cracker thought over the question. Finally, however, he shrugged.

"Anyway, I'm going to beat Sloan now," he told himself. "I'll do that if it's the last thing I ever do!"

From then on Cracker drove as he had never driven before. He took risks, he cut corners in a fashion which time after time threatened to land the stage-coach on its side. But always he succeeded in keeping the coach on the trail.

Gunsmoke City was packed tight with spectators as Cracker hurtled down the main street. Many voices urged him on, but Cracker quickly realised that most of the spectators gave him no chance at all. Cracker only gritted his teeth more grimly. Then he turned his team in the direction of Pinetop.

Through valley after valley wound the trail and then Cracker came out to open country again. He nodded his head in satisfaction, for he had more than halved the distance which had previously separated him from Joe Sloan.

Far ahead of him he caught sight of the river which he crossed every day. He would have to slow down when he reached the one solitary bridge, for it was a very narrow structure of loose planks. Usually Cracker was careful to cross the bridge at a walking pace.

Suddenly, he saw that Joe Sloan was using his whip.

"What's he in such a hurry about?" Cracker muttered, puzzled by his rival's behaviour.

It was the memory of the avalanche he had so narrowly escaped which made him reach into the box alongside the driving seat. Out of it he took a pair of powerful binoculars. With some difficulty he managed to focus them upon the bridge.

He was just in time to see two men scrambling up the far bank of the river—two men who appeared to be hauling on a rope.

Cracker gave an angry gasp.

"No wonder Sloan is in such a hurry," he told himself fiercely. "He's trying to make sure he gets over the bridge ahead of me! If he succeeds, I reckon those two guys I saw through the glasses will pull out some of the planks!"

Cracker's face became even more stern and set. Then, deliberately, he turned his team off the winding trail and set them galloping furiously across country. It was an appalling risk to take. Boulders and hidden potholes might bring disaster upon the stage. But, as Cracker knew that it was the most direct route to the bridge, he paid the risks no heed.

However, luck was with him and soon he was almost up to the bridge. For a moment then it seemed that both stage-coaches would attempt to cross at the same time!

Both coaches raced along neck and neck with Cracker on Joe Sloan's right. Just for a moment Cracker turned his head to glance at his rival. He saw how grimly the man was hanging on to his reins. And then for one long second Cracker's gaze focused on the back of Joe Sloan's right hand. Instantly his eyes widened.

"Well, if that doesn't beat everything!" he gasped. "It—it's the last thing I expected to see."

Cracker took a firm grip upon the reins.

"It may mean nothing," he muttered. "Anyway, my first job is to concentrate on winning this race!"

Next moment, Cracker's horses found an extra turn of speed. They surged ahead. Whitefaced, Joe Sloan suddenly flung all his weight upon his reins pulling his horses almost to a stop. The risk had been too much for him!

And so Cracker went driving recklessly over the plank bridge!

"I'm ahead now," Cracker told himself. "And I'm staying ahead."

Cracker kept his word. He was well ahead when he raced through Pinetop—to the accompaniment of thunderous cheers.

"I'd never have believed it," a spectator shouted. "Cracker's got Sloan beaten after all!"

As his horses charged out of Pinetop, Cracker turned his head for a moment, but he saw no sign of Sloan. Cracker chuckled.

"Seems that I'm well out in front," he breathed.

Time passed. The stage began to enter wooded country.

Then suddenly Cracker's brake was striking sparks from the wheels and all his weight was pulling upon the reins! For lying spreadeagled in the very centre of the trail was the prone figure of a man around whose head a bloodstained bandage had been crudely fastened. A saddled horse stood nearby.

Leaping down from his driving seat, Cracker lifted up the man's head and shoulders.

"What's wrong?" he demanded. "How do you come to be in this state?"

The other's eyes opened and he stared blankly at the stage-coach driver.

"The–the Red Bandit!" he gasped at last. "He held me up, shot me out of the saddle, and he–he took everything I possessed. I managed to tie up my head wound and then–then—"

The man's voice failed him and his head fell back.

And at that moment Joe Sloan's coach appeared, hurtling along the trail. Sloan saw Cracker pulling the man to one side but he made no attempt to pull up. Instead he swerved around Cracker's stationary coach and then increased speed!

Cracker glanced down at the stranger for a moment and then he darted to his driving seat. Taking out his First Aid kit he snatched up a long roll of bandage.

Returning to the sprawling man, Cracker saw that the other had moved slightly. Suddenly he rolled the man over so quickly that once again the man's eyes fluttered open.

"You're a pretty serious case," Cracker told him. "You need attention here and now."

The man tried to sit up.

"Never mind me," he gasped. "I'll be all right. You've got the race to think of and—"

"Just look at the state of your hands," Cracker interrupted.

Next moment, he was winding the bandage around the man's wrists as hard as he could go. Instantly the latter's eyes filled with alarm.

"Hold on!" he gasped. "It's my head that's been hurt, not my hands. I—"

"I'm making a good job of you," Cracker told him. "The better I tie you up the easier you'll ride in the coach."

The stranger kicked out with surprising strength as Cracker grabbed his ankles. But all his efforts were useless. A few minutes later the stranger's ankles were also securely tied together by the bandage.

"I'm not travelling in your coach!" the man gasped, panic showing in his eyes. "I–I—"

"You've got no say in the matter," Cracker told him. "I'm in a hurry!"

Unceremoniously he dumped the trussed up man inside the coach. Then he leapt for the driving seat.

"And now we're going to catch up with Sloan," Cracker muttered. "And we're going to pass him long before we reach River Bend!"

It was then that the smell of wood smoke came to him. He was puzzled for only a few moments.

Seconds later, sweeping around a bend in the trail, he gave a horrified gasp. The forest was on fire directly ahead! It blocked his path completely!

"I get it," Cracker told himself. "It's one final attempt to stop me getting to River Bend! But why should anyone go to such lengths to stop me winning the race for the contract?"

It seemed to Cracker that he was beaten. To the right of him was the great width of the river and to the left a mighty expanse of forest. There was no other trail to River Bend, and he knew that if he tried to work round the forest it would take him days to reach his destination.

Then, even as Cracker began to back the coach, he heard a sudden crackling behind him. He whirled like lightning–and gasped, scarcely able to believe his eyes. The forest behind him was now a blazing mass! Cracker's first impulse was to swing his horses about and charge back through the flames. But he soon realised that such a plan would fail. The horses would refuse to charge through the flames and that would be the end!

Suddenly Cracker snapped finger and thumb together.

"The river," he said fiercely. "It's my only chance!"

Leaping down from his seat, he led his horses through the trees until the coach was standing on the bank of the river. It was obvious that lumberjacks had recently been at work at the spot, for there were several piles of neatly trimmed logs standing on the bank.

"Just what I hoped I would see," Cracker muttered.

He worked with furious energy then. From somewhere he found the strength to roll two of the biggest logs to the coach. The first log he roped to the wheels on one side of the coach as high above the axles as he could get it. Then he secured the second log in exactly the same way on the other side of the stage.

Then, without a moment's hesitation, he drove the horses down the sloping river bank and into the water. It was impossible for the wheels to turn, because of the logs, but they slid easily enough over the damp turf.

Splaaash! The coach entered the water and because of the two logs it kept afloat. Then, helped by the current and the swimming horses, it headed downstream.

Soon the coach was drifting by a blazing wall of fire on one side of the river.

"Reckon I'll still get to River Bend before Sloan!" Cracker told himself. "By taking to the river I've shortened my journey by at least half a dozen miles."

The coach drifted on past the wall of fire and then grounded in shallow water. Cracker set to work at once to cut loose the two logs. Minutes later, he was frantically urging his horses up the bank. He breathed his relief as the coach rolled on to dry land again.

"O. K., now for it!" he cried. "Get going, hosses!"

He had landed at a small ford and now he was able to travel quickly over a narrow trail. His voyage down the river had shortened his journey by several miles and he hoped that when he struck the main trail again he would see Joe Sloan ahead of him.

However, it wasn't until the coach reached open country again that Cracker saw his rival. In the far distance he also saw the town of River Bend.

Cracker leapt to his feet.

"Now for it, my beauties!" he urged. "You've got to prove to everybody that you're the finest horses in the whole of the West!"

Then his whip cracked in the air like a pistol shot.

It was some time later that Joe Sloan turned his head. When he saw the racing coach behind him he stared as though he couldn't believe his eyes. Then he, too, was standing up, and his whip was cracking furiously. Yelling at the tops of their voices cowboys came riding out to welcome the two coaches and to accompany them into River Bend.

"Cracker's going to make it!" one of the riders yelled. "Look at the way he's catching up!"

But even then it seemed that Joe Sloan must win. Fifty yards from the town, he was still in the lead! But suddenly Cracker's whip sounded like a pistol shot and from somewhere his horses found the last burst of speed. They drew abreast of the other coach and then they began to take the lead.

As the stages raced into the town, Joe Sloan tried to gain the advantage once more—by recklessly cutting a corner of the main street. Craaasch! One of the wheels of the stage made contact with a hitching-rack. Next instant the coach was on its side!

And so, unhampered and unchallenged, Cracker pulled up in front of the sheriff's office. Hank Marlow, the sheriff, was there to welcome him.

"Say! You've broken all records in getting here, Cracker," Hank shouted. "You'll get the contract all right. It's yours for all time!"

Cracker slid down from his seat and grinned.

"And I've got something for you, Hank," he said. "You get the Red Bandit!"

Next moment, flinging open the door of the stage, Cracker pulled out the bandaged, trussed prisoner. The man's face was white with fright and beads of perspiration stood upon his forehead.

Jerking his prisoner to his feet Cracker pulled the blood-stained bandage from his head.

"See," he said, glancing at the sheriff, "he isn't wounded at all. It was just a low-down stunt to hold me up so that Joe Sloan could take the lead."

Cracker's eyes narrowed as he turned towards the bound man.

"You'd better start telling all you know about the Red Bandit," he grated. "Some of the bandit's gang must have known you were a prisoner inside my coach but that didn't stop them setting fire to the forest behind me. Obviously they didn't care if you perished with the coach."

Angry, furious words came from the other in a torrent.

"Sloan's the Red Bandit!" he rapped. "He had some of his men stationed between the three towns. They were to stop you at all costs! First of all they were to stage an avalanche. If that failed they were going to dismantle the bridge. And if that didn't succeed in bringing you to a halt they intended to fire the forest ahead of you. That's why I pretended to be injured—we knew that you would pull up at sight of me. It was just a stunt to make sure that Sloan could take the lead."

"Sheriff, I think you'd better get Sloan," Cracker rapped.

Joe Sloan was in no state to offer any resistance for he had been half stunned when his coach had overturned. He was still dazed when he was dragged in front of Hank Marlow.

"How did you get wise to him in the first place, Cracker?" Hank Marlow demanded, glaring at Sloan.

Cracker explained how the Red Bandit had tried to hold him up the day before. He told how he had used his whip to jerk the revolver out of the bandit's hand.

Suddenly, Cracker seized Joe Sloan's right wrist and jerked it upward.

"Look at the back of his hand," he directed. "Look at the vivid weal across it. That was made yesterday by my whip, when it caused the Red Bandit to drop his gun. It was as we raced neck and neck for the bridge that I first caught sight of the weal. I knew then that Joe Sloan must be the Red Bandit!"

Before the day was out the whole of Joe Sloan's accomplices had been rounded up. And by that time the citizens of the three towns were thanking their stars that Cracker Judd had been the driver of their stage-coach. For if Cracker hadn't suggested that great race it wouldn't have come out that Joe Sloan was the Red Bandit.

Of course, if Joe Sloan had been given the contract he would have made sure that the stage was successfully held up every time it carried anything of value!

"Reckon we're proud of you, Cracker," Hank Marlow said that night. "You've got the contract and it's yours for as long as you like to hold it."

"And I reckon that's going to be for a very long time," Cracker grinned. "Thanks a lot, sheriff!"

THE MYSTERY OF THE JUNGLE

DRUMS

Steve Hunter, the big game photographer, was very puzzled when he heard the throbbing of the native drums. But it was only when he fell into an animal trap himself that the mystery of the drums was revealed to him.

_____

Big game photographer Steve Hunter–the "Hunter without guns", as he was known throughout a large part of Africa–was puzzled.

When he had left the last outpost of civilisation, together with his wife Alison, and his son Tim, in order to penetrate into a little-known and only partly explored tract of territory, the local Game Warden had come to see him off.

"You might keep an eye open for a fellow called Malleson while you're up there," the warden had asked. "He's a big-game trapper–catches 'em alive, and sells them to zoos in Europe. I don't particularly like the chap, but I haven't heard anything of him for months, and I hope he hasn't got knocked off by ivory poachers."

Steve thought it might prove a difficult job to find Malleson in the wilds, but to his surprise he had found it quite easy. He had actually come across two natives who had volunteered to guide him to Malleson's camp.

Now he had arrived there, to find Malleson comfortably fixed up in a clearing on the edge of a dense forest. But what puzzled Steve was the fact that Malleson seemed to expect him!

"Hullo, there!" he cried. "You're the Hunters, aren't you? Come along to the camp and make yourselves comfortable. I've been looking forward to meeting you."

Steve looked at Malleson curiously as he introduced him to Alison and Tim. Malleson was a tough, broad-shouldered type of man, who looked capable of looking after himself wherever he was.

"You sound as though you expected us," said Steve. "How did you know we were coming?"

"I've known where you were every day since you left the last trading post." Malleson laughed. "Ever heard of the Bush Telegraph? Listen."

He held up his hand for silence. The Hunters listened. From somewhere just beyond Malleson's camp came the steady throbbing of drums. For a while it continued, then ceased. There was a moment or two of dead silence, then from somewhere far away came an answering roll of drumming.

"I always take native drummers with me," said Malleson. "They're reporting your safe arrival now."

Steve was puzzled. If Malleson had native drummers amongst his bearers—a large number of whom seemed to be hanging around the camp—why hadn't the Game Warden known exactly where he was and what he was doing?

Later, when they were drinking coffee with Malleson, Steve mentioned the matter.

"I don't believe in letting anybody know what I'm doing," said Malleson. "Some of the natives might start interfering. But it's all right now. I'm breaking camp tomorrow and heading back with my catch. When you've finished coffee, come and have a look at 'em."

The camp was quite large. In addition to Malleson's up-to-date tent, and some rough lean-to's for his bearers, there were numerous large crates, all containing various animals and reptiles he had trapped.

To Steve's eyes the space allotted to the animals in the crates seemed extremely small. Steve was a little sickened by the sight, for he hated to see animals in cages, although Malleson explained that when they got to Europe they would be given much more liberty in the zoos which engaged him to trap them.

"Still, I advise you to set up your camp some distance away," said Malleson. "They can be pretty noisy at night, and I guess you Hunters will need a good night's rest. I'll send some of my boys to help you make camp, but I'll expect you back for dinner in my camp this evening at about seven."

Malleson seemed friendly enough, but there was something about him that Steve couldn't quite cotton on to. However, he put this down to his dislike of animal trappers in general.

Alison, however, was a little more outspoken.

"I don't like that man," she said. "I wish we weren't going to see him tonight."

"He didn't impress me much either," said Steve with a shrug. "But he'll be gone tomorrow, so we can't refuse his invitation."

Malleson's native cook certainly served an excellent meal in the cool of the evening, but the Hunters were secretly glad when the animal trapper suggested that they might like to make an early night of it.

Back in their own camp, young Tim went off to his own tent, saying he was very tired and would go to bed immediately. Steve and Alison continued to talk for some time, then suddenly Steve sprang to his feet and leaped forward. For a strange thing had happened. Alison had broken off in the middle of a sentence, and suddenly flopped back upon the camp bed on which she had been sitting. Her eyes closed, and her head dropped forward. Steve caught her just before she collapsed on the floor.

"Alison, what's wrong?" he gasped, but she made no reply.

"She's been *doped!*" Steve gasped. "But how–why—?"

Then the suspicion became a certainty. "Malleson!" he gasped. "This is his doing! He's up to something–I must find out what it is!"

Steve strode into the forest seeking in the darkness for the little game track along which Malleson's "bearers" had guided them earlier that day.

Alison had been drugged all right–and so had Tim. Steve had been unable to wake either of them. Now he remembered that at dinner that evening, both Alison and Tim had finished with coffee. He, too, had been served with coffee, but by accident he had knocked his cup off the table. Malleson had not been there at the time, so Steve had not bothered to ask for more.

At last Steve struck the track. It turned and twisted bewilderingly. It had been a bit of a job to drive the truck along it in daylight. Now, in pitch darkness–for the moon had not yet risen–he kept blundering off the track continuously.

Suddenly he pitched forward, and fell heavily. His first thought was that his foot had become entangled in the thick undergrowth, but the next moment something closed around him in an encircling grip.

Then he was yanked violently upward, his legs twisted under him, and his arms pinned to his side. He was crashing violently amongst the branches of the trees above him. Everything had happened so swiftly that he was completely at a loss to understand how it was that he had been on the ground one moment, and struggling in the treetops the next.

He strove to wriggle his hands free to see what it was that held him in that strangling grip. Then he began to understand.

He was in a net–a net which had closed around him as he fell. It was some sort of ingenious animal trap, and must have been fastened to the top of a tree which had been bent down and fastened there until the trap had been sprung!

"This is more of Malleson's doing!" Steve muttered. "He must have set that trap deliberately in case the dope didn't work."

Why Malleson should go to such extraordinary lengths to make sure he was not spied upon was more than he could understand–unless Malleson was engaged upon something which his animal trapping was just a blind to conceal!

It was then that the moon slid from behind a bank of clouds, lighting up the scene around him. From his place in the treetops, he could see the country spread out below him–including Malleson's camp.

At first it appeared that nothing was wrong there, for he could see no one moving. Everyone appeared to be asleep. Then he suddenly realised that the camp was deserted. Malleson and his men had gone–but where?

It was while he was still trying to free himself from the trap that the question was answered. For Malleson suddenly appeared in the clearing, emerging from the track in the forest. His bearers came after him in single file, each man carrying a cumbersome burden.

One glance at what they were carrying told Steve everything! Each man was laden with elephant tusks–dozens and dozens, perhaps hundreds of them!

"Ivory poachers!" gasped Steve. "So that's Malleson's game! The poachers slaughter the animals wholesale to get the tusks, then Malleson takes over! But how can he possibly get such a cargo out of the country?"

That question was soon answered. For even as Steve watched, Malleson and his men set to work on the crates which held the captured wild animals. They began to prize out boards from the sides of the crates, revealing sizeable hiding spaces in the false sides!

No wonder the animals had appeared to Steve to have so little space! Every crate had a secret hiding place in its walls. And, as each held such dangerous creatures, Customs officials were not likely to subject them to a very close scrutiny. Once out of the country, the ivory would remain safely in its hiding places until the crates were opened in Europe–by other members of this vast smuggling racket!

"So those drums we heard earlier were not to announce our arrival," thought Steve bitterly. "They were to tell the poachers to bring their ivory along so that Malleson and his men could pick it up."

Malleson's natives worked swiftly, but it was not until the first pale light of dawn broke that they were finished, and the false sides of the crates were nailed up again.

Camp was then hastily struck; the crates and their contents were slung up on poles to be carried by the bearers. Then Malleson and the bearers moved off, leaving hardly a trace behind to show where their camp had been!

As the light of day grew stronger, Steve was able to see more clearly what was imprisoning him. The net that held him was a pretty large one, and he realised that it was his own weight which was causing it to close so tightly around him.

If he climbed up inside the net, it would relax the pressure on his arms and legs. With difficulty he began to climb. Soon his arms were no longer pinned in their former helpless position, and he was able to reach the sheath knife he carried in his belt.

The rest was easy. He cut through several of the strands which formed the net, and then set it swinging until it reached the trunk of the palm tree from which it hung suspended.

Clutching the trunk, he disentangled himself from the net, and slithered down to earth.

He raced back to his camp. Alison and Tim were still sleeping, but he could tell that the effects of the drug were wearing off, and he brewed hot, strong coffee. When he eventually managed to shake them awake, the coffee and an antidote from the medicine chest soon had them back to normal. Then he told them what had happened, while he consulted a map of the country.

"Malleson's making for the river beyond the forest," he explained. "According to my calculations, he can't possibly get there until after nightfall. But if we made a detour, we could get there first."

"But Malleson and his men are armed," Alison pointed out. "What could the three of us do against them?"

"We'd have to take them by surprise," Steve answered. "Don't forget that Malleson won't be expecting us to follow him!"

"There's another thing," he went on. "His native bearers don't belong to a forest tribe. They're superstitious, afraid of the forest. If we can put a real scare into them—"

"How are you going to do that, dad?" asked Tim.

"That's where I'll need your help," Steve told him. "I'll tell you my idea later. Meanwhile we'd better get cracking. We've got much further to go than Malleson, but, as he and his bearers are on foot, we might manage it."

It was a tricky journey, for they had to avoid the forest in case they overtook Malleson. It meant a considerable detour, but Steve had learned a great deal about the country before starting off, and the rough map he had drawn stood them in good stead.

They pressed on all day without a halt, and long before nightfall had reached the river, and followed it down towards the spot where Malleson and his men would emerge some time later.

Malleson was already having trouble with his native bearers. It had been a long trek for them through the forest, and carrying crates laden with animals and heavy tusks of ivory had sapped his men's strength.

Night fell and darkness shrouded the jungle. Malleson, leading the little cavalcade, went first, an electric torch helping him to find the forest trail. Casting apprehensive glances over their shoulders, his bearers followed.

The darkness was intense. Then, suddenly, the silence of the night was split by the most unearthly yells and shrieks that echoed and re-echoed from the dense trees. The bearers halted, panic-stricken, and shivering with fear.

The noise grew stronger. It was as though a thousand demons were let loose. Even Malleson stopped dead in his tracks. Then cries of fear broke from the superstitious bearers.

For, blocking the way ahead, was the most fearsome creature they had ever seen!

Two blazing eyes seemed to appear from nowhere. They were of a hideous green colour, and smoke was wreathing all around them. Still the hideous shrieking sound went on, and then the monster moved forward.

It was the last straw! Adding to the uproar with their yells of fear, Malleson's bearers dropped the crates, and, with one accord, raced madly back the way they had come. Only Malleson stood his ground, his heavy elephant rifle in his hands.

The next moment he jumped aside, as the unseen monster swept down on him. The rifle was wrenched from him as someone jumped on to his shoulders, knocking him to the ground.

Then the hideous shrieking noise stopped, and the green eyes of the monster stopped moving.

"Okay, Malleson," said a voice he recognised. "The game's up. Your bearers won't come back here to rescue you–and I've got you covered with your own gun."

It was Steve who spoke. At the same time Alison got down from the truck she had been driving – and from which Steve had made a leap which carried him on to Malleson's shoulders. She whipped off the green shades that had been rigged over the truck's headlights. Tim, grinning, joined his father, and tied the fuming Malleson's hands behind his back.

"Well, Dad, that idea of yours of fixing the record player so that it would play a pop record backwards with the volume turned right up certainly worked! What are we going to do now?"

"We'll load the ivory into our truck," said Steve. "Then, as soon as it's light, we let the animals go. They'll be glad of their liberty–but when the authorities learn what Malleson's little game was, I don't think *he'll* have much of that for a long time to come."

That was the view of the authorities, too, when Steve arrived back at the nearest outpost with the stolen ivory and his prisoner, Malleson.

"It's certainly delayed our little photographic jaunt," said Steve when he had handed the prisoner over. "But I guess it'll warn any other hoodlums in this neighbourhood that it doesn't pay to try to pull a fast one on the Hunters!"

If you turn now to page 213 you will be able to read some more adventures of the Hunter family in Africa.

JET JORDAN, STUNT FLYER

Jet Jordan, who was the leader of the superjet stunt flying team, suddenly found that all the other pilots had disappeared mysteriously from the sky. When he discovered that they had all been hijacked, it was not so easy to get them back.

"Watch it blokes!" Jet Jordan called sharply over his intercom. "It looks as if we're running into an electrical storm."

Jet Jordan was the leader of the Royal Canadian Air Force team of superjet aerobatic pilots known as the Red Bisons. The team was screaming high over the Pacific, heading for a temporary base which had been prepared for it in Australia, where it was to give a series of exhibitions.

Jet had noticed an eerie flicker off the surfaces of his aircraft. An electrical charge was building up. There was no serious danger because the superjet, flying at supersonic speed six miles high, was completely insulated from the earth. But he had to warn his fellow pilots because there was a risk that the instruments might be affected and give false readings.

Jet waited to hear his message acknowledged. Nothing happened. There was complete silence. He turned his head to look behind him through the rear of the cockpit canopy.

He couldn't believe his eyes. The sky was empty!

There was a thin layer of cloud about a mile below him, and his first thought was that the gang were pulling some kind of gag on him, deliberately diving down out of sight. Jet spoke again into his radio.

"Stop acting the goat, blokes. Get back into formation. You know the rules about maintaining contact at all times. Are you trying to get me court-martialled?"

To his exasperation his radio remained dead. The missing planes did not reappear. Angrily he winged over and went slashing down through the cloud. He expected to be through it in a matter of seconds, and to see his team speeding along beneath it. Then something nightmarish happened. Once in the cloud, with swirling mist blanketing his view, he couldn't get out of it.

It was almost as if the cloud had enveloped the superjet and was staying with it. When, at last, he did manage to shake it off, and emerge with a clear, vast bird's eye view of the Pacific, he had travelled about fifty miles from the point where he had lost contact with the team.

Jet circled the area fruitlessly until his fuel began to run dangerously low. He was still convinced that he was the victim of a leg-pull plotted by his team.

"They must have headed for base, expect I'll find them waiting for me when I arrive. I'll certainly skin 'em alive for this," Jet muttered to himself.

The Australian base was almost brand-new. It was in the middle of the Nullabor Plain, where there was unlimited space, huge runways, all the most modern equipment, and the latest in air-conditioned buildings, providing air crews and ground staff with every kind of comfort and luxury.

Jet had been looking forward to spending a few months there. But now everything had suddenly gone sour. He screamed down on to one of the enormous runways. A jeep came out to pick him up. The driver looked at him curiously.

"On your own, sir?" he asked.

Jet, who had been going over in his mind a few of the blistering things he intended saying to his team, smothered a gasp.

"You mean that the others haven't turned up yet?"

"Not that I know of," was the answer.

"Take me to C.O.'s office, and step on it," rapped Jet.

The Commanding Officer gave Jet a baffled look.

"Where are the others?" he demanded.

"I don't know," gulped Jet. "I lost 'em somewhere out there over the Pacific."

"Don't act the goat, Jordan," rapped the C.O. impatiently. "This isn't a matter for joking."

"I'm not joking!" exploded Jet. "I'm trying to tell you–I've lost the Red Bisons. They just dived into a cloud and vanished!"

The C.O. grabbed his phone.

"Get me the security officer!" he yelled, and then went on, "Jordan has just turned up, alone. You'd better put a guard on his plane, then come over here to hear what he has to say for himself."

Then he turned to Jet.

"Go on," he said grimly.

"There's not much to tell," confessed Jet. "I was in front of the team. Suddenly the radio went dead, and when I turned to look for the boys, they'd gone. I thought it was a gag."

"What about this cloud?"

"Funny about that. When I got into it I had the dickens of a job to get out of it again. It seemed to move with the kite."

"A cloud that moved at supersonic speed? It must have been quite some wind up there."

"I know it sounds crazy," admitted Jet. "I'm just telling you what happened. I can't explain it."

A man who had been working quietly in the back of the office, listening, suddenly came out with a curt laugh. He was Flight-Lieutenant Willsby, and he was the leader of the reserve aerobatic team. There was no love lost between himself and Jet.

Willsby reckoned that, given the chance, he could do better than Jet. But Jet and his lads were so consistently good that the reserve team rarely got an opportunity to perform.

"I've been saying for a long time that Jordan was showing signs of strain," he said. "He's been pushed too hard. High-speed aerobatics are tough on the nerves. My team should have been allowed to take some of the responsibility."

"Are you suggesting I'm crackers?" demanded Jet furiously.

Willsby shrugged.

"Supersonic clouds–kites that just vanish–how does it sound to you?"

At that moment the security officer came in. He was holding

a plastic red bison, dangling from a ribbon.

"This was in your cockpit. Where did it come from?"

"I don't remember. Some fan sent it. It's a mascot."

"Mascot!" snorted the security officer. "It's an illegal electronic gadget, a transistorised direction indicator to allow a radio beam to lock on to your kite!"

Jet looked thunderstruck.

"You mean somebody was tracking us?"

"There's another thing. Your flight recorder shows that at one point you were at least a hundred miles off your authorised course. How could that happen to a pilot of your experience? Explain it."

"It must have been the electrical storm. At least, I thought at the time it was an electrical storm. Now I'm not so sure. My instruments were on the blink. And at the speed those superjets shift it doesn't take long to get a hundred miles off the beam."

The security officer gave him a scowling glance.

"I want to talk to the C.O.–alone. Wait outside, Jordan. Go with him, Willsby, and don't let him out of your sight."

"Are you afraid I might run away?" demanded Jet disgustedly. "We're stuck in the middle of hundreds of square miles of desert. Where would I run to?"

Willsby took his arm and steered him outside. The air-conditioned offices had dividing walls which were half glass. Jet could see the men inside, but he couldn't hear them . The offices were completely sound proof. But Jet himself had been trained for special operations. He had done a course in lipreading. He could follow what the security officer was saying.

"This bison gadget. Any good electronic engineer could have devised the circuits, but it would take a genius to pack the miniaturised components into a thing this size. So far as our records go there's only one man capable of doing it. His name's Zorgel. This is his work all right."

"Zorgel? Never heard of him."

"You wouldn't have done. But we've known him for years. He specialises in making gadgets for spy work. Midget microphones, tele-peepy cameras inside coat buttons, transmitters no bigger than a tie-pin – all that stuff."

172

"A dangerous man, if he doesn't happen to be on your side."

"Too true. And according to our information he has defected to a deadly organisation known as CRASH–the Council for Revolution in Asia and the Southern Hemisphere. They are out to put the East in a turmoil. I don't know where our planes and pilots are, but I think we can guess that CRASH has got them."

"But you're not suggesting that Jordan has turned traitor?"

"Frankly, I'm not sure. CRASH has almost unlimited money at its disposal. They say every man has his price. Supposing Jordan had been offered more money than he's ever likely to see in his life? A quarter of a million. Half a million. The superjets would be cheap at the price, and can you say for sure that even a man like Jordan wouldn't be tempted."

At that moment the C.O. turned his back, so that Jet could no longer tell what either man was saying. A few moments later they came out.

"Jordan, you're to go to your quarters and stay there. Willsby will go with you and show you the way," said the C.O.

"Are you putting me under arrest?" demanded Jet grimly.

"Not officially. But it would be very foolish of you to try to leave."

Willsby walked him as far as the door of the living quarters block. Jet paused and looked back before going in to look for the door with his name on it. The airfield seemed quiet, but at either corner of the building stood armed guards, trying to look inconspicuous and unconcerned. They weren't taking any chances with Jet. He went on in, knowing that his cockney batman, Joe Hawkins, would have arrived with the advance party and by now would have everything ready for him. As he opened the door he recoiled, assaulted with a fearful smell.

"What the—?"

The room was occupied by a spectacled, rumpled haired man in an officer's uniform which was scruffy, untidy, and stained with chemicals.

"Boffin Barker!" snorted Jet. "You're in the wrong room. You're even in the wrong block. You should be in the groundstaff quarters across the runway."

Boffin Barker was in the research section. He spent all his spare time on wild projects of his own, hoping to make sensational discoveries that would revolutionise flying.

"I'm sorry," Boffin apologised. "But the chaps with rooms near me are always complaining about the stink. So I thought I could move in here because—"

"Because you thought I'd be in the prison block?" snorted Jet. "News travels fast!"

"I'm sorry, Jet. I'm sure there's been some frightful mistake. Of course, I'll clear out. But you won't mind if I finish what I'm doing?"

Jet nodded, vaguely interested. Boffin had set up a screen of dark-coloured glass. Behind it was a metal plate with wires draped untidily to the light socket. He took a large paper bag and poured some white powder into the plate.

"Flour?" asked Jet in surprise.

"No. I just happened to have a flour bag handy to keep it in," explained Boffin vaguely. "It's some stuff I made which I hope will burn with a tremendously bright light, so that it could be used for signal flares in daylight. That's why I've got the dark glass screen. Watch."

He pressed the light switch. There was a little spark from the bare wires on the plate, a sizzle, then clouds of evil smelling fumes belched up, while the white powder bubbled slowly like lava from a volcano.

"Dear me," mused Boffin, "I seem to have got the formula wrong."

"Out!" yelled Jet. "Back to your own quarters and take all your junk with you. I've enough trouble of my own."

At that moment Joe Hawkins came in.

"What's going on, Mr. Jordan?"

"Open the windows. Clear this muck out!" cried Jet.

When the room was clear he threw himself disgustedly on his bed, and tried to think. He knew he was in a jam, but how was he to get out of it? The only way to clear himself was to find out exactly what had happened to the Red Bisons and their planes.

To do that he would need to start his search in the area where they had vanished. But of course, so long as he was under suspicion they weren't going to let him leave the airfield. And until he could leave the airfield he couldn't start to clear himself of suspicion. It was a vicious circle. He stayed where he was for several hours, hardly aware how the time was passing. Then Joe came in.

"It's tea-time, Mr. Jordan. Will you be going across to the Mess?"

"I'm not allowed to leave here, Joe."

"That's what I thought. So I fixed you a tray to have here. Pot of tea, bread and butter, jam, and something special. This batch of current buns I knocked up myself. Still warm from the oven."

The tea was good. So was the bread and butter and jam. Jet made short work of the plateful, then turned his attention to Joe's buns.

He took a bite, then let out a yell. It felt as if he had broken his teeth.

"It's as hard as stone!" he gasped.

Disgustedly he tossed the bun towards a wastepaper basket. The shot missed. The bun hit the wall. There was a blinding explosion and half the ceiling fell in.

Joe dashed in, to find Jet covered with plaster and surrounded by rubble.

"What happened?" gasped Joe.

"The bun! It exploded! What did you put in it?"

"The usual things," said Joe. "Fat. That bag of flour on the table —"

"That wasn't flour! It's some crazy formula of Boffin's. You baked a batch of bombs. It's a wonder the oven didn't go through the roof!" gasped Jet.

In the distance he heard a siren blowing. Trucks were starting up. Whistles were blowing. The explosion was bringing the security men. They must have thought Jet had tried to stage a spectacular escape. The thought gave Jet an idea.

"Joe. Would you like to help me?" he rapped.

"Of course, Mr. Jordan."

"Then get down on the floor."

Joe obeyed. Jet swiftly covered him with fallen plaster and rubble until only his feet showed. Then he grabbed a rucksack, carefully placed the rest of the buns in it, and slung it over his shoulder. He waited until he heard men running along the corridor. Then he vaulted out of the window. The security officer charged into the room. He saw the buried figure and jumped to the conclusion that it must be Jet.

"The fool. He tried to blow his way out. The stunt backfired on him. He may have killed himself."

As men rushed to drag the figure clear the officer held up his hand.

"Slowly. Lift the stuff off him carefully. He could be badly injured."

They went to work carefully until one of the men made a discovery.

"This isn't Jordan!"

At that moment the officer was almost deafened by the roar of a jeep going across the airfield.

"Jordan. He's making a bolt for it. I guess this proves he was a CRASH agent after all."

Willsby was coming out of the administration block, and was just in time to see the jeep go hurtling by.

"Jordan!" he yelled.

The C.O.'s car was a few yards away. He ran for it and gave chase. The C.O. himself came tearing out, just as the security officer and a truckload of men roared up. A screeching knifed through the air. Everyone ducked. A superjet whistled overhead so low that the slipstream lifted tiles off the roofs. As it passed the men started to straighten, then ducked again as a second aircraft whistled after the first.

"Will somebody tell me what's going on?" yelled the C.O.

"Jordan's made a break for it, the fool," panted the security officer. "But Willsby's after him."

Jet was climbing like an arrow. He heard Willsby's voice in his earphones.

"Don't be a fool Jordan. Turn back. I'm right behind you. I could shoot you right out of the sky."

"You'd do anything to get my job, wouldn't you?" taunted Jet.

It was a bluff. Willsby was jealous of Jet. Willsby honestly believed that he was a better pilot, and would make a better aerobatic leader than Jet, but he wasn't a crook or a cold-blooded killer. Jet knew he wouldn't shoot.

Willsby was helpless to do anything to stop Jet. All he could do was follow. They were high over the Pacific when Jet began to notice the electrical flicker round the nose of his aircraft. He glanced down. There were the whispy clouds again, blotting out whatever might be below.

But this time he was sure that the plane wasn't being affected by an electrical storm. It was some sinister phenomenon resulting from the activities of the agents of CRASH. All at once his superjet dropped by the nose, and nothing he could do would straighten it out. He was plunging helplessly towards the cloud.

Willsby's voice rang in his ears.

"Jordan! I'm out of control!"

"Hit the button!" yelled Jet. "Use your ejector."

At the same time, he followed his own advice. The cockpit canopy blew off. Jet went out like a rocket, and the plane fell away from him. As the chute opened the cockpit seat automatically detached itself, leaving him drifting. He looked up. Willsby was floating down too.

They sank through the cloud and emerged again into daylight.

Jet gasped at what he saw. Below was an island, hidden from observers above by what he now judged to be some kind of artificial fog. The shape of the island struck a cord in his memory.

"Katara!"

It was a name made famous in World War II. The Japs had taken over the island, evacuated all the native inhabitants, and turned it into a fortress airbase of such strength that it had taken the American Marines three months to winkle them out with high explosives and flame throwers. The place had been so devastated that the exile population had never returned. The island had been abandoned.

It still bore the scars. It was cratered, blistered, littered with the stumps of plantations, over which the natural vegetation was even now beginning to put a thin covering.

The runways, Jet noted, had been restored to their original state, and on one of them stood the two superjets which had landed safely, undamaged. Jet touched down and shed his parachute. Willsby landed beside him, looking dazed and baffled.

"How did you know where to come?" he asked suspiciously.

"I didn't. It was just a hunch," Jet answered. "Now get this into your head. There is a dangerous international organisation called CRASH. It is making use of this place–operating some kind of secret weapon. Unless I'm completely off the beam we'll find our kites around here somewhere–and our boys as well."

There was a sudden disturbance in a nearby patch of scrub. Six armed men emerged, and surrounded them. One of them smiled at

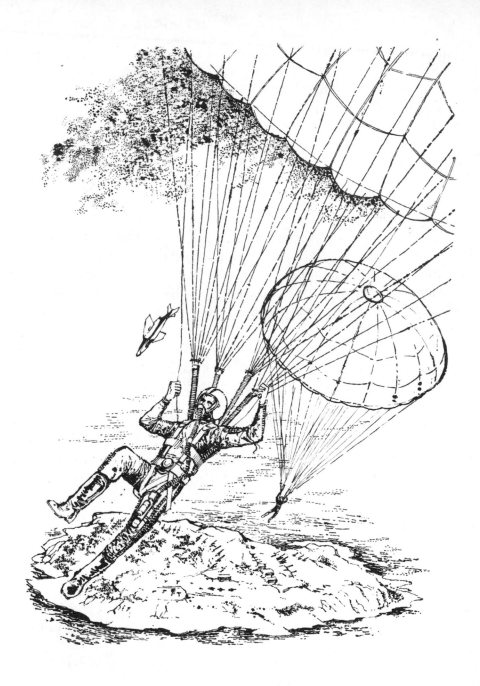

"Katara!"

the two of them mockingly.

"Ah, the too-clever Mr. Jordan. Welcome to CRASH."

The scrub concealed the entrance to a concrete bunker.

Jet and Willsby were forced at gunpoint, and down a stairway into an underground blockhouse, where a big, bullet-headed man in a uniform smothered with gold braid awaited them.

"Search them for weapons," he ordered. "See what he is carrying in that bag."

"Buns," reported one of the captors in surprise.

"Rations. I had to leave in a hurry. Didn't know where my next meal was coming from," Jet said lightly.

The bullet-headed CRASH leader eyed him coldly.

"Why did you come back?" he demanded.

For one thing, to look for a gent called Zorgel, and settle with him for playing a dirty trick on me."

"So! You know about Zorgel!" scowled the other. "How much more do you know?"

"Jordan! Don't tell him anything!" protested Willsby.

"Why not? I'm not giving away any secrets," Jet retorted. "I know that you're operating some kind of radio tractor beam. That's how you pulled our kites out of the sky without damaging them. The electrical charge that builds up on the fuselage, and the clouds, must be some kind of side effect."

"And you have told your security officers all this?"

"What do you think?" hedged Jet.

"It doesn't matter. Because you won't have told them of Katara. You haven't had the chance."

"They'll soon find it," bluffed Jet.

"Fortunately for CRASH, they won't have time. We have devised a means of operating our tractor beam weapon so that it will work in reverse when carried aboard the aircraft you have so kindly provided for us. Airborne, it will create havoc beside which a hurricane would look like a gentle breeze. Tomorrow we launch our first challenge against one of the largest cities in the East. It will be the greatest cataclysm since Hiroshima."

Jet hurled himself forward with a howl of rage.

"Why, you murdering—"

Men fell on him and clubbed him to his knees with gun-butts. Willsby tried to aid him, and was beaten to the floor.

"Put them in with the others," commanded the CRASH boss.

They were dragged along a corridor until they came to a steel barred door which enclosed a cell where the missing aerobatic team were penned. They looked dismayed as Jet and Willsby were booted in and the door clanged behind them.

"Jet!" gasped one. "As long as you were still free we hoped you would do something for us. But this means curtains."

"No," contradicted Jet. "We're getting out of here, and we're getting our planes back."

While the others watched as if he was mad Jet opened his rucksack, took out a bun, carefully broke off a very small piece and jammed it in the lock of the door. Then he sat down and took off his shoe.

"Everyone get back as far as you can," he instructed. "Against the wall. Flat on your faces."

He hurled his shoe at the lock. There was a deafening explosion. The cell filled with smoke. The door fell open.

"Out!" yelled Jet. "Follow me."

They rushed into the corridor. A bunch of men with sten guns appeared at the far end, barring the way.

"Get back inside," yelled one.

Jet threw a bun–bomb.

The flash was almost blinding, and the crash earsplitting. When the dust settled there were motionless bodies on the floor, and an enormous hole in the wall.

"Grab those guns," Jet shouted.

They clambered out into the open.

"Does anyone know where the kites are?" he shouted.

"At the far end of that clover-leaf runway, under the green camouflage."

"We've got a lot of ground to cover, let's get started."

By now the whole island was in an uproar. Running figures appeared, using the scrub as cover. Bullets whistled through the air. Bisons who had managed to arm themselves shot back, firing as they ran.

Jet tossed a couple of bun-bombs in quick succession into a thick patch of brush, and made a tattered mess of a machine-gun position. They reached the camouflaged hangar.

"Get in there and bring your kites out," yelled Jet, posting himself at the entrance. A couple of armoured cars were bowling down the runway. Jet let them get within throwing distance, then lobbed a Boffin special.

It landed between the two vehicles, and blew them both to scrap. Next moment a superjet came howling out, and the slipstream almost threw Jet off his feet. There was a jeep parked near the corner of the hangar.

"Our kites are on the other side of the field. Let's ride over," Jet shouted to Willsby.

They scrambled aboard as a second superjet screamed out. Jet drove. Willsby stood up in the back, cuddling a sten gun and spraying bullets at anything that moved, until he ran out of ammunition.

Jet slipped the rucksack from his shoulder and passed it back.

"There's still a few left. Don't waste 'em," he ordered.

As they approached the waiting planes a tracked personnel carrier burst through the scrub to head them off. Willsby selected a Boffin-bomb and lobbed it thoughtfully. The vehicle and its passengers vanished in a volcano of smoke.

"Bull's eye," congratulated Jet.

They reached the planes. Superjets were screaming to and fro overhead, raising an earsplitting din. As Jet got moving he heard a voice in his earphones.

"Jet. Someone has been monkeying about in this cockpit. There's a lever here that wasn't here before."

At that moment a CRASH anti-aircraft battery opened up on the wheeling superjets. "Use the lever," Jet called back. "Pull it, and see what happens."

About a second later an acre or two of scrub, stunted trees, rock and concealed concrete pillbox fragmented and went straight up into the air.

"The tractor beam! It works in reverse, just like the gent said!" cried Jet. "Somebody get those ack-ack guns."

One of the Bisons came whistling down. He flattened out with shell-bursts popping all round his aircraft.

Then the battery took off, sandbagged wall, operating crew and all, jumping into the air and breaking up into small pieces.

"Let's give 'em a real going over while we're about it," suggested Jet.

The CRASH hideout was torn apart by its own secret weapon. Soon hardly anything could be seen through a great grey pall of whirling dust, but every now and again fresh spurts of rubble jetted up through, spread out, and sank down again. At last, satisfied that they had done enough, Jet gave the order for the Red Bisons to return to base.

Radar picked them up long before they actually reached the field, so that their arrival wasn't entirely unexpected. But when they touched down the C.O. and the chief security officer were out on the runway, hardly able to believe their eyes when they saw the missing planes returning to roost. Jet climbed down from his cockpit, grinning.

"There's a cleaning up job to be done," he said. "Katara Island. That's where CRASH was hiding out in preparation for its bid to gain mastery of the East. We plastered it pretty well, but a task force ought to go out there pretty rapidly to gather up any remnants that we left!"

THE GHOST THAT BLEW BUBBLES

by Mark Grimshaw

How was it possible for a man to be attacked by someone who had been dead for ten years? Once again, Colwyn Dane, the great private detective, had a very great mystery on his hands.

"It's incredible, Dane! A smalltime crook named Logan was attacked and knocked unconscious by a man who has been dead for ten years!"

Detective-Inspector Woods, of Scotland Yard, had dropped in to see his friend, Colwyn Dane, at The Turrets, the famous 'tec's North London home. Seated in an easy-chair in the consulting–room, Woods was telling the ace 'tec about a case he was working on.

"It happened last night," the detective-inspector went on. "A constable on his beat in the East End heard a cry for help. He rushed to investigate, and found Logan lying senseless in the gutter of a near-by street. Logan had been struck on the back of the head by a heavy instrument. Of course, you know Logan, Dane?"

"Yes, I know him," he replied. "He's been mixed up in several smash-and-grab raids, and has just finished a stretch at Bleakmoor Prison."

Inspector Woods continued with his story.

"Logan came to for a few seconds after the constable had phoned for an ambulance. He said he'd been attacked by a spook-the ghost of Rabbit Squitch!"

"Squitch! I remember him," put in Dane. "An old, evil-looking chap who lived near some docks on the River Thames. He had a bad reputation, but you never managed to catch him out at anything crooked. Killed by a bomb in the blitz, wasn't he?"

"No doubt about that!" declared Inspector Woods. "The bomb scored a direct hit on his house. I saw Rabbit Squitch myself when the air-raid wardens brought him out of the wreckage. He was dead all right, and there wasn't a doubt about his identity, either. Yet Logan was certain he'd been attacked by Squitch last night, and Logan ought to know whether it was the old man or not. When Squitch was alive they were as thick as thieves. At least, they were until a few days before Squitch's death," the inspector corrected himself. "Then they quarrelled, and Squitch was heard to say he'd get Logan if it was the last thing he ever did."

"And do you think that the ghost of the old man did attack Logan last night?" put in Dane.

"There doesn't seem to be any other explanation," frowned the inspector. "You see, near where Logan was struck down, we found the weapon which had been used in the attack. It was an ebony walkingstick–the one which Squitch had used in his lifetime. There were fresh finger-prints on it-Squitch's prints!

"Furthermore," the inspector continued, "two other persons have declared that they saw Squitch–or his ghost–last night."

Dane's interest was now fully roused. A ghost seeking vengeance! Or was there more to it than that?

"Have you learned anything more about Squitch's ghost?" he asked.

"Maybe this is just a coincidence," added the inspector. "But work was to start this morning on clearing the site of Squitch's bombed house for a new wharf. Before he was killed Squitch put a curse on anyone who tampered with his property. A lorry taking workmen to the site this morning met with an accident, and three men joined Logan in hospital. Remembering the curse and that Squitch's ghost had been seen last night, the rest flatly refused to have anything to do with the job. There'll be no work on Squitch's bombed house till the strike is settled."

"Anything else?" prompted Dane.

"Yes, there is," nodded the inspector. "See this?"

Unwrapping a brown-paper parcel he'd brought with him into the consulting-room, Woods disclosed a broken house-brick!

"Logan had that in his hand when the constable found him," he explained.

Dane looked thoughtful. Why had Logan carried half a brick about with him? Taking it from Woods, the ace 'tec examined the brick closely. It was just an ordinary brick, and there wasn't a mark or scratch upon it that could tell him anything.

"Got you puzzled, eh?" grinned Woods, getting to his feet. "You're not the only one, Dane. Maybe the brick, like the curse on the bombed site, doesn't figure in the mystery at all. Well, I'll have to be going. See you later."

As the inspector left the house Dane pressed a buzzer on his desk, and Slick Chester, his young assistant, came hurrying to the consulting room.

"Get the car round, Slick," Dane said, after he had told the boy 'tec of Wood's visit. "We're going along to the East End. I want to look at what's left of Rabbit Squitch's house." Half an hour later the 'tecs were in the East End. Having left Dane's sports car at a garage, they walked through riverside streets to the creek on whose muddy banks Squitch had had his house.

There wasn't much left of it now. All that remained were a few heaps of rubble, overgrown with weeds, and a slimy wall disappearing into the black, stagnant waters of the creek.

For some time Dane searched among the mounds of debris, and there was a satisfied gleam in his eyes when at last he turned to Slick.

"It's just as I thought," he declared. "Though Logan was attacked half a mile away, the brick he was holding came from here. It was a hand-made brick–not a common brick. But there are hundreds here like it–because Squitch's house was built of them. And in a crack of the brick was a seed from a rare weed–the same weed that's growing over there. Right! The brick came from here. So how did Logan come to be holding it?"

Slick shook his head.

"And what has it to do with the ghost of Rabbit Squitch?" mused Dane.

Slick suddenly stared at some tall weeds growing on a mound a few yards away. Although there wasn't a breath of wind, the weeds were definitely swaying slightly.

"Somebody's there, guv'nor!" whispered the boy 'tec, nodding to the pile of debris. "It could be a spy!"

Dane said nothing. He was holding a brick he'd picked up. Now he lobbed it over the weeds. From the other side came a gasp and the scurry of slithering feet. Then a man appeared, running for the creek.

"After him, Slick!" snapped Dane.

Tied to some slimy steps at the water's edge was a small rowing-boat. Leaping down to it, the spy ran out the oars. He was disappearing round the stern of a derelict barge when the 'tecs reached the top of the steps. Dane caught only a fleeting glimpse of the man's face. But he recognised him as a member of a gang of crooks to which Logan belonged.

"I want to know what that crook was doing here," muttered Dane. "Maybe he was just curious about us. But he could be mixed up in the mystery of Squitch's ghost! So let's get cracking. There's another boat tied up farther along the creek."

Boarding the boat, Slick cast off the painter, while Dane bent to the oars. A moment later they were skimming across the muddy creek. They rounded the barge, but other shipping prevented them from seeing their quarry.

Suddenly their boat rocked violently, and Slick had to make a lightning grab at the gunwale to prevent himself from taking a header into the creek.

As it was, he was flung forward from his seat, and his chin met the gunwale with a resounding crack. Half-stunned, he found himself looking down at the murky waters. And then an amazing thing happened. From out of the creek rose a black, glistening hand! For a brief instant Slick wondered if his dazed senses were playing tricks on him. Then the mysterious hand's gripping fingers hooked over the gunwale behind Dane!

Before Slick could utter a warning the boat rocked again, more violently than before.

Next moment the boat overturned, and he and his chief were struggling in the water. To make matters worse, the boy 'tec was still feeling half stunned, and so Dane had to swim with him back to the shore of the creek.

In a few breathless sentences Slick told the ace 'tec what he had seen the moment before the boat overturned.

"I know it sounds a bit fantastic, guv'nor," Slick confessed, "but I'm sure it was a hand. I suppose that bloke we chased didn't deliberately lure us across the creek?" he went on thoughtfully.

"What makes you think that?" asked Dane.

"He could have been leading us into a trap," replied Slick.

Dane gazed over the stagnant creek for a long time before replying. Was Slick right? he wondered. Then the famous 'tec stiffened. In the water below him appeared a large bubble. As it burst another took its place a foot or so away. That vanished, and a third bubble appeared, close to the slimy wall that had once helped form one side of Rabbit Squitch's house.

Three bubbles! But they told Dane a lot.

"I don't think you've got the answer, Slick," he said, with a shake of his head. "But I'm beginning to see through this mystery. I know now where to look for Rabbit Squitch's ghost!"

"Well, that throws some light on Logan's movements last night," muttered Dane.

He and Slick were at the hospital to which Logan had been taken on the previous evening. Dane had been hoping to question the crook, but Logan was still lying unconscious in a private ward on the third floor.

Although disappointed, Dane wasn't beaten. He'd got hold of one of Logan's boots, and he was now examining it closely in a room on the fourth floor, peering through a powerful magnifying-glass at some scrapings of mud from the instep.

"There are traces of builder's rubble and river mud," Dane went on. "I'd say that Logan had been hunting round the ruins of Rabbit Squitch's house. My guess is that for some reason he picked up the half brick when he spotted the old man's ghost. He ran for his life, and the ghost went after him."

"And overtook him half a mile away in an East End street," nodded Slick. "That wasn't bad going for a fellow of Rabbit's age. But I wonder why Logan went to the bombed site?" added the boy 'tec. "Looks as if we'll have to wait until he recovers consciousness to learn that."

Dane's frown deepened.

"Logan is conscious already," he said. "He was foxing when we looked at him in his private ward. But I knew it was a waste of time questioning him then. He'd only have told us lies. So I reckoned that our best plan was to stay around here for a while and keep an eye on him."

Dane walked to the window and looked out. Suddenly he beckoned Slick to his side and pointed down at a window on the third floor.

"Logan's room! And that's Logan there now," he added as a man's figure appeared at the window. "I thought he'd be up to something as soon as he was alone."

A small object then fell from the third-floor window, and after a moment the figure there disappeared.

"Come on!"

With Slick at his heels, Dane dashed from the room, and a little while later the 'tecs were hunting on the pavement below Logan's window. From behind a bush growing in a tub Dane drew–a hairbrush!

"Somebody picked it up from the pavement where it fell," he muttered, "and then dumped it here."

Slick stared in bewilderment. Why should Logan deliberately drop a hairbrush from his room? he asked himself. And who had picked it up, only to throw it away?

"One of Logan's gang must have been waiting here," mused Dane. "Logan dropped him a message, wrapped around the hairbrush! You see, there isn't a mark on the brush, though it dropped from three floors on to the hard pavement. The paper cushioned it. The man read the message and threw away the brush as he made off."

"Where do we go from here, guv'nor?" asked Slick.

Dane thought fast. What was in the message? Logan would know, of course, but Dane wasn't going to waste time questioning him. It wouldn't be anything that had happened since Rabbit Squitch's ghost had attacked Logan. But it could concern something that had occurred just before the attack.

"Perhaps we'll find out if we visit the ruins of Squitch's house again," Dane muttered.

The light was fading fast, and it was almost dark when the 'tecs reached the creek. Soon the moon rose over the river, casting sinister, ghostly shadows among the ruins. The 'tecs crouched behind a heap of rubble, where they had an unbroken view of the bombed site.

For a couple of hours nothing happened. Then to Dane's ears came the sound of stealthy footfalls. A minute later half a dozen shadowy figures loomed up in the darkness and halted a few yards from the hidden 'tecs.

"One of them is the spy who got away in the boat, guv'," whispered Slick. "The rest belong to the same gang. And it could be Logan's gang! Gosh, I'll bet they're here because of the message Logan sent wrapped round the brush!"

Dane smiled. It was what he had expected. But why should Logan send the gang there? And how was it linked with Rabbit Squitch's ghost?

He watched eagerly. Three of the men were moving some debris, working quickly and silently, while the others seemed to be keeping guard.

It was plain that they didn't want anybody butting in on them. Little did they realise that the 'tecs were watching their every movement from a near by pile of rubble-until, in his eagerness to get a better view, Slick brushed against a rusty bucket that had been dumped there.

Crash! Clatter! Bang!

The bucket rolled down the heap. The noise created panic among the crooks! Like startled rabbits, they raced away from the site, disappearing in a moment.

"They won't be back in a hurry!" grinned Dane to Slick, heaving himself to his feet.

Bidding Slick to follow, he made for the spot where the crooks had been busy. He dragged away some planking and disclosed a narrow hole, with broken steps leading downwards.

"That's what I thought," he whispered. "Logan found these steps last night. But before he could explore them properly h
by Rabbit Squitch's ghost. And today, being coop
couldn't visit the place. He knew he hadn't an
the workmen were to start clearing the
information to his fellow gangsters."

Slick nodded thoughtfully.

"That means Logan didn't want the demolition workers to discover what is down there," he mused. "And those steps could lead to what were the cellars of Squitch's house."

"And we're going to explore them," put in the ace 'tec. "Come on!"

With Slick following him, Dane descended the steps, gun in one hand and torch in the other. A door at the bottom was blocked by debris, but eventually they managed to force a way through into a cellar, the walls of which glistened with slime.

To Slick's disappointment, it was obvious that no one had been there for years. Dane searched among the mouldering lumber. But there seemed to be nothing that could have interested Logan.

Suddenly Dane dropped to his knees. A minute later he had prised up one of the large flagstones forming the floor. From the inky blackness below came the gurgle of slow-moving water.

As the 'tec flashed his torch downwards it shaved the curved walls of a sewer, with a narrow ledge, rising from the water, right below them.

Lowering himself into the hole, Dane hung on for an instant by his hands and dropped lightly to the ledge. Slick joined him. In single file they edged along the ledge, and suddenly they saw the pale gleam of light ahead. Dane switched off the torch, and they proceeded even more warily.

The 'tecs halted as the tunnel widened into a sort of chamber, half filled with water. The ledge also widened, and the light came from a storm lantern on an upturned box, on which were the remains of a meal. There was no sign of any human occupant, though.

"I'd say there was an outlet to the creek somewhere," muttered Slick, gazing round. "Old Squitch must have used it in his lifetime, so you can bet he was a crook. And—g-gosh, l-look there!"

Slick's hand shook slightly as he pointed towards the pool of water in the chamber. And no wonder! Rising from the black water was the gleaming head of what looked like some monster of the deep!

It wasn't until a minute later that Slick realised the "monster" was man in a self-contained diving-suit! As the man waded from the pool that he wore a polished helmet, and had a supply of oxygen

A diver! The boy 'tec's thoughts raced. Obviously, he had come in from the creek by way of the sewer. So it must have been the diver's hand that had reached up from depths to capsize their boat! And the bubbles Dane had seen afterwards had come from the diving-suit!

But how did the diver link up with the mystery? Slick watched breathlessly as the diver removed his helmet. Then he gasped. The head which was revealed was that of an old man. He had wispy grey hair, shaggy eyebrows, and two protruding front teeth which, with the narrow features, made him resemble a rabbit!

Now he had discarded the black rubber diving-suit, and showed that he was wearing clothes that had been out of fashion for over thirty years!

Slick gasped again. He didn't need to be told that he was looking at the ghost of Rabbit Squitch!

But who ever heard of a diving ghost? What did it mean?

So far the ghost of Rabbit Squitch had seen nothing of the watching 'tecs. But now luck turned against them. A huge rat, scurrying along the ledge, suddenly spotted them, let out a startled squeal, and took a flying leap into the water.

The splash made the ghostly crook whirl. His hand dipped to the pocket of his ancient frock coat and came out gripping a very modern-looking automatic.

Crack!

Quick though Squitch was, Dane was far quicker. His own gun spat flame, even as the old man swung up his weapon. The bullet grazed the other's knuckles, and the automatic, flying from his grasp, landed in the pool.

"Stay put!" Dane barked. "Now reach for the roof!"

The man obeyed, and Dane stepped into the chamber. The ace 'tec handed his gun to Slick, and then stepped up to the diver, flashing his torch into the old man's face. Suddenly Dane shot out an arm, gripped the grey hair, and gave it a sharp tug. The hair came away in his hand. It was a wig!

"I thought as much!" Dane snapped. "Now take out those teeth. And remove those eyebrows."

The crook did so. The change in his appearance was amazing. From an old man he became a snarling, narrow-faced tough, with the slit eyes of a killer.

"Poison Price!" exclaimed Dane, recognising him at once. "That explains a lot. You and Logan's gang are old enemies, but you're all crooks–like Rabbit Squitch. You could have been after the same thing–something that Squitch had in the house before the blitz. As soon as Logan was released from prison the other day he set out to find that 'something'. You got wind of it and trailed him, hoping to beat him to it. Am I right?"

Poison said nothing, but his lips curled. That was enough to tell the ace 'tec he had spoken the truth.

"By posing as Rabbit's ghost you hoped to scare away intruders," Dane went on. "I see you're wearing gloves. My guess is that moulds of Squitch's finger-prints are on their fingers. That was to hoodwink the police, eh? Anyhow, you certainly gave Logan a scare when you found him exploring the ruins last night. Thinking he had the 'something' which belonged to the dead Squitch, you chased him–only to find, when you K.O.'d him, that he was merely holding half a brick he'd picked up to defend himself with."

"And now," rasped Dane, "I'm waiting to hear what that 'something' you're after is!"

Again Price remained silent, but he glanced furtively to his left. Following the crook's glance, Dane saw two rusty kettles on the ledge. They were riddled with holes and worthless, and it was plain that they had not lain there long.

Poison Price could have collected them from the bombed site. But–why?

Suddenly a thought flashed through the ace 'tec's mind, and a grim smile appeared on his face.

"I think I know the answer," he went on. "So now we're going places. Bring the lantern along, Slick, and keep my gun pointed at Price."

Dane led the way back into the sewer. Soon they were standing beneath the trapdoor the 'tecs had discovered earlier. Swinging himself up through it and into the cellar, Dane waited for the others to join him. Then again he rummaged through the mouldering lumber.

Suddenly he straightened up with an old kettle in his hand.

"I saw this here when we were here a few minutes ago," he said.

"This wouldn't be what you were looking for eh, Poison?"

The crook's eyes almost popped out of his head as the ace 'tec thrust a hand into the kettle and drew from it a bundle wrapped in rotting cloth.

The cloth crumbled away, and something glittered in the lantern-light. Dane held it up on one finger.

It was a diamond necklace!

And that wasn't all. In the bundle were several sparkling rings, a jewelled wrist-watch, and some valuable rubies!

"Squitch's loot, eh?" went on Dane. "Yes, I see it all now. He was a 'fence'. And you knew he kept his loot hidden in an old kettle, so you set out to get it. Logan did, too. But it wouldn't have suited either of you if the demolition gang had started work on this bombed site. They might have found the loot. So you spread that yarn about Squitch's curse on the place. One of you could even have caused the accident to the lorry that was bringing the workmen here, and—"

Dane broke off. He'd heard a stealthy sound from the other side of the cellar. Swiftly he turned his head. That was all the diving crook wanted.

Smash!

He drove a kick at the lantern in Slick's hand. Then, as darkness fell, he leapt at Dane like a tiger.

Wham!

A swinging blow to the jaw sent the 'tec staggering backwards. At the same time Poison grabbed the bundle of jewels and sprang down through the trapdoor into the sewer.

The 'tecs had no chance to follow him, for the cellar was suddenly filled with yelling men. Before he could regain his feet two men had piled on to Dane. Others grabbed Slick. Then torches flashed, and the 'tecs got a glimpse of their attackers. As Dane had realised already, they were Logan's gangster pals–the men they'd seen searching in the rubble above!

Thanks to their intervention, Poison Price had got away with the loot. Then Dane saw something gleaming on the floor. It was a ruby, which had fallen from the bundle and been trampled into the mud!

"Look, there's part of the stuff you're looking for!" Dane rapped suddenly to the crooks.

The crooks made a dive for the ruby, and at the same instant Dane went into action, hooking a foot round one man's leg. The crook hit the stone floor with his chin, and a gun slid from his nerveless hand. In a moment Dane had snatched it up.

"Up with your arms!" rapped the ace 'tec. "Right, Slick! Frisk them! Drop their guns down into the sewer. That's it! Now, all of you, get into there!" he went on, pointing to a niche in the cellar wall. "There's just about room for you."

Wedged like sardines in the narrow space, the crooks could do nothing as Dane and Slick piled heavy lumber against the opening.

"You'll stay there till I'm ready to collect you," Dane informed the crooks. "Meantime—"

Dropping into the sewer, he dashed after Poison Price, only to find him gone. But a string of bubbles on the scummy surface of the pool sent Dane into lightning action.

Splash! Diving into the pool, he swam underwater. His groping hands touched something, and he knew it was the crooked diver.

Immediately Price felt Dane's groping hands he lashed out like a madman. The murky waters heaved and threshed.

Dane's lungs were almost bursting, when he suddenly felt his opponent weakening. But Price was only foxing, for a moment later Dane stopped a vicious kick that made his senses reel.

But Dane was determined that Poison Price shouldn't escape. His clasp-knife was in his hand, and he made a slashing cut at the diver's weighty boots.

The keen blade severed the straps securing them as if they had been cotton threads. Next moment the bootless Price shot to the surface–upside-down!

Dane followed him and dragged him out of the pool.

"And that's that!" said Dane as he took the bundle of jewellery from a pocket of Poison Price's diving-suit. "So now I'll get back to lend Slick a hand with those other crooks!"

Another exciting Colwyn Dane mystery appears on page 81. Did you miss it?

POLAR PERIL

Bruce Gaylord was a young naturalist on an expedition in Greenland. Disobeying an order, he took a canoe on to a lake where he was attacked by a wounded walrus. Swimming frantically, he reached an ice floe only to find that a dangerous polar bear was awaiting him and the walrus was about to attack him from the rear.

Four men stood on the barren North-east coast of Greenland, staring out across the bitter sea to a tiny island of rock in the bay. Ice floes drifted slowly past. The arctic wind howled.

Laguk, the Eskimo, shook his head in solemn warning. "No," he said, "it is not safe. We wait for the power-boat. Walrus hunters have wounded a big one, and it will attack on sight."

Between the mainland and the island, dark heads bobbed in the water – a family of walruses.

Young Bruce Gaylord glanced towards Laguk's frail kayak . . .

Nielsen, the big Swede, pulled at his blond beard, and smiled. "No, not in that, Mister Gaylord. You wouldn't stand a chance."

Peters laughed harshly. "He wouldn't even try it – trust Gaylord to figure some way to buy himself across!"

Bruce looked away. The youngest of the party, he knew he was only there at all because his father had financed this expedition to ring the rare Sabine's Gull.

Not for the first time, he thought money a curse. If he were just another youngster now . . . well, he'd be given his chance, the chance to prove his worth. All he wanted from life was to work as a naturalist. But Nielsen treated him with kid gloves – the patron's son must never come to harm. That was bad enough . . . but Peters openly mocked him because he'd always had everything money could buy, and never had to work for his living.

Bruce studied the island through field-glasses. The gulls were there, plainly visible; he had only to cross that bleak stretch of water.

A sudden flurry of snow made Nielsen look up at the leaden sky. "More snow coming," he growled. "We may be too late by the time the motor-boat arrives." He looked again at the walruses. Their powerful bodies could easily upset a boat, and they were certain to attack now. He shook his head, unwilling to risk the lives of his party. There would be another chance later – he hoped.

Bruce lagged behind as they walked back to their tents, feeling the small metal rings in his pocket. If he could slip away somehow, he'd show them . . .

Bruce had his own private tent.

"Only the best is good enough for Gaylord," Peters had sneered.

Peters had come up the hard way. He was a good naturalist; it was a pity he couldn't forget that Bruce came of a wealthy family. Nielsen didn't rib him about that, but he was over-anxious, and never allowed him to go off on his own.

Bruce sneaked a look back at the island, dim through a curtain of snow. It had to be now, or never. "I'll be with you in a minute," he said casually. "Just want to jot down a few notes."

As the others turned into the main tent, he walked towards his own tent . . . ducked round it and ran back to the shore. He launched Laguk's kayak, stepped into the small wood and sealskin craft, and picked up the double-bladed paddle. He pushed off, paddling skilfully, for he had his own canoe at home.

Under a steel-grey sky, he headed for the island between the ice floes. Behind him, Nielsen's angry voice bellowed across the water:

"Mister Gaylord, come back . . . back . . ." His voice was lost in a gust of wind.

Bruce didn't look round but settled to the rhythmic swing of his paddle, keeping a sharp watch for walruses. Through the swirl of snowflakes he saw them, dark heads above the water, two-feet-long tusks gleaming. He shuddered at the thought of their great bodies lunging towards his frail craft. An upset in that icy water and he would freeze solid within seconds.

He watched the herd move. They were coming for him. He was a big one, the leader, with a broken tusk and savage eyes boring in – he paddled faster.

He piloted his canoe between drifting floes. Only a few hundred yards to safety . . . he saw the great head vanish under the surface. Where would it come up? Desperately, he changed direction, took a zig-zag course, paddle flashing as it dipped and churned the water.

Yards off, the walrus emerged, looking round. Then it dived again and swam underwater . . .

Bruce was close to an ice-floe when the water heaved and surged beside him. A massive grey head appeared and red eyes glared at him. Brokentusk's front flippers splashed icy water over him; then one mighty blow stove in the side of the kayak and it began to sink.

Bruce rose and leapt clear in one swift movement. He leapt for the floe and scrambled onto it, slithering over the ice. He heard a frustrated roar from the angry walrus as it heaved itself up after him.

He ran as the great beast lumbered behind. He reached the edge of the floe and gauged the gap he had to jump to the island. He ran on . . . jumped and ran across the second floe. The island was within reach. He jumped again.

Done it! Gasping, he sprawled headlong in soft snow. He had lost the kayak, but Nielsen would come for him in the motor-boat. Meanwhile, he would ring the gulls . . .

As he moved towards the nesting site, snow came down thicker, wet and stinging. All at once, a vast white shadow rose in his path, seven feet of shaggy fur with a black nose and eyes. A polar bear . . . claws extended and rearing to its full height.

Bruce stood quite still, heart beating furiously. Bears were said rarely to attack human beings, but this one seemed suspicious. It ambled towards him, growling.

Something clicked in Bruce's mind . . .

After the bear had gone, Bruce ringed the Sabine gulls on their nests. As darkness came, he burrowed deep into a snow drift and settled down.

In the morning, he heard Nielsen hail him as the motor-boat approached.

"Something clicked in Bruce's mind . . ."

"I ringed the gulls," Bruce said quietly. "I'm sorry about the kayak, but Dad will pay."

Peters seemed about to speak, but only shook his head.

Nielsen tugged on his beard. "The bear, the polar bear . . ."

"I remembered in time," Bruce explained, "that bears have a great respect for walruses. So I imitated the roar of an angry walrus, and it went away."

"We shall make a naturalist of you yet, Mister Gaylord . . ."

Peters interrupted Nielsen. "Naturalist, nothing," he said, holding out his hand. "We'll make a *human* of him!"

ROCKFIST ROGAN

by Hal Wilton

Rockfist Rogan was flying over the Pacific Ocean when he found himself almost out of fuel – so it was quite fun to have to force-land on a desert island. It was not such fun, however, to discover that the natives were cannibals and were getting ready for a feast.

"Where the dickens is the place? Crossbones Island should be around here somewhere!"

Rockfist Rogan, the boxing pilot of Star Airways, gazed down from the cockpit of his flying-boat at hundreds of square miles of empty Pacific Ocean. Then he glanced at the indicator on his dashboard panel. His fuel was getting dangerously low!

"Curly, you fathead, you've lost us!" he exclaimed.

His pal, Curly Hooper, who was navigating the plane, gave an angry snort.

"I've never messed up one of these navigating jobs yet, and you know it! I tell you the island must be right below us! If it isn't, then it must have sunk into the blinkin' ocean!"

Rockfist gave a grim smile. Here they were, right in the middle of the Pacific Ocean and thousands of miles from help! The other two occupants of the plane, Archie Streatham and Dizzy Dyall, the scatter-brained odd-job man, were peering down through the cabin windows. Suddenly Dizzy gave an excited yelp.

"Look at that whale down there!"

"What whale?" scoffed Rockfist. "You're not in the Arctic now, you know!"

"It's got a lot of feathers on its back!" cried Dizzy, pointing.

"Now you're really talking through your hat!" Rockfist retorted.

Rockfist raised a pair of binoculars to his eyes. Then he let out a shout.

"That isn't a whale! That's the island! Yes, it's Crossbones Island all right. And those things aren't feathers–they're palm trees!" He turned and grinned. "Curly, I take it all back. You're a real wizard of a navigator!"

Rockfist grew thoughtful.

"Now remember, we've got an important job to do here, and we've got to go carefully," he warned. "Star Airways have sent us out to build an airfield. And build it we will!"

The big flying-boat was losing height now. The island was no longer a tiny dot. It was increasing in size every minute. It was half-moon shaped, with the twin peaks of two jungle-clad mountains towering up from the middle, and tall palm-tree groves growing thickly along the surf-fringed beach.

Rockfist glanced at his wrist-watch as he circled the plane around the island and prepared to make a landing.

"Right on the dot. To the minute," he declared. "Curly, I'll say it again! You're a wizard!"

Curly scribbled a final message in his navigation log-book, and slipped his fountain-pen into the pocket of his bush shirt.

Meanwhile, Archie was polishing his monocle so that he could get a better look at the island.

"Doesn't seem to be anyone about," he remarked.

Then, with a roar, the flying-boat glided down on to the calm water, throwing up a cloud of spray. Rockfist switched off the engines, and in dead silence they drifted into shallow water. They all jumped out and waded knee-deep through the water towards the lonely-looking beach.

"No one at home," remarked Curly.

"Perhaps the natives have moved to some other island," Rockfist suggested hopefully. "It'll certainly make our job a lot easier if—"

His voice tailed off. He had suddenly spotted a black, tattooed face peering at them from the undergrowth! As he looked, there was a sinister rustling sound. And as if by magic, scores of almost naked black figures appeared and advanced towards the beach. The suspicious islanders, fierce warriors, came creeping on. They carried shields and were armed with spears which were pointed straight at Rockfist & Co.!

"Steady!" Rockfist muttered to his pals. "Remember that we want to give a good impression. We could ruin all our future plans with one false move."

Rockfist walked boldly towards a towering, ugly-looking native who wore arm-bands and leg-bands decorated with feathers which marked him out as a leader.

The boxing airman strode to within a yard of him.

"Greetings!" cried Rockfist, holding out his hand. "We come as friends!"

The natives swarmed forward. There was a babble of shrill talk. Then Rockfist heard Archie's voice raised in protest.

"Don't start any trouble!" Rockfist warned him. "What seems to be wrong?"

"Dash it all, one of these characters is trying to pinch my monocle!" protested Archie.

"Well, let him have it, then," instructed Rockfist. "Remember, we've got to keep on the right side of these people."

Grumbling under his breath, Archie reluctantly obeyed. Then it was Curly who became the centre of a sudden, angry squabble.

"Take your black paws off my fountain-pen, you thug!" Rockfist heard Curly yell.

"Let him have it if he wants it," Rockfist called out sharply. "Remember—"

"I know," Curly said wearily. "We've got to keep on the right side of these people."

With a look of despair he handed over the fountain-pen to the grinning, delighted native.

Rockfist turned back to the huge warrior leader who was making queer, grunting noises, and pointing with his spear at the watch on Rockfist's wrist.

"Hey, steady on!" gasped Rockfist.

"Go on. What are you waiting for?" Curly urged. "Remember? We've got to keep on the right side of these people!"

With a helpless shrug Rockfist unclasped the watch and handed it to the wide-eyed native. It seemed halfwitted handing a valuable wristwatch over to an uncivilised warrior, but at all costs he had to keep the natives in a friendly mood.

Then, suddenly, Dizzy became involved in a wild scrimmage.

"Dyall!" yelled Rockfist. "You heard what I said. D'you want to land us in the soup, you dimwit? Give the man what he wants. We've already had to—"

"It's all very well for you, Captain Rogan!" wailed Dizzy. "But this fellow wants my shorts!"

In spite of the dangerous situation, Rockfist couldn't help chuckling.

"There are some spare ones aboard the kite. Give him a pair of those," he instructed.

The natives were beginning to calm down now, and Rockfist was just about to explain to the native leader that he wished to stay on the island for a while when a new figure came leaping out of the jungle. Strings of human bones with which he was festooned clattered as he capered up and down.

"Him our witch-doctor. Him say you go away quick-quick," the leader said to Rockfist in broken English, a frightened expression on his face. "Magic signs talk along of him. Say you bring much trouble."

"But we aren't going to make any trouble," insisted Rockfist.

"Trouble already begin. Spirits no like you, witch-doctor say. Today our chief die. You no go, worse come. Enemies from next island will come kill us chop-chop," the native replied.

Rockfist thought quickly. If the chief of the island was dead, it was going to add to his troubles because there was now no one with whom he could make a bargain. At the moment the witch-doctor appeared to have more influence than anyone else, and he had obviously decided that he didn't like Rockfist & Co.!

"We can help you against your enemies," Rockfist suggested quickly.

Then, like a flash, Rockfist made a grab for his gun. But he had no intention of using it against the natives. He had just spotted a snake slithering towards the warrior!

Craaack!

Rockfist's gun spurted flame. His shot blew the snake's head off. The warrior spun round, and then his jaw dropped as he saw the headless snake. With a howl of fear he threw himself flat on his face in front of Rockfist. All along the beach the other natives were grovelling in the sand as well. Rockfist's sharp-shooting display had an amazing effect.

The native leader and his followers had decided that a man with a magic "noise-stick" that could kill so strangely was not to be trifled with. Even the witch-doctor looked shaken, although he remained on his feet, glowering.

The leader said nothing more about Rockfist and his party having to leave. By his shot with the gun Rockfist had gained respect, and he meant to make full use of it to settle himself on the island and win over the natives to his side. While the warriors stood around in amazed groups, watching, Rockfist and his pals unloaded supplies from the plane and set up a camp alongside a creek a few hundred yards inland from the shore.

Rockfist glanced up at the sky.

"Better get the tents up first. I think there's a storm coming," he said. "Then we'll light a fire and Dizzy can cook us some grub. I'm starving."

After a while Rockfist discovered that Dizzy was no longer lending a hand with the unloading, and thinking that he was probably starting the cooking, went to see how he was getting on. Then, as he spotted the scatterbrained odd-job man, he snorted with rage.

Dizzy had a fire going, but that was as far as he had got with the cooking. He was seated in a canvas chair at a folding table, and was frowning puzzledly as, with his tongue sticking out between his teeth, he wrote busily on a piece of paper.

A crowd of beaming, excited natives peered over his shoulder.

Rockfist strode across to him.

"What d'you think you're doing?" he demanded.

"Making out my football pool coupon," said Dizzy. "Do you think the supply plane will arrive in time to get it mailed? I've got a feeling that this is going to be my lucky week."

Rockfist looked over Dizzy's shoulder and gave a chuckle.

"Well, there's one wrong for a start," he said, pointing. "You've got the Dazzlers down to lose at home!"

"Ah, but they're not the team they were," declared Dizzy. "They've never been the same since Sandy Murrell got crocked. Their centreforward now is some chap nobody has ever heard of. Danny Robbins or Roberts or something!"

With deep concentration Dizzy added further marks to the coupon, while the natives watched in breathless wonder.

Neither Dizzy nor Rockfist realised the real reason for their excitement. On Crossbones Island an "X" was a magic figure. The island took its name from an old pirate flag which was kept in the village ju-ju house. And the witch-doctor always made a cross in the sand when he began casting "magic" spells. None of the other natives dared to make use of the symbol in any way.

Dizzy suddenly uttered a grunt of annoyance as he realised that he had made a mistake. He screwed up the coupon, intending to start again.

He tossed the paper into the camp fire.

B-booom! B-booom!

As the paper flared up, the first sign of the storm came with a deafening roll of thunder that echoed among the mountains.

This was too much for the natives. They thought that Dizzy had worked some mighty magic, calling up the storm by burning the magic symbols!

Uttering howls of fright, they scattered and raced back to their village as fast as their legs could carry them.

"What do you make of that, sir?" gasped Dizzy.

"I'm not sure," grinned Rockfist. "But I've got a feeling that, whatever it was, it's going to be good for us. They seemed to think you caused that thunderclap. That makes us both wizards!"

Curly and Archie came racing up to take shelter in the tent as a torrent of rain began to fall.

"Looks as if we're going to have plenty of trouble with these natives," Curly remarked grimly.

"I'm not so sure," Rockfist answered. "They've suddenly lost their chief, just when they need a leader. And they're scared stiff of being attacked by enemies from another island. If we can only find a way to make them safe from their enemies they'll be friendly for ever more."

By the following day Rockfist had his camp well established and was doing his best to make friends with the half-frightened natives.

They hung around, watching what was going on, but making no attempt to interfere. Rockfist and Curly then went off together to take a look at the island, leaving Archie working in the tent and Dizzy with various jobs of cleaning-up and cooking to do.

When Rockfist and Curly returned to the camp at midday, having made rough maps of the part of the island they had explored, Archie was still working busily inside the tent, but there was no sign of Dizzy anywhere.

"Where's Dizzy?" asked Rockfist.

"He went off to the village with some of the natives," Archie reported. "He seems to have made a big hit with them. They think he's a master magician!"

"But he's supposed to be getting our lunch!" snorted Rockfist. "I'll crown him when he gets back."

But Dizzy didn't show up. The pals had to cook their own meal. Afterwards, Rockfist and Curly set off again, in the opposite direction to the one they had taken in the morning, to continue their survey. It was almost sundown when they returned, and Rockfist was furious when he discovered that Dizzy still hadn't come back, and not one of the many odd-jobs around the camp had been tackled.

"What does he think he's doing?" Rockfist demanded. "I'll chase him all round the camp when he does return!"

"By the way, we've had a visit from that big native—the first one you spoke to," Archie reported. "His name's Chakkacharralali."

"Eh? Er—O.K., we'll call him Charlie," decided Rockfist. "What did he want?"

"We've been invited to a feast," Archie reported. "Tomorrow night. The natives are holding a big ceremonial blow-out to please the jungle spirits and to obtain their help against those enemy islanders who are expected to attack."

Curly grimaced.

"We'll be expected to eat horrible concoctions like boiled snakes' brains and frog's-egg soup," he protested. "We'll all get dreadful indigestion even if we don't actually get poisoned."

"All the same, we must accept the invitation," Rockfist insisted. "If the natives are willing to be friendly we must co-operate. We're going to need their help when we start hacking down the jungle."

Morning came and still Dizzy hadn't returned to the camp. Rockfist started off angrily for the village.

It was about a mile farther up the creek, and was one of the most fantastic places Rockfist had ever set eyes on. All the houses were built on platforms raised on wooden stilts. Some of them actually stood in the water. The platforms were reached by ladders made out of notched palm trunks, which could be hauled up at the slightest threat of danger.

As Rockfist entered the village clearing he spotted the huge native he had nicknamed "Charlie".

"Where's Dyall?" demanded Rockfist.

"You mean Big-Wizard Thunderman? He up there," grunted Charlie, pointing to one of the houses where two enormous natives stood guarding the door with spears.

Rockfist shinned up the tree-trunk ladder, but the moment he crossed the platform to the door the two guards promptly placed their spears in the way.

Rockfist peered through the door. Dizzy lay sprawled out like a prince on a comfortable palm-leaf couch! Around his neck hung huge strings of beads and he had a crown on his head made out of lumps of coral. He was eating something from a wooden bowl, scooping it up with his fingers.

Piled up all around him were bowls of food and stacks of fruit of all kinds. In a far corner of the room lay a heap of dirty, empty dishes. Two men were running backwards and forwards, picking choice bits of food out of the dishes and trying to tempt Dizzy with them.

Dizzy had a sleepy, contented look. In fact, he looked too full to move!

"Hallo, Captain Rogan!" he beamed. "Gosh, I'm having a wonderful time here. They certainly know how to treat you well."

"What's that stuff you're eating?" rapped Rockfist.

"I don't know," grinned Dizzy. "But it tastes smashing. I've done nothing but eat since I came here. See how fat I'm getting? I won't be able to get through that door soon!"

"We didn't bring you here to stuff yourself like a hog. There's work to do!" gritted Rockfist. "Come on! Back to the camp at once!"

"Oh, gosh—" Dizzy began to protest.

Rockfist stepped forward, intending to lug Dizzy out by the scruff of his neck. But immediately the two guards grabbed him.

"It's no good, sir," grinned Dizzy. "They like me so much they won't let me leave. Every time I try to go out they pull me back."

Rockfist started to struggle in the grip of the native guards, and to shout angrily. Then he realised that Charlie had climbed up on to the platform.

"Make these men understand that Dyall has got to come back to the camp!" Rockfist thundered.

Charlie shrugged and said something that caused Rockfist to let out a yell and struggle harder than ever. He was pushed back across the platform and sent hurtling over the edge. He hit the ground with a terrific thud. Scrambling to his feet, he stared up at the house and drew his gun. For a moment he was tempted to climb back up there and show them who was boss.

But he knew it would do no good. Shooting would only make matters worse.

He turned and raced back to the camp with a grim message for his pals.

"I've got some news about that big feast to-night," he announced breathlessly. "These natives are cannibals!"

Curly uttered a gasp.

"Cannibals? Phew! That's not so good."

"It's even worse than you think," went on Rockfist. "They've got old Dizzy in one of their huts, cramming him with food, fattening him up. Dizzy doesn't realise what's in store for him. It seems that the natives believe that if you really want to get the jungle spirits on your side, you have to sacrifice a wizard. And they're convinced that Dizzy is a super-wizard. If they kill him, they're sure the jungle spirits will send a great storm and sink the enemy war canoes!"

Curly drew a revolver.

"We'd better go up there and rescue him," he gritted.

"No! Put that gun away," rapped Rockfist. "If we try to save Dizzy, the natives will kill him before we can reach him. Besides, if we start a fight here, that'll put an end to our chances of building an airfield. We must settle this some other way."

"But how?" demanded Archie.

"By defeating the natives' enemy so that there'll be no need to sacrifice poor old Dizzy! We've got to move fast!"

Rockfist raced down to the flying-boat. He found that the trip to Crossbones Island had left only enough fuel for a few minutes' flying.

"Just about enough to give me the chance to fly out to the enemy's island and try to spot what's going on," Rockfist decided. "Until I find out what they're up to I can't make any plans of my own."

Rockfist took off on his own, leaving Curly and Archie behind to deal with any further trouble. He hadn't been in the air more than a minute when he saw a flotilla of about forty war canoes coming over the horizon! The enemy had already started out on their attack!

Rockfist sent the flying-boat round in a tight turn and raced back to Crossbones Island. This had upset all his plans. Now that the enemy were actually coming, the natives might decide to kill Dizzy straight away instead of waiting until tonight!

When Rockfist touched down he found the beach alive with natives running up and down in panic, trying to decide on some plan to beat back the invaders. A look-out man on the mountains had spotted the war canoes almost at the same time that Rockfist had seen them and had raised the alarm.

Booom! Booom! Booom-booom!

War-drums beat out madly. Parties of warriors were taking up positions in the undergrowth all along the beach. There was terror and confusion everywhere.

Rockfist hared back to his pals.

"What about Dizzy?" he demanded.

"They haven't sacrificed him yet," Curly declared.

Rockfist sprinted up the beach to where Charlie was screeching orders to hordes of fuzzy-headed spearmen.

"Charlie, if you leave this to me I'll fix the enemy for you. I'll make the biggest storm you ever saw," he promised. "But if you dare to harm Dizzy. I won't help you, and I'll blow your village to bits!"

Charlie looked questioningly at the witch-doctor, who gave a wild leap in the air, contorting his face and chattering crazily. From his expression Rockfist guessed that the witch-doctor was not merely going to refuse the offer of help—he was going to tell Rockfist in native language to go and jump in the lagoon!

Rockfist's hand flashed to his side.

He whipped out his revolver and levelled it at the witch-doctor.

"Listen, you!" he snapped. "You're holding our friend Dyall prisoner. But if he comes to any harm, you'll get what you deserve!"

Rockfist strode back to the flying-boat and hoisted himself into the cockpit. Curly climbed aboard after him.

"Sorry, Curly, but I'm afraid you'll have to stay here with Archie, just to make sure that they don't kill Dizzy," Rockfist ordered.

"But you can't manage the fleet of savages alone! You'll need our help. You've only got one gun!" protested Archie.

"We aren't going to use any guns if we can help it. I'm not going to begin my job here by slaughtering a tribe," Rockfist insisted.

Just then a look-out man perched high up in a palm tree gave a warning whistle. He had spotted the invading war canoes, now only a mile away. Rockfist hustled Curly out of the plane and took off. Flying low, he circled the attacking fleet of over forty long, slim canoes crammed with warriors and oarsmen.

Some of the men stopped to gaze up at the banking plane, then paddled harder than ever. Rockfist shoved the nose of the plane down and hurtled towards the canoes.

Brrrrrrrmmmmmmmm!

As it skimmed the waves the flying-boat hurled up a great shower of hissing water. The natives screamed in terror. They had never seen such a machine before. To them it looked like some horrible, nightmarish monster rushing towards them and thrashing the sea into a mad frenzy.

Rockfist's plane thundered towards them, sweeping a wall of water ahead of it. He swept through the middle of the packed fleet like a knife through butter. The canoes spun round like corks and were thrown helplessly in all directions. Torrents of water pounded down, swamping them.

When Rockfist turned and prepared to make a second run a dozen of the canoes had already been completely swamped and were floating upside down, the natives splashing madly in the water.

Back again thundered the flying-boat, churning the sea into

a frothing tidal wave.

Woooosh!

Canoes stood on end and flung their human cargoes into the water. Zooming, diving, zigzagging, and circling, the flying-boat lashed the sea into a frothy whirlpool. The air was thick with hissing foam, while the thunder of the roaring plane combined with the crashing sound of tons of water formed a deafening uproar.

"Well, that's about the lot, I reckon."

Rockfist saw that his petrol was almost used up. He sent the flying-boat up a bit higher and watched while the terrified natives righted their upturned canoes and scrambled back on board. He gave a smile of satisfaction when they swung their craft round, and, digging their paddles in deeply, headed back the way they had come as fast as they could go, in full retreat.

Rockfist returned to the lagoon to find all the natives dancing up and down, hooting in wild delight over the victory.

"Mighty white wizard, him beat bad men from over sea!"

As Rockfist came ashore the natives crowded round him. Charlie made a hurried speech. Then Rockfist found himself being led to a chunk of coral rock which was formed like a huge seat.

He sat down, and while he was still trying to find out exactly what it was all about, a rusty iron saucepan, circled by a wreath of palm leaves, was placed upside-down on his head with the handle sticking out at the side! The natives gave a lusty cheer, then fell flat on their faces at Rockfist's feet. Suddenly the truth dawned on Rockfist.

The natives, who were seeking a new chief, had decided that he was just the man for the job! Rockfist had just been crowned king of the cannibals!

That night there was dancing and singing and a great feast to celebrate the victory. Instead of being killed, Dizzy sat in a place of honour by the camp-fire–though he wasn't able to eat much. He was too full up already!

HUNTERS WITHOUT GUNS

Tim Hunter and his parents were filming big game in Africa, but Tim fell into an animal trap and was kidnapped. Then he discovered that wild animals were not the most dangerous creatures in the African jungle.

_____

"Right, Dad, keep coming straight, just as you are," signalled young Tim Hunter.

Tim was walking backwards down a ramp from the deck of an African river ferry steamer, on to a wooden landing stage. His father, Steve Hunter, was driving the big motor caravan in which the family lived and worked when they were on their trips, making films of wild animal life.

The arrival of the ferry had brought the sleepy landing stage to life. All around was bustle and deafening confusion, so that when his father suddenly yelled a warning Tim didn't actually hear him, but he saw his alarmed expression through the truck cab's windscreen, and realised that he was yelling.

"Look out, Tim!"

Tim did a quick turn, and discovered that he was walking backwards into the path of a fork-lift loader driven by an African porter. Because of all the noise he hadn't heard it bouncing over the wooden planking of the wharf. The fork-lift swerved. Wheels screeched. The top-heavy load shifted.

Steve was out of the cab and diving forward to grab Tim and snatch him out of the way as a number of wire-bound wooden crates crashed down. One of them burst open. It contained the head and skin of an okapi, a rare animal in which Steve was particularly interested. He was staring at it almost in disbelief, when a luxurious safari wagon piled with expensive equipment drove on to the wharf.

The man who climbed out had spent a small fortune on his immaculate, well-tailored rig-out. His breeches, jungle-jacket, bush hat and high leather boots were almost certainly the most costly that money could buy.

"Sorry about this," apologised Steve. "It wasn't really Tim's fault. But how did you come by the okapi?"

"Bagged it myself. And the trophies in the other cases—water buffalo, giraffe, cheetah," said the other proudly.

Steve raised his eyebrows.

"I hope you had a hunting licence for this lot. Particularly the okapi," he remarked with a hint of anger in his voice.

"Are you a government inspector?" demanded the other. "If so you'd better satisfy yourself by examining the hide. The animal had to be shot. It had been mauled by a leopard."

"No, I'm not an official and it's really none of my business, except that I'm after okapi too. But I'm interested in shooting them with a camera, not with a gun," Steve retorted.

He signalled to Tim to jump into the driving cab. It always put him in a bad temper when he encountered wealthy people who spend extravagantly to equip themselves with every luxury just for the fun of going into the bush to kill wild animals.

He showed his temper by jarring the gears unnecessarily as he drove off the wharf.

"Calm down, Steve," warned Tim's mother, "or you'll have us all in a ditch."

A red earth road twisted ahead of them for mile after mile. They left a billowing trail of dust behind as they wound through hillsides covered with forests of tree-ferns, which gave way to a great sea of tall, rippling golden grass and scrub as the road brought them at last to an isolated town in a high valley.

Here, with the radiator boiling, they halted in a tree-shaded square where hens ran wild. Steve gathered up a batch of official papers to present to the local game warden. Tim got out to stretch his legs.

A battered jeep swung into the square. The driver pulled up and eyed the motor caravan thoughtfully. He got out and walked towards Tim, who didn't care for the look of him. He was fat and swarthy, and his clothes were none too clean.

"Hello, son," he said. "Who's in charge of this outfit? If you're planning going any farther you'll need a guide, so perhaps you'd put in a word for me. My name's Lopez—"

"Thanks all the same but my Dad is the only guide we need," grinned Tim.

"Your Dad? If I could just talk to him—" At that moment Tim's mother appeared.

"Tim's right," she said. "We're driving on from here out to the old tin mine. The company has given us permission to use it as a headquarters. We'll camp in what used to be the manager's bungalow."

A curious light came into the eyes of Lopez. It might almost have been a look of fear, except that it was difficult to imagine what he could be afraid of.

"The old mine? Oh no. That's no place for your husband to take you and the boy!"

"Why not?" asked Mrs. Hunter.

"It's isolated. It could be dangerous, all those old abandoned shafts and diggings, and it's unhealthy," insisted Lopez. "Now I've got a nice kraal across the hills about thirty miles from here. Comfortable, well equipped . . ."

"Thanks, but we're used to looking after ourselves, Mr. Lopez."

"All right ma'am, but if you run into trouble don't say I didn't warn you," muttered Lopez as he turned away.

Meanwhile Steve was presenting his papers to the game warden.

"Glad to have you up here, Hunter. I hope you have a successful trip," said the warden. "If you want to know about okapi in this area you couldn't do better than talk to the local tribal chief."

"I'll do that. I intended calling on him before we moved out of town, to introduce my wife and Tim, and pay our respects," nodded Steve.

The warden handed Steve back his papers.

"By the way, you're not carrying any fire-arms?"

"Only this," said Steve, producing what looked like an elaborate machine-pistol. "It fires tranquilliser darts. I keep it just in case of emergencies. But there's no ban on firearms, is there? I gather you've been permitting a limited amount of killing lately."

"What makes you say that? If I get to know of some animal that is injured or diseased I shoot it, or one of my assistants does. But we don't let trigger-happy tourists use fire-arms."

"There was some dude down at the ferry, shipping home a whole van-load of trophies. Said he'd bagged 'em himself."

"I know the feller. He was pulling your leg. Couldn't hit a barn door at ten paces with a blunderbuss full of rusty nails. He stayed with Lopez a night on his way through, but I'm sure he never shot anything."

"Lopez?"

"That unpleasant type who was talking to your wife and boy just now. Probably trying to sell himself as a guide. Don't have anything to do with him. Came here about six months ago. I don't trust him. I've never been able to catch him at anything illegal but I wish I could. I'd welcome a chance to run him out of my district."

Steve was about to rejoin his family. The warden walked with him to the door of the office.

"Oh, by the way, Hunter, you might keep your eyes open for a balloon. Call me up on your radio if you sight it."

"A balloon? Are you joking?"

"Not at all! We've been asked to keep track of it. It's carrying four Belgian television journalists. Some kind of publicity stunt, trying to cross the continent in a balloon."

"It takes all kinds," chuckled Steve. "I'll just collect my family so that we can call on the chief, and then we'll be on our way up to the mine."

The chief lived in a cool white building, the most imposing place in the town square, in former days the residence of a colonial governor.

He was an impressively tall man, who wore a round leopard skin hat and a voluminous ankle-length robe that looked like a night-shirt that had been made out of a red and white striped bell tent. But what impressed Tim most was the yard-long fly whisk which he carried and flourished with great dignity. He proved to be a charming and hospitable man, eager to help when he heard the reason for the Hunters' expedition.

"You have set yourself a difficult task, Mr. Hunter. Okapi are very timid creatures. They like to stay under cover. But I can give you one useful tip. The okapi likes to feed on the young blossom shoots of flowering shrubs such as acacia. If you come across a wild plantation with the young growth eaten off at a height of about five feet, there are probably okapi somewhere around."

"That's a useful thing to know," nodded Steve. "Are there any such places anywhere near the old tin mine?"

"The tin mine? You're not going there?"

"Why not?"

"None of my people will go near there! Just before the place was closed there was a bad accident. A shaft collapsed. Men were buried. They say it is haunted!"

"Ghosts, eh? It would be a news scoop if we could get some film of them."

"I wasn't joking, Mr. Hunter."

"I'm sure you weren't," apologised Steve. "But don't worry. We're used to taking care of ourselves."

As they walked back to the motor caravan Mrs. Hunter was thoughtful.

"Steve, that man Lopez tried to warn us about the mine, too. Do you think it's wise—?"

"If you're scared we'll change our plans," offered Steve.

"Of course I'm not scared. But I'm not sure it's the sort of place where we ought to take Tim."

"Hey, I wouldn't miss this for anything," protested Tim. "If there is anything prowling round at night I'll bet it's nothing more spooky than jackals. Let's go. I'm anxious to see the place."

The road out to the mine wound through dense forest, teeming with wild life of every kind. Tim sat in the driving cab beside his father, a pair of field glasses in his lap, ready for quick use whenever he spotted any interesting movement in the trees.

At one point they had to cross a shallow but fast-moving river. A brightly-coloured hornbill suddenly flew out of the trees and went honking across in front of them. Tim snatched up the glasses to follow its flight. Suddenly he uttered an excited exclamation.

"Dad, pull up a minute, and look over there."

Steve took the glasses. What Tim had spotted was a clearing, surrounded by a thick belt of gaudy shrubs, the young shoots of which had been heavily cropped.

"You could be on to something, Tim," nodded his father. "If that's a feeding ground for okapi it might be just the place to set up a hide for our cameras. Let's go and take a look."

Mrs. Hunter remained with the van while Tim and Steve went forward slowly and cautiously. Tim moved with a silent skill that was as experienced as his father's.

"Dad," he whispered softly. "I think I see—"

"Ssssh!"

Crash!

There was a sudden ear-splitting din overhead. Small branches showered down on them. Father and son whirled round, startled and bewildered. A rope went swinging past, a few inches from Tim's head. A gaily coloured balloon suddenly came into view just above the trees. Trailing ropes threshed through the branches.

"The balloon! The one the warden spoke of!" exclaimed Steve. "That does it. Clumsy great idiots. If there were any okapi here they'll be away into the next valley by now." The balloon made a bumpy landing in the clearing. Four men scrambled out and began to make the ropes secure. They looked utterly amazed to see Tim and Steve – and even more astounded when the van came bouncing along, driven by Mrs. Hunter, who had headed for the spot in alarm the moment she heard all the noise.

The leader of the party, a young man called Verrier, who was the only one of the four who spoke English, explained their predicament.

A few miles farther down river, where it became a fierce cataract and ran between steep rock walls, treacherous air currents had caused the balloon to drop sharply and the basket had bumped and banged for about a hundred yards along the cliff face.

"The bottom has started to fall out of our basket," Verrier explained ruefully. "A lot of our supplies dropped into the river and were washed away. We were in danger of falling out too. We shall have to make ourselves secure here while we do our best to make repairs to the basket."

"We've got plenty of gear and food," Steve said. "You'd better join with us and make the mine your headquarters. It isn't far."

The stranded balloonists gratefully accepted Steve's invitation, and everyone piled into the van. When they reached the abandoned mine they found the whole place wild and overgrown, but the manager's bungalow, for which Steve had been given the keys by the owners, had been left in good order, neat and clean, with a cooking stove in working order, and some bunks and furniture. By the time everyone had lent a hand unloading the gear Tim's mother had the place looking invitingly homely and soon had their first appetising meal ready.

Tim had slipped off to do a bit of exploring. Hidden in the tall grass he found the remains of an old railway, and some rusted tubs. There were bits of abandoned machinery scattered about. There were entrances to mysterious looking shafts and tunnels, which had been carefully boarded up.

"This is a wonderful place," he reported when he came back. "I'm going to have fun exploring."

"You'll do nothing of the kind," his father warned. "We've got free use of the bungalow but nobody is to go poking round the old workings. It could be dangerous. You could get trapped by a cave-in, or fall into some shaft where we'd never find you. No exploring. Promise?"

"Promise," agreed Tim reluctantly.

That night, when he rolled into his sleeping bag, Tim found it hard to sleep. Normally he was never disturbed by the strange croakings, the shrieks, the eerie chatterings and bubbling cries of nocturnal creatures that kept up a chorus all through the hours of darkness in the bush.

It was gone midnight, and everyone else was sound asleep, when Tim sat up sharply, listening intently, trying to sort out the sounds. There was one he couldn't identify at all. An eerie, intermittent groaning. No creatures he had ever come across made such a sound. He was still listening to the sound when he fell asleep.

Next morning Steve joined Tim on an exploration of the area surrounding the mine. Steve had covered about a hundred yards when he realised Tim wasn't still walking behind him.

Tim was about a hundred yards away, standing stock still at the foot of a tree, staring into a dense clump of giant fern.

"Tim!"

Tim made no move except to raise his hand as a sign of caution. He had spotted something interesting. There was a sudden crash, a wild bellow, and a great horned head smashed into view. The creature was a buffalo, and it came charging out as if it was maddened beyond endurance.

It made straight for Tim. Then it appeared to stumble, as if its forelegs were entangled. It crashed down, bellowing, giving Tim time to scramble into the tree.

The buffalo picked itself up, blundering and roaring, and turned on Steve, who just had time to snatch his dart pistol from the cab seat. He fired. The great beast came blundering at him with its murderous horns, stumbled, got up, then went down again.

Steve stood for some moments without moving, making sure that the dart had done its work. Tim slid out of the tree, and as they went forward cautiously Steve's eyes hardened in anger. There was a wire noose tight round the buffalo's neck. The creature must have been half strangled and in great pain. Yards of loose wire trailed from the noose, making an entanglement which had snared and slashed the animal's legs.

It was the buffalo's groaning that Tim had heard the previous night.

"You know what this means," Steve said grimly. "Someone is setting snares to trap the animals illegally. This one managed to tear itself free."

Carefully he unwound the tangle of wire from the unconscious beast.

"I've seen wire twisted like this somewhere before, and recently," he said thoughtfully.

"That's right. Don't you remember?" cried Tim excitedly. "The ferry. That dude with his trophies. His crates were fastened with exactly this kind of baling wire."

"It's beginning to make sense, Tim," Steve nodded. "The man said he'd shot those trophies, but the warden said it was impossible. Somebody trapped them for him–illegally."

"They said he stayed with that man Lopez, Dad."

"Of course. Lopez! He also warned us against coming here! He's the one who wants us out of the way."

"Are you going to radio the warden?"

"Not yet. A length of baling wire isn't much in the way of evidence. We need more proof, Tim, and I know just how to get it."

It was several hours before the buffalo recovered from the effect of the tranquillising dart.

By that time Steve had driven the van some distance up a steep incline, and was watching patiently through glasses. The buffalo picked itself up unsteadily, and then made its way slowly off through the bush and scrub.

"There's a waterhole tucked away, nicely secluded, down there," Steve said. "I think it might be an ideal place to get some good film."

"Okapi?" asked Tim.

"Are you kidding?" grinned Steve. "We're after bigger game."

They went back to the mine to collect some gear. Tim spent the rest of the day helping his father to build a cleverly camouflaged hide near the waterhole. Then they went back for an evening meal that Mrs. Hunter had prepared for them. The four balloonists had also returned, famished and eager to do justice to Mrs. Hunter's cooking, but satisfied with the progress of their repairs.

When the meal was over Steve nodded to Tim.

"You can help your mother with the washing up–then off to bed."

"But Dad–you're going to the waterhole. You'll need help—"

"Not this time, Tim. This is something I've got to do on my own," Steve insisted firmly.

Tim turned away, disappointed and anxious.

"Can I read for a while?" he asked.

"Of course, but try not to fall asleep with the light on."

Tim went to his room and lit a lamp. He closed the door. The light from the lamp showed beneath it. But he had no intention of staying in his room. He was worried. He could imagine all kinds of things going wrong. His father might need someone to help him out of a tight spot. He raised his window silently and crept out. He ran silently to the van, heaved himself up on to the roof and threw himself flat.

A little later Steve came out, and drove off, unaware that he had a passenger on the roof. He drove to within a mile of the waterhole, and then parked the van in thick scrub, out of sight. He sat listening for a long time before he decided that no one had heard him arrive. Then he moved off silently.

Tim slid down from the roof, and followed, trailing his father as he glided like a shadow through the forest until he reached the thicket where the hide was concealed. Steve vanished inside. His camera was already set up and loaded.

The rest must be a matter of patience. He might have a useless vigil. Even if he was right about Lopez being a big game poacher the man might not be operating tonight, or he might not be using the waterhole.

Tim was creeping along with all the caution of a jungle animal. Suddenly the ground gave way beneath his feet. He crashed into a shallow animal trap. He heard an excited voice say:

"We've got something!"

A light flashed, faces peered down at him.

"It's the Hunter brat!"

A man dropped down on top of him. A hand was clapped over his mouth before he could yell. A noose was slipped over his arms.

Steve heard the commotion and saw the flashing lights, but was too far away to see what had happened. He supposed that the poachers had trapped some kind of animal. Then he heard a banging and clanging, accompanied by more blazing lights, and shouting. Beaters were driving a pair of kudu towards the snares.

Excitedly, Steve set his camera running. The waterhole became a scene of wild confusion. Lopez and his men were closing in on their prey. Suddenly there was a fresh sound. The roar of a prowling leopard. Guns roared. The kudu, more frightened of the leopard than of their human persecutors, turned, and charged through the line of beaters.

Steve kept his camera going until he realised that the alarmed animals were charging blindly, straight at the hide. He got out in the nick of time, salvaging his camera, but leaving the rest of his equipment behind as the hide was trampled to pieces. He raced away, back to the van, started up the engine, reversed out, and drove like mad back to the mine. Back by the waterhole Lopez was examining the scene under portable floodlights. The trampled ruins told their own story.

"Hunter's been taking pictures of us," he roared.

Steve drove back to the mine.

He grinned triumphantly at his wife and the four balloonists.

"I lost some gear, but it was worth it," he annouced. "We were right about Lopez. He and his gang are bootlegging big game trophies, selling at high prices to tourists who buy them to take home and hang up in their dens so that they can boast to friends that they bagged them themselves. Well, this is the end of the line for Lopez. In the morning the warden will get this film. Lopez will either have to clear out of the country at top speed, or risk being put behind bars."

He suddenly noticed the light under Tim's door.

"I'll bet he's fallen asleep over his book," he chuckled.

He opened the door, saw the empty sleeping bag, and the open window.

"Tim's not here!"

There was a sudden sound of breaking glass. The living room window shattered. An arrow whizzed across the room and buried itself in the wall.

Steve yanked it out. A sheet of paper had been speared on the arrow shaft. A message was scrawled on it.

"Hunter, you've got something I want, and I've got something you want—your son Tim. Send your wife, alone, to the ford at first light, and we'll arrange a deal. Don't do anything reckless, or you may never see your son again."

"He wouldn't dare to harm Tim!" gasped Mrs. Hunter.

"I'm not so sure," Steve gritted. "The thing is, do we let him get away with it?"

"Tim would never forgive us."

"We've got until dawn to think of something. The big question is, where is Tim?"

"Lopez said something about a kraal—"

"I think I know the place," Verrier said quickly. "Can we help? Five of us ought to be able to handle that mob. We could get there in under an hour in your van."

"No good. They'd hear us, in the dead of night, when we were still miles away! If we're to stand any chance we've got to move silently—"

Steve broke off. "What about the balloon? Is it fit to use? Could we get there—?"

"If the wind is right, and I think it is," Verrier broke off and looked at Steve's wife. "But it is really up to Mrs. Hunter. Is she willing to let us try it?"

"Are you sure you could get Tim away from them, without him coming to any harm?" she asked.

"I don't think Lopez has the pluck to risk any serious harm coming to Tim. He'd pay for it with his life, and he knows it."

Mrs. Hunter was silent for a long time. Then she brushed her hair back from her face with a worried gesture.

"All right, Steve. We'll do it your way."

"You follow us with the van. Use your own discretion, but don't let them see or hear you too soon," said Steve. "Let's get moving."

It took almost an hour, on foot, to reach the balloon, and another thirty minutes to get it into the air.

They drifted silently and, to Steve, with agonising slowness over the moonlit jungle.

"I think we're going to come out dead right," whispered Verrier at last. "See, over there, the big thatch-roofed building on stilts? That's the kraal."

Verrier stood at the edge of the basket, giving low-voiced instructions. His crew dropped trailing ropes. One, with a grapnel on the end, spun over the treetops.

For a moment it looked as if it was going to miss the building. Then the swinging fluke dragged into the thatch, and tore a great chunk off, letting a shaft of lamplight through from below. It caught again, this time in an exposed rafter, and the balloon stayed anchored. Steve went swarming down the rope, and plunged through the hole in the roof. As he did so he heard Tim's voice.

"Look out, Dad."

Lopez was charging up a ladder with a heavy hunting rifle. Steve had armed himself with the dart pistol. He hit the floor as the gun went off with a deafening roar.

Tim huddled in a corner with his wrists and ankles tied, rolled himself over and hit a table holding a pressure lamp. The table overturned and the lamp exploded. Flames shot up and the battered thatch overhead started to burn.

Lopez was crouching for another shot. Steve whirled round and fired the pistol. The heavy dart drilled through Lopez's shirt and buried itself in his shoulder. It contained enough dope to stop an elephant. It seemed to Lopez that his rifle suddenly weighed a ton. He pulled the trigger. The bullet went through the floor.

Lopez took a couple of wobbly steps and tumbled headlong down the ladder like a runway truck over a cliff. Steve grabbed up Tim and scrambled down the ladder while the burning building caved in overhead. Men were racing about in the light of the flames. Steve heard yells, the sound of blows, and the crash of panic-stricken men in flight.

Verrier and two of his friends had slid down the ropes, leaving the other man in the basket. Lopez's gang of beaters were in full flight.

"Let them go," said Steve. "We've got the man we want."

Headlights added their glare to the brightness of the flames as Mrs. Hunter drove the van, thrusting forward along a narrow, overgrown trail.

"Tim, are you all right?" she cried.

"Right as rain," grinned Tim. "But that's more than you can say for Lopez. You should have seen the way Dad nailed him."

Steve heaved the inert form of the poacher over his shoulder and lugged him towards the van.

"A present for the warden in the morning," he grinned, "I think it would be only fair if we delivered him tied up with his own baling wire."

Then he turned to Verrier.

"Thanks for all your help. I suppose you'll be moving on tomorrow. It's going to be quiet. After this, the job we came to do, stalking okapi, is going to be rather tame."

"I'd like to be able to believe that," said Mrs. Hunter, looking at her husband and son, "but life is never tame with you two around."

BEAU FORTUNE AND THE WITCH'S
SECRET

Beau Fortune, the friend of George III, was really the Masked Rider in disguise. After meeting an old witch, he outwitted all his pursuers by a series of tricks and escaped the gallows yet again.

Beau Fortune, the celebrated dandy and man of fashion in the days of George III, languidly raised his quizzing glass to his eye as he stepped out of his coach.

Fortune was a long way from his usual haunts. The country place to which the coach had brought him was far removed from his favourite clubs and the fashionable drawing-rooms in London's West End.

The road, full of deep pot-holes and ruts, which had caused the horses to stumble at every step and the coach to sway and creak as if it would break an axle at any moment, led through an untidy, overgrown wilderness of heath and woodland.

An unhealthy, brooding silence overhung the lonely, sinister spot. There was no bird song. There was no sign of life anywhere. It was as if some dreadful spell had been placed upon the spot to blight it. Fortune's coachman and valet, Robinson, looked at his master uneasily, finding himself thinking of witches and black magic. He couldn't think what had possessed Fortune to come to such an evil place. It would scarcely have surprised him to see an old hag riding a broomstick flitting among the tree-tops.

Fortune uttered a sudden exclamation of satisfaction.

"Ah!" he said, and pointed with the gold-knobbed cane he carried.

A thin spiral of smoke was rising above the trees, evidence that somewhere in this deserted wilderness there was a human being, though why anyone in his right mind should choose to live in such an uncanny spot was a complete mystery.

"Come, Robinson," drawled Fortune, stepping carefully, so as to avoid as much as possible soiling his highly-polished riding boots.

"M-must we, sir??" gulped Robinson, with a regretful glance back at the safety of the coach.

"We have urgent work to do," Fortune assured him.

Robinson shook his head helplessly. He, alone in the whole world, knew that his master was not just the foppish, idle fashion-plate that his society friends believed him to be. He shared a startling secret with his master. He knew that Fortune had another side to his character, and that he was none other than the dashing, baffling figure known as the mysterious Masked Rider, whose reckless and bewildering exploits were the talk of all London at the time.

But what strange motive could have brought Fortune here was beyond Robinson's imagining, accustomed though he was to his master's fantastic behaviour.

Beating a way through a tangled undergrowth of briars with his gold–knobbed cane, Fortune came in sight of a thatched cottage, the chimney of which was sending up the smoke.

It was a crazy, haunted-looking place, with mildewed fungus sprouting from the thatch of its twisted, sagging roof, and windows thick with dirt. It was set in a neglected and overgrown garden - a stagnant waste of weeds which matched the decayed air of the cottage.

Fortune picked his way delicately along the filthy path and rapped on the door with his stick. For a long time there was no response. Robinson was beginning to hope that there was no one within, and that they would be able to get away from this horrible place.

Then Fortune knocked again, and from the other side of the door came an impatient muttering and snarling, followed by the creak of rusty bolts being slowly drawn.

Robinson flinched when the door began to open on squeaking hinges, fearful of what horrid secrets this ghost-haunted hovel might conceal.

Two gleaming, suspicious eyes peered out of the shadows at the elegant visitor. Then a bent figure shuffled forward into the light. The man was unwashed, unshaven, dressed in patched and ragged old clothes.

"What is it you want?" he asked in a voice that rasped like sandpaper.

"My fool of a coachman lost the way," Fortune said loftily, and Robinson smothered a gasp, for he had been ordered to drive here and would never have found the place if Fortune had not directed him.

"We are hungry and thirsty," Fortune went on. "Can you oblige us with food and drink? We scarcely expected to be so lucky as to find a house in such a spot, but, by great good fortune, we spied the smoke from your chimney."

The man eyed him watchfully.

"Folks don't come visiting me often, your honour," he sneered. "They're frightened of meeting my brother."

Robinson shuddered. If the man's brother was more terrifying and repulsive than he was himself, an unpleasant shock was in store.

"I shall be delighted to make your brother's acquaintance," Fortune assured him casually.

The man suddenly bared his teeth in a savage grin.

"I wouldn't be too sure. Wait until you've seen him. My brother Ebenezer is different from other people," he said.

He chuckled, with a suggestion of horrible relish, as if enjoying some private and grisly joke.

"Come in, if you've a mind to," he invited. "We're just going to have supper, my brother and me. You're welcome to a share of what there is."

"Charmed," drawled Fortune. "My name is Fortune. May I be permitted to know to whom I am indebted for this kind hospitality?"

"Folks call me Mad Jack. They think I'm crazy. *He-he-he!*" Fortune took the information without twitching an eyebrow, but Robinson gulped as he followed his elegant master over the threshold.

The cottage had a strong, unpleasant odour of mustiness and decay. Mad Jack pulled three chairs up to the table, and laid out four plates and spoons.

"Sit down," he invited. "Supper will be ready in a moment."

"Only three chairs?" commented Fortune. "What about your

brother Ebenezer. Won't he need one?"

"He eats standing up," leered Mad Jack. "He hasn't been able to sit down since he had his - misfortune."

Mad Jack went out into the adjoining kitchen. No sooner had he gone than Fortune began to prowl round the room, prying into corners, peering into ornaments, opening cupboards and drawers with mysterious stealth. Fortune silently opened the drawer of a small chest, and his eyes lit up at the sight of several golden guineas. With a nonchalant air, he picked up one of the coins and put it in his pocket.

Robinson looked outraged.

"Mr Fortune!" he hissed. "Must I remind you that you are a guest? How can you lower yourself to rob this poor . . ."

Fortune put his finger to his lips. Mad Jack was coming back with an iron pot filled with boiled carrots. He filled the plates with a large ladle, and then went back into the kitchen.

"Eb!" he shouted. "Supper!"

Robinson had already been badly shaken, but it was nothing to what happened next. His hair stood on end. There was a clattering noise in the kitchen, and a small donkey walked into the room.

"This is my brother Eb," exclaimed Mad Jack. "Eb, this is Mr Fortune."

The donkey walked to the empty place at the table, and stood there calmly while Mad Jack tied a cloth round its neck.

"I have to do this for him. He gets food all over himself," explained Mad Jack in a matter-of-fact way. "He still can't get used to being the way he is, though he's been like this for six months now. Wicked, ain't it?"

He drew up his own chair and tackled his plate of carrots as if there was nothing unusual in sitting down to supper with a donkey.

Robinson grew red in the face and glared at Mad Jack.

"Sir, this is an outrage! Mr Fortune is a gentleman. He is one of the most respected people in society. He is a friend of the Prince of Wales. He cannot be expected to eat in the company of this - this creature!"

Then came the most shattering moment of all.

The donkey looked up and spoke.

"Carrots again!" it snarled. "I'm sick of carrots!"

Robinson went rigid. His eyes bulged. He came to his feet.

The inn-keeper came bustling forward, breathless and overcome by the honour that was being done his house.

"You are Mr Fortune?" he asked eagerly. "The famous Mr Fortune? The celebrated Mr Fortune?"

"There is only one Mr Fortune," the Beau told him loftily. "I wish to be provided with rooms for myself and my man, and to have a hot bath prepared at once."

The inn-keeper was deeply impressed.

In those days, ordinary people never dreamed of washing themselves all over. Hot baths were a new-fangled fad enjoyed only by the very rich and fastidious.

"It shall be attended to immediately, Mr Fortune."

"By the way," drawled Fortune, as if struck by a sudden after-thought, "have you ever heard of a lady who is called the Widow Skelton?"

The inn-keeper winced and turned pale.

"A fine gentleman like you has no call to be interested in such things," he said in a shaking voice. "Widow Skelton is," he looked round, lowering his voice as if afraid of being overheard, and finished in a hoarse whisper - "a witch!"

"So I have been told," murmured Fortune. "I have lately had an interesting encounter with your neighbour, Mad Jack, and – ah – his brother Eb. The one with four legs."

Fortune's flippant manner made the inn-keeper tremble, and the rustic customers of the inn eyed the dandy furtively, those nearest to him edging away. These simple country folk believed firmly in demons, spells and black magic. They stared watchfully at Fortune, as if expecting to see him struck at any moment by a blue flame that would change him into a two-headed newt or a block of stone as a punishment for his flippancy.

"You really believe that this donkey is Mad Jack's brother?" asked Fortune.

"The donkey will tell you so himself. Isn't that evidence enough?" asked the inn-keeper.

"A most profound remark," agreed Fortune. "But I see I have unwittingly struck a chill upon the company. My apologies, gentlemen. Warm them, landlord. Drinks for everyone. Robinson, bring the bags from the coach."

Fortune was conducted to his room, Robinson following with the baggage. A maid clattered in, trundling a large, round, iron bath, bowling it like a hoop. Two other servants followed, carrying yokes on their shoulders from which hung large wooden buckets filled with steaming hot water.

Fortune hooked a finger into his vest pocket and drew out the guinea he had taken from Mad Jack.

"I forgot to pay for the drinks," he said. "Carry this to the inn-keeper."

The valet went downstairs again with the coin.

"With Mr Fortune's compliments," he said.

The landlord took the coin and dropped in into his till. Instead of landing with a ringing sound, it made a flat noise. Silas Crow darted from his post at the fireplace and snatched up the coin. He turned swiftly on Robinson.

"Where did you get this?" he demanded. Robinson was taken by surprise.

"I don't understand!" he gasped.

The Thief-Taker shook him roughly.

"Speak!" he cried. "What do you know of the Masked Rider?"

Robinson felt his knees turning to jelly.

Then, from across the room, a cold voice spoke:

"Is someone looking for me?"

Silas Crow whirled.

In the doorway stood a tall, impressive, masked man, wearing a high-crowned beaver hat, a triple-caped riding coat, and mud-spattered riding boots.

In each hand he held a pistol.

"The mysterious Masked Rider!" cried the Thief-Taker. "How did you get in here? How did you pass my men unseen? This time you shan't escape! You are well and truly trapped!"

Silas Crow, the Thief-Taker, uttered the words triumphantly as he faced the masked figure across the inn parlour. Robinson, valet to the celebrated dandy Beau Fortune, had his heart in his mouth as he stood, a silent spectator of the scene. For he alone knew that Beau Fortune, man of fashion and bosom friend of the Prince Regent, son of King

eorge III, was none other than the elusive and daring Masked Rider.
Again Robinson found himself puzzling over the same bewildering
questions.

What had induced Fortune to stick his head into a noose? Why had
he travelled so far from London just to visit a fantastic character called
Mad Jack, who claimed that his brother had been changed into
a donkey by an old witch called Widow Skelton? Fortune, alias the
Masked Rider, advanced recklessly, his pistols pointing threateningly
at the Thief-Taker.

"You had better surrender," advised Silas Crow in a quavering
voice. "My men are surrounding this place. You cannot escape."

"Do not be so sure, my friend," advised the masked man. "Did
anyone see me come in? Then why should they see me leave?"

Silas bared his teeth.

"I don't know by what trick you got in," he snarled. "But you
certainly won't get out again."

Fortune chuckled softly. His boots and riding coat were spattered
with mud, giving him the appearance of a man who had just ridden fast
and far, but the simple explanation, which Silas Crow completely
overlooked, was that he had merely assumed his disguise and walked
down from his room upstairs.

He slipped one of his pistols into his pocket, but kept the other
pointed at Crow's head. Then, reaching towards the bar, he snatched
up the golden coin which was lying there, and dropped it into his
pocket. For a moment he stood as if pondering whether or not to blow
out the Thief-Taker's brains.

Then he gave a spring and a whirl. His greatcoat billowed out. He
darted out of the door through which he had come, and slammed it
behind him.

Crash! The sound of the slamming door spurred Silas Crow to
action.

"Men! Stop him! Don't let him get away!" he screamed.

He darted out into the courtyard, where Bow Street Runners in
scarlet waistcoats were coming from all directions.

"Where is he? Who has seen him? Which way did he go?" screamed
Silas Crow wildly.

There was confusion everywhere. But out of the confusion came

"Fortune, alias the Masked Rider advanced recklessly"

one certain fact. No one had seen the Masked Rider after he had slipped through the door. Somewhere along the short passage to the courtyard, he had just melted into thin air. It seemed impossible, yet, if he had escaped, he must have been able to make himself invisible.

Silas Crow's eyes narrowed cunningly.

"If no one saw him go, he must still be in the house," he snarled. "Search every room in the building."

The Runners went through the inn like an invading army. A mouse could not have hidden from them; but, when every room except one had been searched, there was still no sign of the Masked Rider.

"Whose room is this?" snarled Silas.

"Mr F-F-Fortune's, sir," stammered the inn-keeper, terrified that his important guest was going to be insulted.

"We will search it!" snapped the Thief-Taker.

"Wait!" cried Robinson desperately. "You cannot go in there. Mr Fortune is taking a bath!"

"That makes no difference," Silas Crow snapped, flinging open the door.

The room was full of steam. In the middle of the floor stood a large iron tub filled with hot, soapy water. Fortune was near the door, wrapped in a towel.

"How dare you, sir!" he cried indignantly. "What does this intrusion mean?"

"I'm sorry. We're looking for the Masked Rider. We have searched every other room in the house. He must be hidden somewhere in here," snarled the angry Thief-Taker.

"I give you my word that I am alone in here," Beau Fortune said stiffly.

"He may have slipped in while your back was turned," insisted Silas. "We must search."

Robinson's blood ran cold as the Runners began to peer and probe. Fortune had been very smart in getting undressed so quickly, but what had he done with the clothes he had worn in his disguise as the Masked Rider? He must have hidden them hastily somewhere. When the searchers came upon them, the game would be up. Fortune's reckless and daring double-life would be exposed at last.

Silas and his men searched every cupboard. They peered under the bed. They dragged back the bedclothes. To the valet's astonishment and relief, they found nothing. In some amazing way, Fortune had been too clever for them. Silas was covered in confusion.

"Well, sir?" Fortune demanded angrily. "You have intruded on my privacy. You have doubted my word. You have refused to treat me as a gentleman. And to what purpose? The Prince Regent shall hear of this, sir."

"Mr Fortune, please! A thousand apologies! I was only trying to do my duty," pleaded Silas, distracted and almost weeping in frustrated rage. "Sometimes I fear that devil the Masked Rider will drive me mad. He isn't human!"

"Sometimes your repeated failures to catch him make me doubt that he even exists," remarked Fortune dryly. "And there is another matter on which I am angry with you, Crow. You alarmed my servant by accusing him of being in some way associated with this Masked Rider. Explain yourself."

"It was in the matter of the guinea with which he paid the landlord the reckoning, the guinea which the Masked Rider took back just now," stammered Crow. "The coin was a false one. I have reason to believe that it came from the Masked Rider in the first place."

"Fellow, I gave him the coin myself," insisted Fortune. "Perhaps you would accuse me of being the Masked Rider? A pretty tale indeed for the ears of the Prince Regent."

"A thousand times no!" cried Silas, aghast at the thought. "But how did you come by the coin?"

"Crow, you are a stupid oaf," Fortune protested wearily. "I have so much money. How should I know how one particular guinea piece came into my pocket? And now, if your business here is finished, kindly take these minions of yours away and allow me to dry myself in peace. I am beginning to shiver."

"A million apologies, Mr Fortune," whined Silas as he backed out of the room, bowing.

Fortune suddenly turned and caught his valet's wrist.

"Robinson, you have a wart on your hand," he exclaimed.

"Yes, indeed, sir," the valet admitted, wondering what new quirk had came into his master's mind.

"Oh, landlord," said Fortune, "touching on this Widow Skelton who, as they tell me, changed Mad Jack's brother into a donkey. Think you that she can also charm away warts?"

"I haven't a doubt of it, your honour," gulped the inn-keeper.

Fortune beamed at his valet.

"I think you should call upon this Widow Skelton," he suggested. "It might prove a profitable visit. The landlord, doubtless, will be able to tell you where to find her."

The valet's jaw dropped. The inn-keeper had hastily followed Silas Crow in leaving the room.

"Something is bothering you, Robinson?" asked Fortune.

"The clothes, sir. What became of the clothes?" Robinson asked distractedly. "I was in terror that they would be found."

"Ah, yes, the clothes," murmured Fortune. "I almost forgot."

He went to the bath-tub and plunged his hands into the bubbling soap-suds. He drew out of the water first the hat, then the boots, then the sodden greatcoat.

"You had better order a big fire to be lit in here," Fortune said. "Otherwise, we may not get these things dry by the time that we need them again."

Robinson looked at his imperturbable master helplessly.

"Mr Fortune, why have you taken such risks? Why, when you knew that Crow and his men were here expecting the Masked Rider to appear, did you deliberately give them a chance to catch you?"

Fortune chuckled softly.

"My good Robinson, in a place such as this, news of unusual happenings travels fast. I think it will not be long before Mad Jack gets wind of the affair, and, when he does, I expect some interesting things to happen. By a fortunate chance, this window commands a view of the path which leads to Mad Jack's cottage. I propose to keep watch."

A servant was soon summoned to kindle a fire in the huge hearth, and, while Robinson hung up the sodden clothes to dry, Fortune settled himself at the window and surveyed the countryside through his quizzing-glass. A long time passed before his patience was rewarded.

"Robinson, tell me what you see out there," he exclaimed.

"A man riding a donkey, and in some haste," declared Robinson.

"It is Mad Jack and his - er - brother," murmured Fortune.

"Unless I am sadly mistaken, he is on his way to consult the Widow Skelton. Things are moving at last. Robinson, I have a task for you. Hire a nag from the ostler and ride at once to Widow Skelton's, to ask for a potion to charm away your warts."

Robinson gulped and his eyes bulged as he stared at his master.

"The widow Skelton - the witch?" he said in a quavering voice. "You mean, sir, that I must go alone? You are not coming with me?"

He was filled with horror at the idea of facing, alone, the frightful old witch who was supposed to have changed Mad Jack's brother into a donkey. Yet such was his loyalty to Fortune, he was prepared to do even that, if his master commanded it.

"I shall be joining you later," Fortune assured him. "It will be your task to detain the widow and Mad Jack until I arrive. I have reasons for thinking that they plan flight."

"Very good, sir," said Robinson.

Fortune drew a coin from his pocket.

"The widow will expect a fee. Pay her with this."

"This is the false coin, sir!"

"Precisely," nodded Fortune, "and, on your way out of this place, arrange for a fast horse to be waiting by the back door. I shall have need of it."

The way to the witch's home led over a wild, rocky waste. The old woman's hovel was a wooden shack built in front of a cave. Robinson could not repress a superstitious trembling as he dismounted and knocked on the door. A shrill voice bade him enter.

The place was dark and foul. A stuffed alligator hung from the rafters. Over the fireplace, a mummified cat and two owls stared out from glass cases. On shelves there were bottles containing pickled toads and snakes, dried herbs and mysterious-looking potions. An iron pot bubbled on the hearth, and by it squatted the witch herself, wearing a high, pointed hat, and dressed all in black. She turned a wrinkled face towards Robinson. She smiled, and her pointed nose almost touched her sharp chin.

"Come in, pretty gentleman," she said in a croaking voice. "What can old Widow Skelton do for you? Don't be shy. Tell me your troubles. You want me to put a spell on somebody? You want me to strike them cross-eyed, or bow-legged? Or perhaps you want them to

die, eh? He-he-he!"

"Nothing of the kind, madam," gulped Robinson. "It is merely a matter of these troublesome warts."

The witch took his hand in her own skinny claw, and the valet shuddered.

"I have charmed thousands of warts," the witch assured him. "I have a sure remedy, which I brew myself, from newt's oil, chicken gizzards, crushed beetles, and . . ."

She broke off. Someone was riding towards the hovel. It was Mad Jack.

As the newcomer dismounted from his donkey, he stared sharply and suspiciously at Robinson.

"What are you doing here?" he snarled.

"We have met before," Robinson bowed politely. "I trust I see you well - and your brother, too."

"I'm perfectly well," brayed the donkey.

It wasn't the first time that Robinson had heard the donkey speak, but he still couldn't get used to it. He shuddered and wished Fortune would hurry.

Meanwhile, at the inn, events had suddenly begun to move fast. Silas Crow heard a sudden yell, and the clatter of hoofs in the yard.

"There he goes!"

The Thief-Taker rushed to the window. He saw the Masked Rider riding madly for the open road. Fortune had got away to a flying start. Glancing back over his shoulder, he saw horsemen gathering far down the road. Then his horse swerved.

Two Bow Street Runners, on foot and armed with cudgels, had suddenly appeared ahead. Fortune tugged at the reins. The horse cleared the nearest hedge and pelted across country.

At the Widow Skelton's hovel, Robinson was in trouble as he offered the false coin in exchange for a box of black, evil-smelling ointment. Mad Jack's face contorted with sudden fear and fury. He suddenly drew a pistol.

"Tell me where you got this!"

From the doorway, a voice said:

"I think not. It is time for a reckoning between us, Mad Jack."

Fortune, masked and armed, stood in the doorway. For a moment

there was a tense silence. Then, behind Fortune, the donkey spoke.

"Drop your pistols, Masked Rider." Fortune remained unmoved.

"That trick won't work, my friend. You can throw your voice very well to make people believe the donkey is talking, but your skill is wasted on me. Whatever you may have made others believe, I know that your brother Eb was never bewitched. He was hanged - hanged at Tyburn for being in possession of false coins. It would have been none of my business, except he tried to put the blame on me. He told the law officers that I was the coiner."

From across the heath came angry shouts as Crow and his riders came into view. The witch suddenly tugged at the chain from which the brewing pot hung. Part of the rear wall of the hovel slid back to reveal the entrance to a cave.

Mad Jack and the widow scuttled for the secret opening, just as Silas Crow and his men came surging in at the door.

"Quick!" cried the Masked Rider, pointing with his pistols. "There's your coiners' den. After them!"

Silas and his men dashed into the cave. Fortune darted to the fireplace and tugged the chain. The secret wall closed again. By the time that Robinson had worked the secret opening again, and Crow's men stumbled out with their struggling captives, the Masked Rider had gone.

"You blundering fool!" snarled Crow. "Why didn't you hold him?"

"Oh dear, oh dear!" protested Robinson. "You can hardly blame me when you and all your men have failed to catch him."

It was the landlord of the inn himself, bubbling over with excitement, who brought Fortune the news when he carried in the breakfast tray.

"And what of this rascal the Masked Rider?" yawned Fortune.

"Escaped again. And to tell you the truth, your honour, I can't say I'm sorry. He is an engaging rogue."

BIFF BAILEY – FIGHTING FURY

by John Marshall

Biff Bailey, the British heavyweight boxer, expected the fight of his life when he met Dark Dynamite, but he did not reckon on seeing an eerie face at the window of his room. What was the mystery behind this?

Biff Bailey felt a tremendous thrill as he gazed down from the window of the air liner in which he was travelling. The plane had just crossed the Sahara and tropical equatorial Africa, and was about to land on the magnificent airfield at Kiman.

Biff was a British heavyweight boxer. He was on his way out to West Africa with his manager, Terry Watts, and his trainer, Sam Tubb, to prepare for a bout with the heavyweight champion of Kiman, Dark Dynamite. Kiman was a go-ahead country which had recently gained independence. It had a dazzling modern capital of white skyscraper buildings flanking wide streets teeming with traffic, where half a century ago there had been nothing but jungle.

With the rapid modernisation of Kiman there had grown up a tremendous interest in sport–football, cricket and, above all, boxing. The boxing fans of Kiman were thrilled and excited because in Dark Dynamite, for the first time, they had a local champion good enough to be included in the world rankings, good enough to attract opponents from overseas.

Biff's visit was causing a stir, because he was the first important heavyweight ever to come to Kiman for a match against a local fighter.

The plane touched down. The passengers waited while the gangway was wheeled into position. Biff glanced from the window and saw reporters, photographers and film cameras waiting below. He stood back modestly to allow some of the more important passengers to go first.

First down the steps was a famous movie star, escorted by his personal manager, his secretary and his valet. At the bottom of the steps he paused and looked around for a microphone.

"I am glad to be in Kiman," he declared dramatically. "It has been the dream of my life to visit your beautiful country. I am here for location shots for my new pic—"

He broke off as he suddenly realised that no one was listening to him.

A portly and well-groomed figure, a famous politician, good-humouredly nudged him on one side.

"Sorry, old man. I think I'm the chap they want to hear from," he said.

He took a firm grip on the microphone and cleared his throat impressively.

"I am sure that with goodwill on both sides, our governments will achieve a mutual understanding which will be of lasting benefit to both—"

Someone wrested the microphone from his grasp. By now the impatient reporters were almost storming the steps.

"Where's Biff Bailey?" one of them cried. "We want Biff Bailey!"

The movie star and the politician exchanged dumbfounded looks.

Terry Watts grabbed Biff, who was still hanging back.

"Come on, Biff, it's you they're waiting for," Terry insisted, pushing Biff towards the door.

A vast roar of welcome went up as Biff descended the steps. The crowd surged round, clamouring for autographs. Biff posed for his picture and answered the reporters' questions as best he could, but it took a police patrol to get him out of the milling throng and into a waiting taxi.

They drove to their hotel, a vast, many-storied building in the latest luxury style, where there were more interviews and press receptions. By the time it was all over Biff felt as exhausted as if he had just fought fifteen rounds, and went to bed early.

So great was the interest in Biff's arrival that next morning the papers were full of reports, interviews and pictures. The arrival at the same time of the movie star and the politician gained only small mention on the inside pages.

Terry ordered meals to be served in their own suite to gain a little peace and quiet for Biff, and to escape the attention of the fans they had to leave the hotel by a back door when they drove to the gym where Biff was to do his training.

As there was only one gym in the city sufficiently well equipped to satisfy the needs of a star boxer, Biff and his rival were sharing it, using it at different times each day. Biff discovered that almost everything he would need had been provided in advance, even to a punchbag of extra heavy weight which he favoured.

Biff used a very light ball for speed, and a particularly heavy bag to build up the strength of his wrists. A group of sparring partners had also been lined up for him, so that he could engage the men he wanted.

After he had made his choice, one of the men he had rejected sidled up to him rather furtively.

"Mister Bailey, it would pay you to engage me," he whispered. "I could help you a lot. I can give you lots of tips about Dark Dynamite. I used to work for him!"

Biff eyed the man suspiciously. This kind of thing had happened often enough before–shifty-looking men offering to give him secret information about an opponent in exchange for money or employment. Usually the information was worthless, but even if it did have some value Biff was not the type to try to gain an advantage over an opponent by having dealings with shady sparring partners.

"If you've worked with Dark Dynamite, why do you want to help me?" questioned Biff.

"That's my affair," said the other craftily. "Look, I'll give you a hint. Dark Dynamite wins his fights by frightening the wits out of his opponents."

Biff almost laughed out loud.

"I don't think he'll frighten me," he declared. "I've met some pretty tough opponents in my time."

"Dark Dynamite is different. I tell you he's clever. He can make a nervous wreck of a man."

He paused. Biff waited.

"Well, go on," he urged.

"How much will you pay me if I tell you what I know?" asked the other.

Biff's temper started to rise. But before he could put his contempt into words a frightened look came into the other man's eyes. He seemed to be staring at a spot behind Biff's back. Next moment he turned and bolted through the nearest door. Biff turned round to see the owner of the gym coming in. He walked swiftly up to Biff.

"That fellow you were talking to—what was he up to?" he asked.

"He offered to tell me how to beat Dark Dynamite—at a price," grinned Biff. "I was just going to tell him what I thought of him when he bolted."

"He's a crook. That's why Dark Dynamite had to fire him. He's been barred from this place, and I warned him that if I ever caught him on the premises again, I'd hand him over to the police."

"No wonder he ran when he saw you," smiled Biff. "Let's forget him. I want to thank you for the way you've got everything ready for me."

"Glad to have the opportunity. Perhaps you don't realise yet what a great thing you've done for boxing in Kiman by coming here to meet our champ," answered the gym proprietor. "And talking of the champ, he's outside. He says he'd like to meet you."

"Bring him in," grinned Biff invitingly.

Dark Dynamite came in with his manager. He was big, soft-spoken, lazily genial in his manner, but every inch an athlete. He was obviously no simple thug, but an educated and exceptionally intelligent sportsman.

"I'm very pleased to be shaking hands with you, Mister Bailey," he said. "This is a great day for boxing in Kiman."

Biff took an immediate liking to him. Dark Dynamite, for his part, appeared to be thoroughly genuine in his welcome, but they both knew that this wasn't going to prevent them from trying to knock the daylights out of each other when they met in the ring.

Biff's visitors departed after a few minutes, and he got down to his first morning's training. He finished at noon, to leave the gym free to his opponent during the afternoon. He was driving in a taxi back to his

l with Terry and Sam when suddenly, through the window, he
something that brought a grin to his face.

hey were passing the stadium where the fight was to be staged.
ge posters advertised the bout. Standing beneath them was a street
endor with a tray holding pairs of boxing dolls, one black, one white,
o represent Biff and Dark Dynamite. He was doing a brisk trade in
them.

"The whole city seems to have gone crazy over this fight," chuckled
Biff as they drove past.

Once again they slipped into their hotel by the back entrance. They
rode up to their suite in the elevator. Terry unlocked the door and
walked in, only to recoil with a swift exclamation of disgust. "My
stars! What on earth's that?" he gasped. "Biff–it looks as if you've
made an enemy of someone–and he's been here, in this very room!"

Biff pushed past Terry into the room. His eyes narrowed angrily.
Dangling by a cord from the light fitting in the centre of the ceiling was
one of the little boxing dolls of himself. A tiny spear, fashioned from
a bodkin, had been driven through its head.

"If this is somebody's idea of a joke," snorted Terry, "I think it's in
pretty poor taste."

"I don't think it's meant to be a joke," Biff retorted, cutting down
the doll and holding it in his hand. "This is a piece of African black
magic. The idea is that if you make a doll to represent someone, and
you damage the doll, it's the person the doll represents who feels the
pain."

"That's just silly superstition," Terry protested.

"I know. But I think someone is trying to frighten me," Biff
declared.

"But that's nonsense," scoffed Terry. "Who would want to do
that?"

"Remember that chap who tried to get money out of me in the gym
this morning? He said that Dark Dynamite wins his fights by turning
his opponents into nervous wrecks–before they even reach the ring."

"You can't seriously believe that he has anything to do with this!"
protested Terry. "You've met the man. He's obviously a grand
sportsman. Besides he's educated, civilised, intelligent. I don't think
he's got anything to do with it."

"I hope you're right, because I'd like to think that too," Biff ag
"Dark Dynamite certainly didn't strike me as the type of chap
would go in for cheap tricks like this to help win a fight."

Biff tossed the doll into a wastepaper basket and made up his m
to forget about it.

He had almost dismissed it from his thoughts by the time he wen
bed that night. He pulled back the sheet, jumped in, and almost
quickly jumped out again, letting out a yell.

Terry came running from the next room. Then he pulled up with
a gurgling sound in his throat. His face went as white as a sheet.

In the middle of Biff's bed was a hideous creature, black and furry,
that looked like a giant spider except that it had three eyes and only
four legs.

Sam dashed in and joined them. He backed to the wall.

"Wh-what is it?" he asked huskily.

Biff grabbed a rolled-up newspaper and swatted at the thing. But it
didn't move.

"It looks dead," Biff remarked.

He prodded it cautiously and turned it upside down.

"In fact it's never been alive," he went on as he examined the
three-eyed creature more closely. "It's just a faked-up thing."

Thoughtfully he crossed the room and rang the service bell. In a few
moments the bell-boy came into the room-an alert, smartly uniformed
coloured lad.

"Are you easily frightened?" asked Biff.

"I don't think so, sir," answered the bell-boy with a puzzled smile.

Biff stepped aside to let him see the ugly thing on the bed.

"Did you ever see one of these things before? Do you know what it
is?" he asked.

The bell-boy chuckled.

"I saw one or two when I was living in an upcountry village," he
said. "It's a Kiman Dream Demon!"

"What is it supposed to do?" Biff asked.

"You get a witch doctor to put a spell on it, then hide it in the bed of
someone you don't like. It's supposed to give him nightmares,"
explained the bell-boy. Biff thanked him and the lad departed. Then he
settled down for the night.

In the morning he woke with a splitting headache. Terry took one look at him and let out a yell.

"You've got a headache! By gosh. That doll with the spear through the head. Could it have any connection with that? Could sticking the spear through that doll's head have had the effect of giving you a headache?"

"Nothing of the sort. It's coincidence. A coincidence that Dark Dynamite–or whoever planted that doll–was counting on. I'll bet you've got a headache, and so has Sam."

"Well, now you come to mention it I have," muttered Terry.

"Me, too," agreed Sam.

"There you are. It's the sudden change of climate, the different food, the crowds, the excitement. The doll had nothing to do with it," Biff insisted.

"How did you sleep? Any nightmares?" asked Terry cautiously.

"I slept badly, for the same reason that I woke with a headache," Biff rapped. "The heat takes some getting used to, and the last two days have been all rush and tear. Don't worry. None of these tricks is going to frighten me into losing this fight."

Biff had two weeks in which to prepare for the fight, and he planned to build himself up steadily so that he would be in peak form on the night he stepped into the ring.

Everything he did was carried out under a blaze of publicity. The newspaper filled columns every day discussing the outcome of the fight. Biff accepted all the attention with quiet good humour, and refused to let himself be worried by all the notice he was getting.

There were no more threatening displays of black magic and Biff came to the conclusion that he had shown everyone–including Dark Dynamite–that such tricks weren't going to upset him and were not worth trying.

On the night before the fight he went to bed early. He was awakened, round about midnight, by a curious tapping at his window, as if someone was trying to get in.

He opened his eyes, still half asleep, and blinked in the direction of the sound. Then, suddenly, he was wide awake and sitting up in bed. A man's face was moving about outside, peering in at him through the glass. A hideous, terrifying face!

Biff slipped quietly out of bed without turning on the light and padded through to the adjoining room to rouse Terry and Sam. He whispered to them to follow him back into his room.

Terry uttered a strangled gasp as he saw the eerie face at the window.

"What the dickens is that?" he gulped.

"Don't get the wind up!" begged Biff. "There can't possibly be anyone out there. This room is at least fifty feet above street level and there's nothing out there that a man could stand on. No balcony, no ledge, not a thing!"

"But we can see him," argued Terry. "If there's nothing for him to stand on, he must be walking on air, floating fifty feet up!"

"The face moves, but the expression doesn't change," Biff said. "It isn't a man. It's a mask. A witch doctor's mask."

"That still doesn't explain how it comes to be floating fifty feet above the street," shuddered Terry.

"It must be hanging from a cord," declared Biff in a matter-of-fact voice. "Someone is working it from above."

He rapidly donned track-suit trousers and a pair of canvas shoes.

"Come on. We're going to do a little investigating," he said.

He slipped out, with his pals behind him. He ran lightly up the stairs to the next floor and went swiftly along a corridor until he reached the door of a room directly above his own.

"If I'm making a mistake we're going to have some awkward explaining to do," he whispered, putting his hand on the knob. "But here goes!"

He flung the door open. The room was in darkness. He heard a gasp of terror from the direction of the window. He switched the light on. A Negro was leaning out of the open window, the end of a cord in his hands.

It was the man who had tried to sell Biff information about Dark Dynamite, in the Kiman gym. He turned in wild-eyed alarm and tried to let the cord go as Biff leaped at him. But he wasn't quite quick enough. Biff grabbed the cord and pulled it in until the mask came over the sill.

Biff looked sternly at the cowering sparring partner.

"I suppose you were responsible for putting the doll and the dream demon in my room, too?" he asked.

The man nodded wordlessly, terrified now that he had been caught.

"Well you can go back to Dark Dynamite and tell him that his cunning scheme didn't work. It was a neat idea of his to try to make me think you were against him, so that I'd fall for his cheap tricks," Biff said hotly.

"Oh no! Dark Dynamite doesn't know anything about this," stammered the cowering man. "It's just that when you turned me down I got mad, and decided to get my own back on you this way."

"You low-down trickster!" exploded Terry. "We ought to hand him over to the police, Biff."

"Don't be silly. We're not going to do anything to him," retorted Biff, and turned to the trembling sparring partner. "Tell me, have you worked these black magic tricks on anyone else?"

"Oh no," gasped the other. "This is the first time I ever tried it."

"Then I hope this'll be a lesson to you and it'll also be the last time you try it," said Biff, grimly. "Now get out and don't ever let me see you again!"

The relieved man scuttled away. Biff and his pals returned to their own room.

"I'm mighty glad we've got to the bottom of it," Terry declared. "Especially now we know that Dark Dynamite had nothing to do with it."

"I'm glad for that reason, too. But something else is bothering me," Biff declared. "What sort of shape am I going to be in after a broken night's sleep? I've got to be in tip-top form for beating Dark Dynamite–here's hoping I'll be on my toes despite this trick."

The fight was the most spectacular sporting show ever organised in Kiman.

Biff's bout with Dark Dynamite came as the grand climax to a programme of matches which had starred the pick of the country's boxers at all weights.

The preliminary matches had worked the fans up to a pitch of terrific fervour. The ring stood empty, and a hush of anticipation fell over the packed audience. Suddenly, dramatically, the lights went out. The stadium was plunged into darkness.

Through the darkness swelled the stirring notes of a fanfare.

As the last notes died away a brilliant spotlight speared down from the roof, and focused on Biff, standing at the top of the gangway, waiting to make his entry.

The fans gave him a tremendous welcome as he walked towards the ring, followed by Terry and Sam. The spotlight tracked them so that they moved in a pool of light amid the surrounding darkness.

The light remained on Biff when he reached his corner.

Then the trumpets rang out again. A second light blazed down from the roof, to illuminate Dark Dynamite at the door.

The roar which had greeted Biff had been rousing enough, but it was nothing to the frenzied, delirious acclaim with which the fans greeted their local hero.

Then all the lights came on. The preliminaries were gone through, and the battle was on. From the start Dark Dynamite glided out of his corner with all the stealthy ease and menace of a black panther.

The way he moved was deceptive. His lithe movements gave the impression that he was taking everything in a leisurely stride, when in fact he had the speed of a striking viper.

He slid towards Biff at a tremendous pace, his gloves poised perfectly, his every movement suggesting that he was about to let loose a terrific storm of punches.

His gloved fists darted out towards Biff's head. Instinctively Biff backed off a little, lifted his gloves a little higher, and tucked his chin well down on to his chest so as to be ready for the attack.

But the fierce onslaught never materialised. Dark Dynamite, without outwardly seeming to alter his pace, suddenly seemed to slow up.

Instead of letting loose a barrage of shattering punches, he just sent a few light, swift jabs home to Biff's unprotected body.

Biff thought he had been outsmarted, and so lowered his gloves again to protect his body. He had already formed the opinion that in Dark Dynamite he had a very shrewd opponent. The din and the wild enthusiasm would have been enough to unnerve a challenger less experienced than Biff.

But he was used to big occasions, and had learned to shut out everything from his mind except the important job in hand, that of dealing with his opponent.

For all the effect the racket had on Biff, he and Dark Dynamite might have been alone in the stadium. The crowd, almost to a man, were cheering on the local favourite, and if Biff had allowed that overwhelming support to unnerve him, the effect would have been disastrous.

He gave the appearance of being cool and composed, alert and watchful as he and his opponent circled each other, weighing each other up. It didn't take Biff long to discover that he had taken on a formidable and clever opponent. Dark Dynamite was first class, good enough to hold his own anywhere.

Even when he was just quietly moving round the ring he had the air of being charged with menace. But it was a menace that never quite materialised. Dark Dynamite was a riddle. He fought in a style that Biff had never met before. He seemed all the time to be threatening an attack which never came, to be preparing some kind of trap for Biff which was never sprung.

It seemed that the sparring partner who tried to sell Biff information hadn't been far wrong. Any man with less strong nerves than Biff might have been made a nervous wreck!

Biff was alert, watchful, and baffled. At last, tired of waiting, he launched an attack of his own. At once Dark Dynamite unleashed a terrific counter. It missed by a hair. The narrowness of his escape shook Biff.

They mixed it. They exchanged blows, but the big attack, always threatening, never came off. His patience wearing thin, Biff charged in a second time and tried to jolt his opponent into making his big effort. Again came a succession of tearing counter-punches which threatened destruction but just missed. This time Biff got the distinct impression that the narrow misses had been deliberate.

By the end of the third round Biff was inwardly jittery. He wasn't frightened, but the constant strain of being kept at full stretch waiting for something that never happened together with his lack of sleep the previous night had brought him almost to screaming point.

Suddenly the truth dawned on him. This was the secret of his opponent's style. Dark Dynamite fought a war of nerves. He softened his opponents by reducing them to a state of shaken bewilderment before turning on the heat.

"Round Four"

It was a style that could be followed only by a man who had superb ringcraft, and Dark Dynamite certainly had that.

Round four! Dark Dynamite glided in, gloves poised, threatening destruction. Biff, from the experience gained in the previous rounds, decided not to be held at bay by the threat and went in.

It proved a wrong guess. His opponent outsmarted him. He threw fast punches, and they met Biff as he was coming in.

Biff backed off, his ears ringing.

Rapidly he decided that there was only one way to handle Dark Dynamite, and that was to match him with tactics that would get *him* guessing.

Biff retreated. He slid against the ropes, ducked off, and let his gloves fall to waist level. Dark Dynamite thought he was groggy, and leaped in like a panther.

Biff allowed him to come in close, then his gloves flashed up. He weaved, slipped the punches that were thrown at him, and countered. Dark Dynamite was caught unprepared, on the wrong foot. Leather hammered in his face. He was driven back. He stumbled his way out of trouble, a puzzled expression in his eyes.

They went two more rounds of fast action that kept the fans in a ferment. Dark Dynamite had abandoned his kidding and was resorting to solid fighting.

They reached the seventh round. They clashed in a tremendous exchange of mighty blows. A thundering fist connected with Biff's jaw. He reeled backwards. His knees were giving way. His gloves felt like ton weights. His fists dangled and his arms lacked the strength to bring them up.

The fans yelled at Dark Dynamite to go in and finish him off. Had he done so he would certainly have put Biff down for the count. But he hung back. He couldn't make up his mind whether to risk it, and he lost his chance.

Biff was able to recover and get his second wind. When his opponent did rush him, he was ready. Biff halted him with slamming body blows, and followed through with a hook to the jaw. Dark Dynamite went back on shuffling feet.

Biff hit him again. He went down. But he was a gallant fighter. When the count reached the halfway mark he made a superhuman effort to get off the floor. He almost succeeded. Then he crumpled back to a kneeling position, and was counted out.

The tumult died down, and an ominous silence fell on the stadium. The fans sat dumb, dismayed and disappointed. Their hopes had been bitterly shattered.

It was an ugly moment. Biff could feel the hostile tension building up. Anything might have happened.

Dark Dynamite sensed it, too. He pulled himself to his feet. He stood at Biff's side, grabbed his arm and held it high for everyone to see.

The sporting gesture broke the tension. The fans stood up and cheered. They cheered the winner and cheered the loser impartially for having provided them with such a thrilling fight.

Grinning at each other, arms round each other's shoulders, the two battlers left the ring together.

"Thanks," panted Biff. "You got us out of an awkward situation."

"You mustn't blame them for being disappointed," answered Dark Dynamite. "But they'll soon get over it. They'll forget the defeat and remember only that the finest boxer who ever came to fight in this ring was—Biff Bailey!"